An Unwelcome Interruption

"Look, Susan," said Mr. Campion firmly, "this is the first food I've had since I got home. Let's eat it, and forget our own and other people's troubles just for half an hour, shall we?"

Susan smiled. "Grand girl," said Mr. Campion, and raised his glass. He put it down again untasted, however: advancing down the room towards him, with a purposeful nonchalance which stamped "police" all over him, was Superintendent Yeo.

On the whole, Mr. Campion went quietly.

"I won't keep him a moment, miss," said Yeo to Susan. "I only want a word with him. I'll send him back in no time. Sorry, I'm sure, Mr. Campion."

"Gestapo!" said Campion, as they entered the passage behind the service door.

"No need to be abusive," said the Superintendent mildly. "You're going to be very interested in half a moment."

"That's nice," said Mr. Campion. "What'll you bet?"

AGATHA CHRISTIE

Death on the Nile
A Holiday for Murder
The Mousetrap and Other Plays
The Mysterious Affair at Styles
Poirot Investigates
Postern of Fate
The Secret Adversary
The Seven Dials Mystery
Sleeping Murder

DOROTHY SIMPSON

Last Seen Alive
The Night She Died
Puppet for a Corpse
Six Feet Under
Close Her Eyes
Element of Doubt
Dead on Arrival

ELIZABETH GEORGE

A Great Deliverance
Payment in Blood
coming soon: Well-Schooled in Murder

COLIN DEXTER

Last Bus to Woodstock
The Riddle of the Third Mile
The Silent World of Nicholas Quinn
Service of All the Dead
The Dead of Jericho
The Secret of Annexe 3
Last Seen Wearing

MICHAEL DIBDIN

Ratking

LIZA CODY

Stalker
Head Case
coming soon: Under Contract

JOHN GREENWOOD

The Mind of Mr. Mosley
The Missing Mr. Mosley
Mosley by Moonlight
Murder, Mr. Mosley
Mists Over Mosley
What, Me, Mr. Mosley?

RUTH RENDELL

A Dark-Adapted Eye
(writing as Barbara Vine)
A Fatal Inversion
(writing as Barbara Vine)

MARIAN BABSON

Death in Fashion
Reel Murder
Murder, Murder, Little Star
Murder on a Mystery Tour
Murder Sails at Midnight
The Stalking Lamb
coming soon: Murder at the Cat Show

DOROTHY CANNELL

The Widows Club
Down the Garden Path
Mum's the Word

ANTONIA FRASER

Jemima Shore's First Case
Your Royal Hostage
Oxford Blood
coming soon:
Cool Repentance
The Wild Island
Quiet as a Nun
Slash of Red

MARGERY ALLINGHAM

Police at the Funeral
Flowers for the Judge
Tether's End
Pearls Before Swine
Traitor's Purse

PEARLS BEFORE SWINE

Margery Allingham

BANTAM BOOKS
NEW YORK • TORONTO • LONDON • SYDNEY • AUCKLAND

PEARLS BEFORE SWINE

*A Bantam Book / published by arrangement with
Doubleday*

PRINTING HISTORY

*Doubleday edition published May 1945
A Selection of Detective Book Club, July 1945
Bantam edition / December 1984
4 printings through April 1990*

ISBN 0-553-24548-1

Published simultaneously in the United States and Canada

*Bantam Books are published by Bantam Books, a division of Bantam
Doubleday Dell Publishing Group, Inc. Its trademark, consisting of the
words "Bantam Books" and the portrayal of a rooster, is Registered in U.S.
Patent and Trademark Office and in other countries. Marca Registrada.
Bantam Books, 666 Fifth Avenue, New York, New York 10103.*

PRINTED IN THE UNITED STATES OF AMERICA

KRI   13 12 11 10 9 8 7 6 5 4

PEARLS BEFORE SWINE

1

THE MAN AND the woman carried the body cautiously up the stairs. Although it was still early evening, the narrow way was grey and shadowy, and it was very cold, colder even than it had been outside amid the thin traffic of a wartime London.

The two who were alive in that grim little group which writhed and breathed so hard in the gloom were both elderly people. They were an unexpected couple in any situation; the man was a large, blank-faced Cockney without any pretensions and the woman was out of place beside him, her delicate aristocratic grace accentuating both his clumsiness and the horror of her present task.

All they had in common was the job in hand and a sense of nightmare, and as they plodded upward with the dead weight between them their feet trod the carpeted stairs without feeling them and they strained their muscles without noticing the strain.

Mr. Lugg, who was in his disreputable Civil Defence uniform, reflected that he had to hand it to the old girl even if she was a marchioness, she was showing very game.

"One more flight," he muttered.

"Hush," said Lady Carados, adding breathlessly: "oh, *can't* we keep her feet off the ground?"

Meanwhile in the apartment above, Mr. Albert Campion, who was in that particular state of ignorance wherein it is downright idiocy to be wise, was taking a warm bath.

He lay in the soothing water utterly at ease for the first time since his long journey home had begun some eight weeks before. For the first time he was entirely happy, and his only worry in the world concerned the possibility of his dropping off to sleep and so missing his train. For a long time

1

he kept perfectly still, his lean body relaxed and content. He had changed a little in the last three years; the sun had bleached his fair hair to whiteness, lending him a physical distinction he had never before possessed. There were new lines in his over-thin face and with their appearance some of his own misleading vacancy of expression had vanished. But nothing had altered the upward drift of his thin mouth or the engaging astonishment which so often and so falsely appeared in his pale eyes.

Just now he was barely thinking. His mind was ticking over very slowly—pop pop, pop pop, pop pop. He had just worked out with enormous mental effort that he had fifteen and a half minutes to lie thus, twenty minutes to dress, twenty minutes to potter about remembering the things he might have forgotten, and twenty minutes to catch his train. From his present viewpoint this simple programme possessed beauty, luxury, civilization.

He had been back in London exactly one hour and ten minutes, and as yet had had no time to form any real impression of the changes in the great city. But already it had spread its ancient charm about him and he knew from the very smell of it that it was still safe, still firmly respectable, still obdurately matter of fact. He was immeasurably relieved; from the tales he had heard abroad he had expected worse.

For three years he had been at large on two warring continents employed on a mission for the Government so secret that he had never found out quite what it was, or at least that was the version of his activities which it seemed most prudent to give at the moment. Meanwhile he was certainly damnably tired.

At this point he thought he heard a curious shuffling noise on the other side of the bathroom wall, but he quietened his over-alert senses by reflecting that he was home again in London where shuffling noises had prosaic explanations. Lying in the water he stirred slightly, moving his hands like fins, and remembering how as a child he had enjoyed playing "sleeping fish" in the bath. Life was very good and very quiet. Six weeks' leave was due, and he was prepared to enjoy it in a leafy peace which yet promised a gentle excitement of its own. However, just now, just at this very moment there was at last time to waste.

He heard the latch of the front door and the subsequent scuffling without undue surprise. He took it that Lugg had got the wire he had sent from the port. Well, that was nice, it would be good to see the old villain who had served him so faithfully if so truculently for so long. He had clearly done his best by the flat, too. The blitzed windows in the bedroom were neatly pasted up with cardboard, and the whole place was cleaner than one might have expected.

Campion was just about to shout a greeting when he became aware of a new, and more unlikely series of noises; swift footsteps raced up the main staircase, the front door shuddered open just as someone on the inside was closing it, there was a muttered expletive, and finally an entirely unfamiliar feminine scream.

Mr. Campion sat up slowly.

Another unfamiliar female voice, but older this time and very close at hand, said pleadingly:

"Be quiet, dear, oh, be quiet."

Then more scuffling, followed by whispering, and afterwards a second door opening and closing.

Mr. Campion's impulse was to lie down again and to pull the soapsud blanket over his head, but he dismissed the idea as unworthy and clambered out gingerly. Draped in a towel he stood listening. Evidently the Reception Committee, or whatever it was, had moved into the sitting-room across the passage; he could only just distinguish the murmur of voices.

He began to dry himself reluctantly. He was disappointed, of course—not, as he reflected between rubs, that he was averse to some small token of welcome on his return, on the contrary he had been looking forward to a reunion with his old friend and knave; but why the man should have thrown a party, and of what it could possibly consist, he could not imagine.

He had no dressing-gown in the bathroom, and so, uncomfortably girt about with towels, he tiptoed into the hall, intending to fetch one from the bedroom. The sitting-room door was closed, but he could hear the steady whisper of voices within. He opened the bedroom door very quietly and made straight for the hanging cupboard. Since most of the window space was boarded up, the room was in semi-darkness, and he found what he sought before he noticed anything unusual. It was when he turned again and was tying the girdle tightly about his lean ribs that he first saw the shape on the bed.

His first impression was that it was a roll of carpet which lay there so stiffly, and he was annoyed with himself for being so startled by it; but as he came forward to lean over the foot of the bed he saw the thing for what it was, and a wave of mingled incredulity and apprehension passed over him, leaving him suddenly cold.

It was a woman, and she was dead. There was no possible question about it. In life she had been a birdy little creature, bright-eyed no doubt, and even pretty in a faded, possibly over-excitable fashion, but now her eyes were hidden, her mouth was set in a dreadful narrow O, and the high, thin bone of her nose rose like a knife-blade about to cut through the livid skin.

She was clad in a black silk nightdress under a long grey squirrel coat, while on her bare feet hung little wedge shoes of grey-and-black leather, very square and serviceable. One of her legs was twisted unnaturally, the knee turned outwards and raised an inch or so from the coverlet on which she lay. She was dead, rigor was well advanced, and her hands folded on her breast looked formal and absurd.

Campion stood staring at her blankly; she was a complete stranger to him. Moreover, ten minutes before when he had turned on his bath she had not been there. Whoever had brought her was presumably in the next room now, whispering. The first definite thought which reached him amid the firework display of question marks in his mind was that whatever had happened, whoever this pathetic little bundle might turn out to have been, he must not permit her to prevent him catching his train. That train was important. The reward it promised him had been most hardly earned.

All the same the present situation could hardly be ignored. Twitching his bright dressing-gown more tightly round him he stepped lightly down the passage, and opened the sitting-room door. He did not enter it, but stood back taking the elementary precaution by force of habit.

"Oh, my God!"

The cry which greeted the silent swinging door was purely superstitious. He recognized the panic note instantly, and walked in, to find himself confronted by three frightened people: Lugg, in Heavy Rescue uniform, and two of the most striking women he had ever seen in his life.

It was the girl who had cried out, he could tell that by the grey pallor of her skin and the fear in her wide-open eyes. All the same, she was lovely, very fair with unusually vivid blue eyes, and long slender bones. It was her youth which impressed him most at that first glance; she was downy with it, twenty at the very outside, he judged, and at the moment she was shocked and too horrified even to cry.

He glanced past her at the older woman and was surprised by a sudden conviction that he ought to be able to recognize her. It was clear that she expected to be recognized. She was frightened now, set with resolution and hardened out of the normal, but there was no mistaking her for what she was, an Edwardian beauty still young in everything but years. She was still alive, still adventurous, still emotional, and she wore her age ruefully, as if it were an unbecoming garment of which she was determined to make the best. She was a personality too. Struggling to place her, Campion found to his disgust that he was thinking of the portrait of Mrs. Siddons by Sir Joshua Reynolds.

She made no attempt to speak, but stood looking at him woodenly, nothing in her eyes.

Campion turned to the only member of the group whom he had met before and made a discovery which alarmed him more than any of the others. Mr. Lugg was frightened also; he was shaking, and downright uncompromising disbelief was written plainly across his great white egg of a face. Campion met his eyes, and the three years' separation between them vanished, so that in spite of himself a flicker of his old smile passed over Campion's face.

"Is the lady in my bedroom staying long?" he enquired.

Lugg opened his mouth and closed it again without speaking; he glanced round with a helplessness which was not typical of him and finally confronted his old employer with an expression which was no longer truculent.

"I didn't know you was back," he said devastatingly.

"Oh well, then, that's all right." Campion appeared relieved. "I'm just going, anyway. I only dropped in for a bath between trains. You just go on as though I weren't here."

"No, wait a minute, guv'nor." Lugg put up a fat hand appealingly. "I'd like to have a bit of a word with you. It's lucky you come along, reely. 'Ere, come into the kitchen a minute, will you?"

They might have retired, but at this point the woman who reminded Mr. Campion of Mrs. Siddons collected herself and intervened.

"Oh, this is Mr. Campion, is it?" she said graciously. "I'm afraid we're imposing on you terribly. I don't think we've met, have we? But I've heard my son John speak of you many times—Carados, you know."

It was a very fair effort. The great drawing-rooms of the early part of the century had been a severe training ground and some of their stoic gallantry reappeared for a moment in her quiet voice and unshakable ease of manner. Mr. Campion was astounded. If John, Marquess of Carados, was her son, then she must be Edna, Dowager Marchioness, one time the lovely Edna Dawlish, daughter of old Henry G. Dawlish, cotton king in the golden age before the wars. No wonder he had fancied he recognized her, he ought to have done. Her photographs had taken the place of Mrs. Langtry's when the Jersey Lily had first begun to fade. They had appeared in every magazine and shop window in the country. As a young bride she had swept London society off its feet, and her wealth, her vivacity, and the romantic tales about her had become fabulous in a year.

As soon as he had digested this piece of information the utter unbelievableness of the present situation struck him afresh, and he pulled himself together with difficulty.

"Why, of course," he said stupidly. "Please use the place as much as you like. Tell me, is Johnny about?"

At this moment the nods and grimaces in which Lugg had been indulging for some time gave place to audible noise, and Lady Carados turned to look at him. The fat man was more pallid than ever and his small eyes were imploring.

"I would like to 'ave a bit of a word with 'im," he said. "I brung you 'ere, you see."

She sat down. "Do," she said. "Do. You explain everything, Mr. Lugg, will you? I don't want to hear it again. I'm afraid we need help."

Lugg made no comment on this last observation until he

and Campion were in the dressing-room beyond the bath-room where the traveller had left his clothes. Then he expressed himself forcibly.

"The fact is, cock," he added more calmly, when he had relieved his feelings, "we're up the old-fashioned creek. You've come just in time, that's about the size of it."

Mr. Campion emerged from the shirt he was pulling on, his hair dishevelled, but his expression firm.

"Don't you kid yourself, my lad," he said mildly. "I'm catching a train in fifty minutes and a thousand corpses all in coronets won't stop me. You—er—you only have the one at the moment, I take it?"

"Yus, only the one," Lugg agreed absently, adding reproachfully, as he recovered himself, "now's not the time to be funny, neither. You've 'ad your fun abroad, I dare say. This is serious. A stiff is still a stiff in this country. There'll be a lot of questions asked."

"So I should imagine," murmured Mr. Campion dryly. "However, compared with mere warfare, you all seem to have toughened up considerably. What the hell are you doing, Lugg? Who is that woman?"

"We don't know," said Mr. Lugg surprisingly, "that's 'arf the trouble."

Campion glanced up from the shoe he was tying, his face unusually serious.

"Suppose you come across," he suggested.

Lugg still hesitated.

"Well," he said at last in a burst of confiding, "it's like this. I've been sitting in the square for about a year now . . ."

"Carados Square?"

"Yus. I'm on duty there, see? We've 'ad our ups and downs, but for a lot of the time I 'aven't 'ad a lot to do, and me and my old girl 'ave been bored some of the time."

"Your old girl?"

"That's my pig—we keep pigs, us 'Eavy Rescue chaps."

"In Carados Square?"

"Yus. 'Elping the war effort."

"I see." Mr. Campion concentrated on his other shoe.

"You're out of touch," Lugg explained magnanimously, "but you'll pick it up."

"Yes, I hope so. Carry on."

"I am carrying on. You keep your mind on what I'm telling you, 'cos it's difficult, some of it. Now, this 'ere Lady Carados, wot's in the next room, she lives in the square, on the side wot's still standing."

"The other three sides are not so hot, I suppose?" Campion could not forgo the question, for he had a sudden picture of the graceful houses with their slender windows and arched porticos, which used to stand like guardsmen round the delicate green of one of the city's finest gardens.

"Most of the other three sides is cooler now than wot they was," said Lugg succinctly. "But a part of the 'ouse where 'is nibs, 'er Ladyship's son, used to live, that's all right, and that's wot we're coming to."

Johnny Carados's house and only part of it all right. In his mind's eye Campion saw again the Carados mansion, which George Quellett had redecorated in his Bakst period. It seemed impossible that it should not still exist. It was the Music Room he remembered best; it had been at the top of the building, so probably it had gone, and its Indian red hangings, its gilt and its green, all reduced to a mass of blackened spars.

All the same, it had been worth doing, even for so short a life. It had been from that room that Johnny had conducted his remarkable activities. Of course, as a man with such a background and with such a fortune, Carados had had every opportunity to give his genius full rein, but he had never wasted those opportunities; he had been a great patron. It was Johnny who had financed the Czesca Ballet, Johnny who established the Museum of Wine, Johnny who had put the Pastel Society on its feet, who had given Zolly his first half-dozen concerts in London, and who had rebuilt the Sicilian Hall.

Moreover, he had always fostered his own art, and was, incongruously, one of the leading amateur fliers of the age. Campion remembered him as an inspiring figure with the power to draw brains round him, and who had had, despite his youth and his money, very little trace of the dilettante in his make-up. He had held his friends, too. Peter Onyer and his wife Gwenda had lived with him, Campion remembered, Peter managing his financial affairs and Gwenda acting as her husband's secretary. There had been other members of the household also—that queer little fish, Ricky Silva, who had existed solely to do the flowers, as far as anyone knew, and the plump cheerful girl who was the social secretary, whose name Campion had forgotten; not to mention the silent Captain Gold, who ruled the servants and did the housekeeping. It had been an odd, interesting outfit, the members all of an age and all highly intelligent. Together they had formed one of the most closely knit of all the little gangs which had characterized the social life of pre-war London.

Carados had lived his own life in his own magnificent fashion. Evangeline Snow, the revue star, had never married him, but she was always there amongst them, and Johnny was faithful to her as far as anyone knew.

The brilliant picture of the past faded into the dust and rubble of the present, and Mr. Campion blinked. The war must have split them up, of course, he reflected. He thought he remembered hearing something about Johnny getting himself into the R.A.F. at an age which at the time had appeared fantastic; his record as an amateur had stood him in good stead, and it had been arranged. The move must have taken him clean away from his old surroundings, and now, most of the house itself had gone.

Campion turned to Lugg. "Where is Carados now?"

" 'Is Lordship? At 'is 'ome, I 'ope. They've got the two lower floors and the basement going. He was just due there when we got the stiff away."

His large white face was growing more and more lugubrious. "We've got ourselves in a mess and no mistake," he said. "The girl coming in so unlikely, not to mention you—that's torn it. I was going to manage it all quiet, you see."

"I don't, quite," said Mr. Campion frankly, "not yet. Go on from where you were sitting in your pigsty."

Lugg was hurt. "It's not only a pigsty," he said, "it's a whole depot. A.R.P., you know, 'eroes of the Blitzes. It's right in the middle of the square where the grass used to be. That's where I picked up 'er Ladyship. All through the Blitz she ran a voluntary canteen there, a real old sport, she is. Not a nerve in 'er body. Me an' 'er always 'ave got on very polite. So when she got 'erself in this spot of trouble it was natural she should turn to me. Also, she knew I was still working for you in me spare time, and p'raps that 'ad something to do with it. You've got a reputation, you know, and I've come in for a bit of it."

He paused and regarded his employer defiantly. Campion's expression was not helpful. Lugg sighed.

"When she come to me I 'elped her," he said. "I felt it was my duty, and I 'elped 'er."

"Yes, well, let's hope you haven't helped the nerveless Marchioness to jug," observed Mr. Campion pleasantly. "You say you don't know who the dead woman is; has your distinguished confederate any idea?"

"No. She don't know neither. That's wot's made 'er so wild, if you ask me."

Mr. Campion put on his coat. "Do you know how the woman died?"

"Oh, that's all right, don't worry about that. It's nothing fishy." Lugg was unexpectedly confident. "That's O.K. I've taken care of that. You know me by this time. I wouldn't mix myself up with nothing dangerous."

Campion regarded his old friend with respectful astonishment.

"I don't know how carefree the old country has gone in my absence," he said, "but you seem to be considerably more casual with your corpses than is the fashion elsewhere. Are you telling me you've got a doctor's certificate for that body? What are you doing? Just throwing a small funeral from my flat?"

"No, cock. No. Not yet."

Lugg was uncomfortable, and again the unusual gleam of alarm showed for an instant in his small eyes. "We ain't 'ad a doctor yet, as a matter of fact. But I was goin' to, of course. It was suicide, if you want to know—straight suicide. Bottle of muck by 'er side, and everything."

Campion remained unimpressed, and Lugg went on earnestly:

"We 'ad to move 'er, you see, because she was in 'is bed. It didn't look the article, especially with 'im due any minute for the wedding. That's going to be the day after tomorrow."

Mr. Campion sat down slowly on a chair which was fortunately behind him.

"Whose bed?" he enquired.

" 'Is nibs'."

"Carados's?"

"Yus, I'm telling you."

"Whose wedding?"

" 'Is, of course. Don't you see no papers where you come
from?" Lugg's voice was becoming appealing. "There's been
pictures of them both in all of them; 'im in his uniform with
'is ribbons up, and 'er looking about fourteen and all very
nice. I'm going to 'and round at the reception," he added
shyly, "if I get out of this."

Mr. Campion struggled to adjust his mind to the facts so
startlingly presented. One complete incongruity in the story
stuck out and he commented on it casually. He was very fond
of Evangeline, he said, but he could not believe she could
look fourteen. The Heavy Rescue stalwart appeared puzzled.

" 'Er name's Susan," he said, adding brightly, "Oh, I get
you, cock, it's not the same girl. No, he ain't marrying Miss
Snow, he's got one of my ambulance drivers, Admiral's
daughter. The bloke wot got himself in the papers by sinking
the *Prince Otto*. You've seen 'er, she's in the next room.
That's the trouble, or some of it," he added gloomily.

"How did she get into it?"

"By a ruddy mistake," said Lugg with feeling. "Nothing's
gorn right with this thing from the first. I shouldn't be
surprised if it's going to be unlucky. I 'ope it's goin' to be a
lesson to us all. No, well, you see, it was 'er time orf from
duty this afternoon. She 'asn't got a deputy now as things 'ave
been quiet for a bit. When she's away I mind the ambulance.
To tell you the truth, things is so quiet I'm pretty well alone
at the depot most afternoons."

Mr. Campion began to understand.

"You brought the body here in an ambulance," he said. "In
fact, Lady Carados made a confidant of you because you were
the one man who could get hold of a vehicle without being
questioned. That's a relief, the woman isn't quite mad after
all."

Lugg looked hurt. "She confided in me because she knew
she could trust me," he said. "But I'm not saying the ambulance might not 'ave 'elped. You can't trust a taxi to 'old 'is
tongue, and no one's got a car running these days. It was a
very good idea of 'ers, and it would 'ave worked, too, if the

girl 'ad not come into the square just as we were slipping out of it."

"She followed you, did she?"

"Yus, she did." Lugg was torn between admiration and exasperation. "She's a conscientious little beggar—some of these kids are; and when she saw 'er ambulance being drove orf by a woman (I was in the back, you see, with the corp), she thought the vehicle was being pinched, and I suppose she 'opped in a taxi and followed it. Anyway, she came barging in the door right on top of us, and when she saw wot we'd got, she was frightened. We was just tryin' to argue a little reason into 'er, when you come in."

Mr. Campion made no comment. He glanced at his watch, noting that he had twenty minutes before he need start for the station. The situation was so macabre, the possibilities so unpleasant, the characters so illustrious, and the explanations so humanly silly that it left him speechless.

Lugg was watching him under heavy white lids. No voices sounded from the sitting-room, and there was silence in the flat.

Lugg stirred uncomfortably. "It wasn't 'alf so barmy when we started out," he said. "Left to ourselves, me and the old lady might have brought it orf and not a soul been the wiser. Now that the girl's in it—not to mention you—it's not going to be so easy."

Mr. Campion eyed his old companion steadily.

"And there are the others," he said. "All the hundreds of others who are bound to hear the story in confidence. My dear good chap, you don't imagine that you can keep a thing like this quiet? Just think . . ."

He broke off and sat listening. Someone was coming up the stairs; light, purposeful footsteps advancing upon them steadily; on and on, they came, nearer and nearer, neither hurrying nor hesitating, but coming ever closer to the door.

2

THE KNOCKING WAS gentle at first, almost timid, but the quiet sound echoed round the flat like thunder or the noise of guns. In the sitting-room the urgent whispering ceased abruptly, and Campion caught an echo of the thrill of fear which went through those others who heard it. Beside him, Lugg was standing stiffly. He was frowning, and the veins on his forehead stood out clearly under the skin. No one moved, and the knocking came again. It was more resolute this time; still nobody answered.

From outside the faint rumblings of the traffic floated up to the silent flat. These were homely, ordinary noises, hootings, the squeal of brakes, and the cries of paper-sellers shouting the news. But they were far off, belonging to another world.

Within the flat there was silence. The four who lived were as quiet as the one who lay so stiffly on the bed.

The third bout of knocking was violent. The summons was angry and the bell rang shrilly like an alarm, while the knocker shook the panels of the door. Immediately afterwards, as there was no response from within, the lock rattled savagely and there was an ominous noise as someone put a shoulder to the wood.

At this new sound Mr. Campion raised his head and glanced sharply at his companion.

"I'm afraid that means business," he murmured. "Wait a moment," he called amid the noise, "what's up? What's the excitement?"

He pulled the door open but did not step back, so that the visitor's face suddenly appeared within a foot of his own.

The very young lieutenant of the United States Army who stood on the doorstep appeared to be as astonished by Campion as his host was to see him. He fell back a pace, but there was no suggestion of retreat in his square shoulders and serious pink face.

"I'm very sorry," he said gently, "but I think Mrs. Shering is here, isn't she? I'd very much like to see her, please."

He conveyed patience and studious politeness, but also the confident determination of a tank. Campion regarded him dubiously.

"I don't quite know," he said at last, "unless . . . Tell me, what is she like?"

The boy's face flushed a deeper crimson, and his pleasant grey eyes grew angrier.

"She came in here about fifteen minutes ago," he said. "I want to see her at once, please."

It was a very small hall, and he was a very large youngster. Mr. Campion showed no signs of moving and some sort of impasse appeared imminent when the sitting-room door burst open and the girl who had screamed came running out towards them. Her eyes were unnaturally bright and she was very pale.

"Oh, Don," she said desperately, looking past Campion. "Oh, Don, take me away."

He went over to her as though there were no one else in the world, much less in the room. It was a peculiarly youthful movement and Mr. Campion experienced considerable sympathy for him.

"Susan, my dear, who is this?"

Lady Carados did not come out into the overcrowded lobby and did not appear to raise her voice, yet the effect of her personality was by no means lessened by the fact that she spoke from half-way across the sitting-room. She dominated the group immediately, and Mr. Campion began to understand a little more of the present extraordinary situation. He realized that here was a woman who never from babyhood had expected any consideration whatever to stand in the way of her desires. It was not that she was particularly ruthless, but simply that things to inconvenience her had not been allowed to occur. She was frightened now, but he guessed that she was finding the experience invigorating.

"I think everybody had better come in here," she said. "Now, Susan, who is this?"

Young Mrs. Shering took a firm hold of herself, and

Campion, who was watching her closely, decided that his first impression of her had done her less than justice. He was astonished to find that she had been married; she looked not only younger than he had thought, but even more lovely. She stood up to the older woman very well, and it occurred to him that Lady Carados was her prospective mother-in-law, so that in view of the revealing expression on the face of the youngster at her side the position must be very difficult for her, quite apart from the alarming secret in the next room.

It was a considerable kettle of fish all round, he thought, and he eyed her curiously to see if she betrayed any answering feeling for the boy. At the moment her face told him nothing; she was schooled and impassive, her young mouth guarded and her eyes shadowed.

"Why, of course," she said. "Darling, let me present Lieutenant Don Evers. Don, this is Lady Carados."

It was naturally done, but all the same it was not quite an ordinary social introduction. Both pairs of eyes were wary, and the woman took in everything the boy's face had to tell her. He was not disguising much, and she had plenty to read. His bewilderment kept him silent and she was the first to speak.

"I'm afraid I don't quite understand," she said, and waited for him to explain.

"Don's been waiting downstairs for me," Susan cut in quickly. "When I saw my ambulance we were together, you see. We'd been out to lunch and he was bringing me back to the depot. I changed into my uniform there. But when we turned into the square I was a minute or two late and I considered myself technically on duty, so when I saw the ambulance being stolen, I followed it."

"Yes, that's so," said Evers, in his slow, deliberate way. He was still very doubtful of the position, but he was keeping his end up gallantly. "That's so," he repeated. "When Sue saw her ambulance flash by with a strange civilian at the wheel she felt it was her responsibility; so I sent our taxi after it—we were in a taxi when we saw the ambulance."

Lady Carados was ignoring the girl, but she kept her eyes fixed on the young soldier.

"Did you see anyone leave the ambulance here?" she enquired abruptly.

Again it was the girl who answered.

"We saw it turn into the cul-de-sac, but we were held up for a minute or so by the lights on the corner. When we saw it again it was standing outside here, empty. I would come up here alone, but Don insisted on waiting for me. It wasn't until I got into the flat that I saw . . ."

"That you saw us all, Susan," said the elder woman firmly.

The two looked at one another, and again it occurred to the watching Campion that young Mrs. Shering possessed un- usual determination. Either that, or she was at the end of her tether. All the same, it was she who first gave up the silent battle. She turned to the boy again and repeated her first abrupt request.

"Don, take me away from here."

"Sure," he said, closing in on her and taking her arm, adding apologetically as he glanced round the company, "I'm afraid I don't quite get what's going on around here yet, you know."

Mr. Campion could have shaken his hand, and very nearly did so absent-mindedly in the warmth of his fellow- feeling. But meanwhile Lady Carados was pursuing her own line.

"Do you know," she said, with a flicker of her early charm, "I don't think I want either of you to leave here at the moment."

"But I must," the girl insisted, "I must. I'm on duty, for one thing, and for another, I can't stay here a moment with . . ." She broke off helplessly.

"What exactly *is* this?" said Evers.

Lady Carados ignored him. "My dear," she said, putting her hand upon Susan's arm. "I'm so sorry, but you must wait here—both of you—until Johnny comes. I've 'phoned my son, Mr. Campion," she went on, turning to him. "As soon as Mrs. Shering arrived so unexpectedly, and then you came in, I realized that I'd done a very silly, dangerous thing. So while you were dressing I telephoned my son's house. Fortu- nately he'd just got in, and he's coming round at once. I'm afraid I've been rather foolish, but I did what I thought best in an intolerable situation."

She made the admission as if she were relinquishing a

responsibility rather than accepting one. Don Evers looked at her blankly.

"Is Carados coming here?" he enquired.

"Yes," she said placidly. "At any moment now. It'll all be all right when Johnny comes. We've only got to wait."

Mr. Campion only hoped she was right; for his own part he was not so sure.

Meanwhile Evers, who alone of them all was unaware of the main dilemma, appeared to have one of his own.

"I don't think I want to stay, Sue," he said simply.

The girl did not answer him but she took his arm, and her expression answered one of his questions concerning her. These young people were in love with each other; well, that was another mystery. He glanced at his watch. In fifteen minutes he must go—whatever happened there must be no question about that. In thirty-five minutes he must be in the train.

A laugh on the stairs outside cut into his calculations, and he heard a woman's voice raised in amusement. He glanced at Lady Carados.

"Did you tell Johnny?" he enquired.

She was listening also, and the look she gave him was as startled as his own.

"No, not everything. Of course not. Not on the 'phone. I simply told him to come here immediately."

"I see," said Mr. Campion, adding as someone beat a lively rhythm on the knocker, "I rather think he's here now, you know, and I fancy by the sound of it he's brought Evangeline Snow with him."

3

LUGG OPENED THE door to the new-comers, and they trooped into the room looking both enquiring and sympathetically apprehensive as do those who have come to give unspecified aid. There were three of them: Lord

Carados, Evangeline Snow, and the cheerful girl who had been the social secretary in Carados Square in the days before the war, and whose name Campion could never remember.

His first impression of Johnny Carados was that he looked younger than ever. He was a big man, not particularly tall and certainly not fleshy, but wide and long-armed, with a strong chin and serene smiling grey eyes. He glanced round the room as he came in, raised his eyebrows affably at the sight of Susan, smiled reassuringly at his mother, and stared at Campion in amazement.

"Hello," he said, "I thought you were out in the blue. What are you doing here?"

"I live here," said Mr. Campion mildly. "I just looked in, you know. It's my flat," he added, by way of explanation.

"That's right—of course it is." Carados grinned disarmingly. "I knew the address was familiar. I said so to Eve, didn't I? I say, darling, do you know everybody?" He was talking without thinking, his eyes taking in the curious assortment of people, as he strove to get some line on the situation. He was embarrassed, too; not unnaturally, Mr. Campion reflected, and he glanced at Eve Snow with interest.

She met his eyes and nodded to him, her unbeautiful, unforgettable face breaking into its famous smile. She was the same Eve, he noticed with pleasure, still incredibly chic in her plain clothes, still valiant, still exquisite of form and absurd of face, still the most lovable comedienne in the world.

All the other women in the room had some pretension to beauty, while she had none; yet she took the colour out of them all and her vivid honey-coloured eyes sized them up and conquered them one by one.

Meanwhile Carados was making the introductions in the hasty, casual fashion of one whose mind is elsewhere. Susan Shering looked no more than surprised at the name of the celebrity when she was presented to Evangeline, but Campion received the impression that the two women had met before. It occurred to him that young Mrs. Shering was remarkably ignorant of her fiancé's history.

The most acutely miserable person present, Lugg always excepted, was Don Evers. He was a straightforward, decent youngster, and he was very unhappy. He stood resolutely by Susan's side, nodded when it was required of him, and did not smile at all.

The cheerful girl who had come with John and Eve was introduced at last, and Campion remembered her name at once—Dolly Chivers. She was a fair-haired, thundering English rose, a jolly young woman who clumped about putting everything right with a big, frank smile. For once he was delighted to see her; in his opinion this was one of the few occasions which merited her sort of treatment, the sooner the better, too; after all he had his train to catch.

The moment everyone present had at least a vague notion who exactly everybody else might be, Lady Carados took matters into her own hands. Sitting down gracefully, she took out a small handkerchief and began to cry into it quietly. Johnny and Miss Chivers hurried over to her, and Campion found Eve at his side.

"Darling, for God's sake," she said in her familiar squeaky whisper, "what's up? Can't we go in the kitchen?"

It is a human instinct in times of other people's stress to find the most disinterested person present and get in a huddle; and Campion, having seated his guest on the draining board in the kitchenette, perched himself on the dresser and kicked the door shut with a certain amount of relief.

"It's all highly peculiar," he added, after retailing the story as far as he knew it. "Lady Carados would appear to be one of those women who have an original view of law and order, all probably based on the fact that she used to tip the Home Secretary half a crown when he was at Eton. My own bet is that she's been frightened for the first time in her life, and that she's lost her head. By sheer bad luck the man she picked to help her is one of the few people on earth who are used to doing the unconventional when so directed. Lugg's got a bee in his bonnet about the aristocracy—they go to his head."

"Like wine," she said absently. She was not listening to him any more. She had pulled off the ridiculous lavender fez she had been wearing, and the narrow yellow curl in the front of her dark hair shone in the grey light.

"Where is the—the thing, Albert? In the next room?"

He nodded. "On my bed. Lugg swears it's suicide, so I

take it that angle is healthy, but the whole thing is madness—horrible madness."

"Very," she agreed, her head still bent. "But it's dangerous, too, isn't it? I mean, one ought to get right away at once, oughtn't one, before one gets in the papers? And one would, of course, if it wasn't for old Johnny."

He glanced at her curiously, but she was not going to enlarge on that angle, or at least not much.

"She looks a nice child, doesn't she?" she remarked. "She was married at nineteen, you know, and widowed in a week."

"Susan?"

"Uh-huh. But all that is rather overshadowed at the moment, isn't it? My dear, what an unspeakably awful thing to happen. You say nobody knows who the poor beast was, and yet she was found in Johnny's bed the morning before he was due to come home to be married?"

Mr. Campion slid off the dresser. He had caught a sound outside in the passage.

"That's the tale at the moment of going to press," he said; "but I rather think there are developments." He opened the door cautiously and looked out. Johnny, very broad and solid in his blue-grey uniform, was backing away from the bedroom door. Dolly Chivers was behind him, and for once the ready smile had been wiped from her wide, fair-skinned face. Lugg in the role of guide was still in the bedroom. Carados turned to the woman and said something. She nodded, and he caught his breath; then, seeing Campion, he came forward into the kitchen. He looked amazed; shocked and worried also, but mainly amazed.

"Who is it?" said Eve.

"Do you know her?" Campion demanded.

"Yes. Yes, I do." He looked round at Miss Chivers, who had followed him. "It is the woman, isn't it?"

Dolly Chivers nodded again, her mouth stiff with alarm.

"Who is it?" Eve asked again, her head held on one side and her light brown eyes narrowed.

"Her name was Moppet," said Carados, unaware of any incongruity. "Moppet . . . Moppet . . . Harris, was it? No, Lewis. That's right. Mrs. Moppet Lewis. Remember her, Eve?"

"No." The star hesitated. "No, I don't unless . . . oh, not that little crow of a woman who . . . not . . . oh, Johnny!"

The man looked at her helplessly, and as he met her eyes a faint mischievous smile appeared at the corners of his mouth.

It occurred to Campion, who was looking at him, that much of the charm of the man lay here.

"Yes, that's the girl," he said. "If it wasn't so damned awful, it would be terribly funny. She's got in at last."

Eve shook her head at him and at herself also, for a gleam of shocked amusement had crept into her own eyes. "That's fantastic," she said, and turned to Campion.

"She was a little gate-crasher, oh, years ago," she went on. "Johnny always did collect fans, and she was one who took the whole gang of us too seriously altogether. I forget who brought her round, but she got into the house once and I remember Gwenda trying to stop her trying on all our clothes. She thought we were all too 'sweet and brittle' for words, and actually said so, I believe, to someone like Peter. Where are Gwenda and Peter, by the way? Due to arrive tonight, I suppose. Oh, tomorrow—well, it doesn't matter, I only thought by the look of things they ought to be here. Well, let me see, where was I? Oh yes; well, we got rid of Mrs. Moppet in the end, or rather Gwenda did. You never had an affair with her, did you, Johnny?"

The final question came out directly and without affectation, and for a moment they were all transported into that other world before the war when little affairs were fashionable, and no one seemed to have very much to do. The query appeared to startle Carados.

"Why, no," he said. "No, of course not. I may have taken her out to lunch once or twice, you know."

"To lunch? Once or twice? Darling, I thought she was only in the place once or twice, and that we were all rather beastly to her. Wasn't she the one who was always offering to get things for us wholesale? That was the one, wasn't it, Dolly?"

"Yes, that's the woman. I remember her perfectly." Miss Chivers was forthright as usual. "A bit of a trial, nosy, and possessive. You hated her, I remember."

Johnny shrugged his shoulders.

"All the same, I took her out to lunch three or four times about seven years ago." He spoke firmly and flatly, and the rest of the gathering did not look at him. Eve drew up her long dancer's legs, and sat with her arms round her knees.

"Before we decide what to do, let us know exactly what happened," she said. "How did she get into the house last night, or whenever it was?"

"That's what I don't understand," said Dolly Chivers quickly. "I was in the house until about six yesterday. I took a brief look round to see that everything was all right before I left, and I imagine I locked up after me. I think so, anyway, and I went home in the ordinary way. Rogers has got leave, and insists on coming back, bless him, just for the seven days, so that Johnny will have someone to look after him, but he won't be here until tomorrow morning, and meanwhile there were no servants in the place or anything."

She stood thinking, and her heavy but by no means un-handsome face was clouded.

"This morning when I arrived, Lady Carados was there doing the flowers. I didn't go in the bedroom and she sent me off to do one or two things she wanted done, and I only got back just now when you and Johnny arrived, Eve. As far as I can gather Lady Carados went in the bedroom and found this woman with a glass and a medicine bottle by her side. Then she seems to have gone out of her mind, thought it would be convenient if the body were found somewhere else, and simply decided to move it. Upon my word I never heard of such a thing—whatever next! It's all these air raids, you know, people aren't afraid of the unconventional any more."

"The row frightened her," said Carados. "The Edwardians got the fear of scandal under their skins. It was the same sort of thing as the funk the Victorians had of cholera, and we have of poison gas. It was the worst that could happen in those days, I suppose."

Eve Snow caught his eye. "Not jolly now," she said. "The stink will be considerable, Johnny. Not nice for anybody. We're not quite the gay don't-cares we used to be, are we, any of us?"

"No," he said seriously. "No, my dear, that's what I've been thinking for the last half-hour. It all looks so damn bad that it looks like a frame-up, doesn't it? Everybody knows how I feel about my job, and everybody knows about my prospective father-in-law. The old boy's been a sticky conventionalist all his life, and was having it knocked out of him. Then he goes and fights an old-fashioned sea battle in precisely the way he said sea battles ought to be fought, and its success has confirmed him in all his other opinions. He's a hundred per cent Victorian heavy father, at the moment. That's why this thing is so hopelessly damaging. Why on earth should the woman do it? After all, she had nothing very much against me."

"It looks," said Dolly Chivers, who appeared to be one of those people who have the misfortune to cross all their t's and dot all their i's, "as though she were as much against your marriage as—well, as most people are."

She flushed violently after she had spoken, and looked wildly after the careless words, and it was at this point, while the air was still tingling, that Mr. Campion, noticing his watch again, decided that the time had come.

"But, Albert, you can't." Eve was vehement, and every ounce of her lively personality went into the protest. "You can't go off and leave us all like this. What on earth shall we do?"

The tall, thin man peered through his spectacles at the group in the tiny kitchen. "My dear people," he said, "there is only one thing you can do. Take the advice of an old practitioner; go to the police; go in a body; go in a great conscience-stricken huddle of innocent, foolish persons, each bearing a powerful well-known name. Pour in on the suspicious but at heart all too human police, make no more mystery. Hide nothing. Confess to the borrowed ambulance, the body-snatching, and the takings out to lunch. Put yourselves wholeheartedly in the hands of old uncle Oates, who as far as I know is the new chief of the C.I.D., and then pray. The Press is mercifully short of space and there's bigger news about than you. As for me, I'm sorry but I'm going. For nearly four years I've been thinking of catching a train at Euston, and this is the great afternoon. I'm catching it." He paused and grinned at them. "That's about the lot, I think," he said.

There was silence for a while after he had spoken, and it was Eve who made the first comment.

"Yes, well," she said at last. "That's the voice of reason,

isn't it? All the same I wish you would stay and shepherd us through it, Albert. I mean, you are used to this sort of thing."

Mr. Campion was affronted. "Not at all," he said. "You've been reading escapist literature. This is not at all the side of the fence to which I'm accustomed. Besides," he glanced at his wrist again, "I can't," he added. "Sorry, my dears, but I can't. In fact I daren't stay another moment. Good luck, and good confessing."

"I'll take you down the stairs, guv'nor," said Lugg from the passage, but Johnny forestalled him.

"No," he said. "No, you stay here. I'll get you into your cab, Campion. Nobody move till I get back."

Mr. Campion made no objection, and as they went down together Carados laid a hand on his shoulder.

"Look here," he said, "this is an imposition on you, I know that, and I'm sorry. But meanwhile I can trust you, can't I?"

The hastening traveller cocked an eye at him.

"My dear chap," he said mildly, "at this moment my only interest on earth is to catch my train. Do what you must, of course. I've given you my advice and apart from that I have no further finger in the pie. I shouldn't do anything really silly, though, if I were you."

"Who's to tell what is silly?" said Carados slowly, and Campion glancing at him saw a curiously bewildered expression on his strong face. "I'm living in two worlds, Campion," he said suddenly. "Two utterly different worlds. I shall tell the police, of course, but I'm not sure if this is the time."

They had reached the narrow hall and Campion did not comment. He was fishing in his pocket for the key of the porter's small office which since the war was uninhabited.

"I've got some kit in here," he said. "It's heavy stuff which has been waiting for me for about eighteen months; I'd like to take it with me."

There was little time to waste and Carados went off to get a taxi. He came back almost at once, very pleased with himself. "Found one," he said. "Providential—you're in luck. Let me give you a hand. Very well, then, old boy, I can rely on you. I'll use my wits and you keep quiet."

Campion did not answer him immediately, since he was negotiating the luggage, but as the driver was settling the two crates beside his seat, he leaned out of the cab and took Johnny's proffered hand.

"You can rely on me to all reasonable lengths," he said, "but in my opinion you're up against the impossible. Too many people."

Carados nodded gloomily, but there was grimness in his bright blue eyes. "Yes," he said, "but I'm getting married the day after tomorrow, and I don't want anything to muck it up. I don't want any trouble for forty-eight hours. I say," he added suddenly in a lower voice, "who's the American, do you know?"

"I don't. The name is Evers."

"Did he come along with Sue?"

"Yes, I rather think he did."

"Oh!" For a prospective bridegroom Carados seemed only casually interested on that score. "A boy friend? I mean, someone she knows fairly well? Not an acquaintance?"

"A farewell, I think," Campion ventured. Carados opened his eyes and his mouth twisted into a grimace of self-derision.

"And then Eve and I came barging in," he said. "God! We never get any older, do we? Life's very difficult. I believe I'm mad, Campion."

He spoke very seriously. It was impossible not to be curious, but Campion had caught a glimpse of the time again.

"Now's the time to be as sane as hell, if I may say so, old boy," he said. "Good-bye, er—happy funeral. Euston, driver."

The cab started with a small explosion and as Campion picked himself out of the leathery depths and glanced out of the small window behind his head, he saw Carados going slowly back to the house. The small box of an ambulance still stood where Lugg had left it against the kerb, just outside the empty building which had once been the old Bottle Street Police Station. It looked pathetic and slightly sinister, as ambulances do.

Campion was still speculating on the exact nature of Johnny Carados's madness when he noticed that wherever the cab was taking him at the hoppety, rabbit-like speed of the London taxi in a hurry, it was not to Euston Station.

4

IN THE TAXI Campion peered out of the window at the fast darkening town. He was confused to discover that many of the familiar landmarks had vanished, to leave new squares and avenues of neatly tidied nothingness. But when he suddenly caught sight of the uniquely horrible bronze group depicting Wealth succouring Innocence squatting unscathed against the bland face of the M.O.L.E. Insurance building, in what was presumably still Sabot Lane, he knew he was going astray. He rapped on the glass and shouted:

"Not Waterloo, Taxi. Euston, my lad. Euston."

The driver took no notice whatever, and his fare was trying to slide back the connecting window when he became aware of an eye peering at him through the driving mirror. It was only one eye, and not an attractive one, but there was a shrewdness in it that was unmistakable.

Mr. Campion was both astounded and aggrieved. He had good reason to believe that all his more recent enemies were on the other side of the Channel, at least, and it seemed very unfair that some of his old ones should not have forgotten him. He noted the time again, and a futile rage possessed him. On attempting to open one of the doors he made a second discovery. Neither had any handles on the inside.

Since the situation had now become obvious, Campion took steps. He wrapped his coat round his arm, and pulling off a shoe took careful aim at the near-side window. The reinforced glass starred but did not break, and at the same moment the cab swerved sharply through an archway, jolted over the cobbles of an ancient yard, and plunged into the darkness of a building.

Campion took another swipe at the glass. This time his shoe-heel went all the way, but before he could slip his hand

26

through the hole, the door behind him was jerked open and long arms seized him round the shoulders. He hunched instinctively, making himself wide, but he knew as soon as he felt the grip tighten that the advantage was with the shape in the gloom. He braced himself against the seat, pitching his weight backward on to his adversary, and gained a moment's advantage. But the next moment the door with the broken glass was swung open, and a pad with a nauseating smell was clamped over his mouth and nose. He struggled violently, aware even in this extremity of a sensation of outrage and injustice. His last conscious thought was that he had missed his train.

He was still thinking about his train when he opened his eyes again. He was aware of pain and nausea, cold, and a light which was too bright to be borne. This last shot towards him in a long, straight blade from between two dark pillars. It hit him in the eyes, and he closed them.

Once again he remembered the train, and a sense of desolation spread over him. He had missed it. This was sunlight, the train had gone. Missed it; missed it by hours. He could have wept, he was so angry and so helpless.

Presently a new procession of pictures began to undulate through his head. These were visions which possessed all the inconsequence of nightmare. He saw Eve Snow sitting on the draining board in the kitchenette in his flat; she was looking at him with her head held on one side and a strange, tragic expression on her attractive but ridiculous face, which was meant only for comedy.

Then he saw a boy, a pleasant, stalwart boy, in the olive green of an invading army. He looked resolute but puzzled, and desperately unhappy. A second woman jostled the young soldier out of Campion's waking dream. At first she was only a vague, recumbent outline and his memory focused on small wedge shoes, grey and black, the square toes turned up like a doll's.

Through the mist he struggled to comprehend the significance of this final picture. There was something odd here, something very wrong. He ought not to have seen the soles of her shoes, he thought, unless . . .

He opened his eyes again. That was right; there was something wrong with her, very wrong. She was dead, he remembered now. Her name was Moppet somebody, and she was dead.

He stirred as the shaft of light broadened, and he saw that the twin pillars were walking towards him, stout blue pillars they were, very dignified and solid. He tried to sit up and a policeman bent over him.

"Feeling better, sir?" he enquired. "The ambulance is on its way, but the Chief said we were to wait for him."

Campion blinked at the man, and turning stiffly, looked about him. He was in a small garage, through the half-open doorway of which bright sunlight streamed. There was no car about, nor yet any sign of one. The place had been used as a storeroom for some time; there were old picture frames against the wall and a heap of electric-light fittings, and some decorative iron-work in the foreground. Between him and the door was a pile of debris, which he took some time to recognize as portions of his own luggage; its contents were strewn about the floor as if some mad Customs official had made hay there.

Campion eyed the policeman. "Did you do that?" he enquired.

"No, sir! Nothing's been touched since I found you, except that I opened your collar and propped you up. I got your name from your papers in your wallet. You've still got plenty of money there, sir; you don't seem to have been robbed. I've got a glass of water here. Will you have some?"

Campion was sitting up sipping, when once again the sunlit shaft was disturbed as a melancholy, elderly person in a flapping raincoat came striding in. There were a couple of other figures behind him, but at the entrance they dropped back, and he came on in, alone.

The Chief of the Criminal Investigation Department, Stanislaus Oates, was never a wit, nor was gaiety his province, and Campion's first impression on seeing his long face after three years' absence was that the world catastrophe had cheered the old boy up. At any rate, a faint sad smile spread over his drawn face as he recognized his friend, and his cold eyes roved over the scene of desolation.

"Hello, Campion," he said. "Got yourself a welcome home, I see."

"A pity the Police Department didn't assist in the festivities." The lean wreck in the corner spoke acidly.

"Oh, I don't know. I don't know." Oates was still glancing about him, his inquisitive eyes taking in everything. "What are you grumbling at—you've been found, haven't you?"

"Where am I?"

"Number twenty-seven, Goldhawk Mews, North One— what's left of it. This is practically the only building with a roof for a mile. Is that where you thought you were?"

"No. They put me out on the other side of London."

"Humph." Oates continued his terrier-like sniffing, and finally sat down suddenly on an upturned suitcase. He looked hard at the other man. "Well, how are you?" he enquired.

Campion told him.

"I see. Like to see the Doc?"

"No, I don't think so. I want to catch a train. Any objection?"

"Well . . ." The Chief scratched his ear with the same earnest misgiving with which Campion remembered him scratching it when a mere Superintendent. "That rather depends, don't you know. As a matter of fact, Campion, I'm supposed to be holding you. You looked in at that flat of yours yesterday, I believe."

"Yes." Campion's pale eyes narrowed. "Yes, I did."

"Ah, well, there you are, you see." The Chief's seat was low and he rubbed his knees, which were stiffening in their unusual position. "We found a corpse there, you know. A woman. She had been murdered. I'd just got the report on the P.M. when this constable 'phoned up to tell me you had been found."

Campion stared at him. In that moment it was the girl he thought of first, the pretty girl who was so young and so much in love with the man she was not going to marry. The girl with the old-fashioned father, the conscientious girl who had followed her ambulance. This was going to hit her as hard as anybody.

"Murdered? Are you sure?" he asked stupidly.

"As sure as I am that you've got to talk," said the Chief.

5

JUST FOR A moment as they came through the city Mr. Campion forgot his train. It was a moist, grey-and-yellow morning with a hint of sun behind the mist and great, round drops of moisture dripping silently from the plane trees. The river was busy and warm, and the hollow bellows from the tugs sounded sadly through the traffic's noise. The old sense of haste was there, too. The police chauffeur drove purposefully; there was work to be done, people to see, points to be raised, mystery to be unravelled; he was home again.

Oates was quiet. It is rare for a man who has begun his career as a police constable to end it as Chief of the Criminal Investigation Department, but the miracle does occur. The grey man wore his honour stoutly; if he knew he had enemies he also knew just how much they mattered, enough to make him watch his step, not enough to cramp his style.

At this moment by carrying Campion off personally he was breaking one of the prime rules of police etiquette, which is rigid and considerable, and although he did this he was careful not to question him until they were safely in the Senior Superintendent's room overlooking the glassy river.

Superintendent Yeo was waiting for them, and Campion's sense of home-coming was made acute by the sight of that square, bullet-headed man. He regarded the circular dark eyes, and the snub nose which lent the full face such a misleading air of comedy, with affection and respect. Yeo was a policeman in a thousand, but he was a policeman in soul; he was dependable, exact, conventional and tenacious, but he liked Mr. Campion and, moreover, admired him if somewhat against his will. He came forward now with genuine welcome.

"I'm glad to see you," he said, sounding as though he

meant it. "You've landed head first in something pretty hot, I'm afraid. What's he got, Mr. Oates?"

"I don't know yet." The Chief's cold eyes rested lazily on the Superintendent's face. "I thought we'd hear him together."

Yeo coloured with satisfaction, and he expanded. "That's just what I'd like," he said, "just the plain story. We can take the statement later. There's been an awkward little development, and I'll want your advice, Mr. Oates. But at the moment a straight tale would help. It's a straight case of murder and it fits in with the other matter."

He checked himself abruptly as though he had said too much, and added cheerfully:

"You look all in, Mr. Campion. Sit down over here, will you?"

"What about the Inspector in charge?" said Oates. "That's Holly, isn't it?"

"Holly's got his hands full at the moment, sir." Yeo looked uncomfortable and Oates became studiously incurious.

"Right," he said, seating himself. "Now then, Campion, no omissions and no theories. Just the straight facts."

Mr. Campion was not a fool nor had he any illusions about the true place wherein his loyalty lay. There are some crimes which are serious and murder is not the least of them. Oates was right, the time to talk had arrived.

He went through the events of the previous evening very carefully, and the others sat watching him, Oates with approval, Yeo with growing concern. From time to time they made notes and when Campion had reached the end of the kidnapping, an episode which struck him as more fantastic the more he came to consider it, the Superintendent was fidgeting.

"This is going to be very awkward," he said suddenly, "very awkward indeed."

It was an unexpected comment, and when they stared at him he turned to the Chief.

"We had the Assistant Commissioner in just after you left, Mr. Oates," he said. "He didn't want to influence you in any way, of course, but as far as I could see he was in a bit of a fix himself. It appears the Minister had phoned him to say that a lady who was a very old friend of his had come to him with a story which she felt she ought to tell the police. She appears to have acted insanely, he said, but he also said he was sure she couldn't have realized what she was doing, so he was sending her along at once with a secretary of his. Everyone is a bit hot and bothered, if you ask me."

Oates swore a little. It was not his habit and Yeo was placatory. "I know, Mr. Oates, you won't have interference, and of course you're right, but if I may say so in this case I don't think the gentlemen could have done much less for her. They both acted in a strictly proper way and they have put her into our hands. She's not the sort of person you'd expect to be mixed up in this sort of thing. It's the Dowager Lady Carados. She's not the ordinary sort of party you'd expect to be found in a Police Court."

"How true," agreed Mr. Campion fervently. "Have you had her up yet?"

"She's here now," said Yeo. "Holly's got her downstairs. She's made her statement, and the trouble is, it's not quite the same as yours, Mr. Campion. The differences are rather serious, as a matter of fact."

Oates sighed. "Oh, my Gawd, these silly old women," he said wearily.

Yeo cleared his throat. "There are two main discrepancies," he said. "In Mr. Campion's statement he records that he understood from the man Lugg that the body had come originally from Number Three, Carados Square, which is the house of the Marquess of Carados, where it had been found in the owner's bed just before he was due home on leave. However, Lady Carados deposes that it came from her own house, Number Twenty, on the other side of the square. I must say she's got it very circumstantial. She says it was in a basement room which before the war was used as a footman's sleeping quarters. There's still a bed there. In her opinion the woman was a vagrant, and as the basement door is always unlocked in the daytime and there is only one maid left who is frequently upstairs, Her Ladyship says she doesn't see that it is at all unlikely that the woman should have walked in on her own. That's her story, anyway. She's got it quite clear in her own mind, I will say that for her."

"The first vagrant I knew to have a black silk nightshirt," said Oates. "Go on."

Yeo glanced appealingly at Campion. "We mustn't forget

this first point is open to question," he said. "Mr. Campion admits that his version is based on hearsay, but this second point is more difficult. Mr. Campion has just said that Lady Carados phoned her son and that he came along, bringing Miss Evangeline Snow and his social secretary, Miss Dorothy Chivers, with him, and that between them Lord Carados and Miss Chivers identified the body as a Mrs. Moppet Lewis whom Carados said he'd not seen for five years. That's her name, certainly, but I don't see it gets us much forrader.

"Lady Carados has got this very differently," he said. "According to her, when she phoned her son he wasn't there, but she was answered by a Major Peter Onyer who used to be an adviser to Carados. According to her story it was Onyer and his wife who came round with Miss Chivers and she says that neither of them had ever seen the woman before. That's point-blank, isn't it? We shall take statements from them all, of course."

"The fools," Campion burst out helplessly. "The silly, silly fools. They don't realize it's murder."

"She does," said Yeo unexpectedly. "We told her that at once, we've been very careful."

"Then she's mad," said Campion. "You treated her with more consideration than you did me, by the way. How did this wretched woman die?"

"She was smothered," said Oates, before Yeo could speak. "She was given a strong opiate, and then when she was all out a soft cushion or pillow was held firmly over her face until she stopped breathing. Roder-Whyte did the P.M. and he's got it very clear as usual. The cause of death was suffocation and there was fluff and stuff in the larynx. Anybody might have done it."

"Anybody," echoed Yeo. "Not a lot of strength was required, you see, it just needed nerve."

Campion shivered. The homeliness of the method and the deliberation it required were very unpleasant. "When was this?" he enquired.

"According to Roder-Whyte, some time on Monday evening," said Oates. "About twenty-four hours before you saw her."

"You were on the water then, Mr. Campion." It was clear that Yeo intended the information to be reassuring and Campion grinned at him.

"Yes," he said, "that's right. It's the Coroner's pidgin and yours. Not mine, thank God. I catch my train now, don't I?"

"No." Oates spoke flatly, adding as he turned to Yeo: "I think it'll be enough if they just meet each other accidentally in the passage. Don't you? No need to make a set-out about it."

Mr. Campion objected vigorously, but without hope of success. Yeo spoke briefly to Inspector Holly on the house phone and soon afterwards they went downstairs.

The two witnesses met in the main corridor by an arrangement which had been made many times before. Campion and his two guardians turned the corner at the exact moment when Lady Carados and Chief Inspector Holly came out of a door at the far end of the alley. For some seconds the two parties advanced slowly towards each other. In spite of his discomfort, Campion was curious to see Lady Carados. He was not sure when it was that she first noticed him, afterwards he was inclined to think that recognition must have been instantaneous: She came on briskly, her carriage splendid and her head, which was still lovely, held high so that they could see her smile. It was a gracious smile, happily self-confident; the smile of a woman who knew she was at her best, there was nothing even brave about it, she looked as if she had had a satisfactory interview with a properly attentive listener.

At first Campion thought she was going to pass him without a sign, but as they neared each other she met his eyes and stopped immediately.

"Oh, it's Mr. Campion, isn't it?" she said. "My dear man, I am so glad to see you here. Now you can bear out everything I've been saying."

The tone was not quite casual, and he was not sure it did not contain a note of command. It was the last line he expected her to take and it knocked the breath out of him. He stared at her anxiously, but if she noticed the appeal she did not respond. Her smile was still friendly and contented as she passed on with Holly, tall and immaculate, striding behind her.

"That's that," said Oates, as they returned to the Superintendent's room. Yeo shut the door.

"She's got something like a nerve. I could admire a woman

like that, you know. Unless . . . ?" He paused, and glanced at the other policeman.

Mr. Campion considered them both with interest. Yeo, he noticed, was sweating a little.

"It's a possibility, of course," said the Superintendent, "but in view of everything—*everything*, Mr. Oates, I can't believe it."

The Chief returned to the bewildered Campion. "Just sit down for a moment," he said. "I want you to answer one or two questions very carefully. In your story you do not mention that you telephoned the police last night to report the discovery of the body, yet you did telephone them, didn't you?"

Mr. Campion was unprepared for this inquisitorial approach and he looked at his friend in amazement. Once again it occurred to him that something very much more than an enquiry into an ordinary murder was afoot. Clearly Oates and Yeo had some secret which they were not prepared to share at the moment.

"I did not phone at all, I went to catch my train," he said.

"Now, think, Campion." Oates was persuasive. "It was a thing you ought to have done, a thing you'd do almost instinctively. Someone phoned a local police station last night and he gave your name. That was what put us on to the whole thing. Are you sure it was not you?"

Mr. Campion became slightly amused. "I'm sorry," he said, "I thought you could do your own dirty work; I had a train to catch."

"There you are, you see." Oates persisted in his new, slightly unconvincing manner. "You're obsessed by that train. Tell me, how do you think we knew you were ever at your flat yesterday?"

"You saw it in the old police crystal," said Campion, whose sense of humour was failing him. "I don't know. Spies everywhere, I suppose."

"No. This is very important. How do you think we knew?"

"Have you forgotten little Acres, Mr. Campion?" murmured Yeo, sounding as though he thought he was cheating.

"Little Acres?" Campion was becoming annoyed and his eyes narrowed. Oates was looking at him with incomprehensible coldness.

"You've forgotten," he said. "You've forgotten you spoke to a plain-clothes man on Victoria Station yesterday. You told him where you were going. Can you remember anything about it?"

Mr. Campion began to understand, and for a moment he was very angry indeed. It was a rare emotion with him, and he kept silent. Oates went on.

"Probably you can't. It makes all the difference, Campion. I've never believed you've ever quite recovered from that business at the beginning of the war. You were working for a week in a state of amnesia. Oh, I know the Foreign Office is very pleased with your work abroad, but to my mind that other case did you a permanent injury. You do see what I'm driving at?"

The suggestion was so completely unfounded and absurd that Mr. Campion was temporarily silenced. It was true that on the last occasion on which he and Oates had worked together he had, for a short period, lost his memory, but over four years' gruelling work had not provoked a return of the trouble. It occurred to him very forcibly that something very odd indeed must be up to make Oates take this line. He smiled.

"Victoria was like a cup final," he said. "As I fought my way out I did see a little prehensile snout with a gingery quiff above it. A piping voice hailed me and asked me where I was going, and I told him home to wash. Then the waves of blue and khaki carried him away. I do admit I forgot the incident. The snouty redhead is a plain-clothes man called Acres, I take it."

Oates remained suspiciously obstinate. "All the same . . ." he began.

"All the same," agreed Mr. Campion firmly, "if you are hoping to infer that I can't tell the difference between Johnny, Marquess of Carados, and Peter Onyer, and might even when drunk, drowned, or in a coma confuse Eve Snow with Gwenda Onyer, you're just unlucky. Don't be silly, old boy. You can't muck about with the facts, I saw them."

"I don't know," said Oates desperately. "I don't know. The mind plays tricks. I've never felt the same myself since that business four years ago. I was unconscious for a week and you were out on your feet for three or more. It's no good, Campion, we can't afford to take your unsupported word for it at this juncture. I mean," he added awkwardly, "we don't want to, just at the moment."

The younger man got up with care.

"You're right. I shall go away and nurse myself," he said. "This is a job for somebody else. I can have my luggage, I suppose?"

"No, I don't want you to do that." Oates was still speaking very carefully. "I don't want you to leave London for a day or two. You can get at these people much more easily than we can."

Mr. Campion's smile became genuinely amused. "Scotland Yard employs mental defective," he suggested.

"Scotland Yard holds material witness, if not accessory after the fact," said Oates. "I tell you frankly, if this is what I think it is, it's a most unpleasant, difficult incident in one of the most extraordinary crimes I've yet met, and if this good lady is lying, as you suggest, then it's going to be very awkward."

"I think she's lying, and I think I know why," said Campion carefully. "She's lying because she doesn't know it's serious."

"She was told," Yeo repeated.

"Yes, I know. But even so, it hasn't registered. This is a woman who is absolutely sound and wide-awake in her own sphere, but murder is outside that sphere. She's never come up against anything remotely like it."

Oates sniffed. "She's got a lot of nerve and she admits moving the body. If she's lied as well, I don't see why she shouldn't have done the whole thing."

"Nor do I," agreed Campion, "except that I don't see why. Also I don't see how she could possibly have arranged my kidnapping. I don't see the point of that, either, unless she had some good reason for not making her statement before this morning, and in that case who phoned the police last night?"

"Why should your kidnapping have anything to do with the case at all?" enquired Oates. "As I see it that was something entirely fortuitous."

"That's what I think," put in Yeo, looking up. "That incident must be something separate. That's revenge; someone who had a grudge against Mr. Campion was lying in wait for

him." He cocked an eye at Campion. "You don't think so?"
he suggested.

The tall, thin figure by the chair shrugged his shoulders.
"Not a very good revenge," he observed mildly. "Why should
anyone carry a man off to one garage, put him out, and then
carry him off to another where he leaves him after strewing
his belongings all over the place? He irritates him possibly,
but he doesn't do him much harm."

"All the same, it doesn't seem reasonable to me that the
Carados Square lot could have had anything to do with it,"
Yeo persisted, "and they're the people in whom we are
primarily interested. They're all being interviewed, of course.
The first thing is to make certain where the killing took place,
and if they are all going to lie like troopers, that isn't going to
be so simple with Lugg out of the way."

Mr. Campion wheeled round. "Lugg out of the way?" he
enquired.

"Yes, I'm afraid so." Yeo was apologetic. "He seems to
have taken the ambulance back to the depot last night, fed
his pig, and then vanished. We shall pull him in eventually,
of course, but meanwhile there's just the two conflicting
statements, yours and Lady Carados's."

"Here, Campion, where are you going?" Oates demanded.

Mr. Campion, who was already in the passage, put his
head round the door again. "To find him," he said, "you
didn't tell me it was serious."

He came out into the watery sunlight in evil mood. He was
dirty and stiff from his night's adventure, exasperated with
Oates for what appeared to be an easy if ingenious temporary
way out of an admittedly awkward position, and genuinely
alarmed for Lugg. He turned out of the gateway, and was
walking along considering his next move when an elegant
khaki-clad figure dropped into step at his side. He looked
round to find Peter Onyer's narrow, dark eyes on a level with
his own. Campion was not pleased to see him; not that he
had any aversion to the man himself whom he knew but
slightly, but he had no desire to find himself running with
both hare and hounds. He had experienced that nightmare
before.

"I take it you've been waiting for me?" he said acidly.

"Oh, not very long." It was typical of Onyer to assume an

apology. "I came down with Edna Carados and a lad from the Home Office. They've gone back now with an Inspector. She said you were here, though, so I thought I'd wait and collect you."

"Decent of you," said Campion.

"Not at all. I wanted to see you." He lowered his sleek, handsome head a little. "It's a most unfortunate business; Edna's so impulsive, she's quite old, too. She doesn't understand what she can or can't do."

"She can't get away with murder," said Campion brutally, "if she's a hundred and two. She must know that."

"Murder?" Onyer stopped in his tracks, pulling Campion round to face him. There was no colour in his cheeks, and his graceful elegance dropped from him like a garment leaving the essential, intelligent core of the man exposed. It might have been the discovery that a guilty secret had been uncovered, but Campion was inclined to diagnose straight astonishment.

"Was that woman Moppet . . . ? I mean, do the police suggest . . . ? Good God, how did she die?"

Mr. Campion told him. He whistled, and as they walked on together, made a very extraordinary remark.

"I knew there would be hell to pay over this wedding," he said, adding presently, and as if he were thinking of something else, "women do do such incredible things, don't they? I think we'd better go along there at once, Campion. Do you mind?"

6

APART FROM THE fact that half the house was down, the famous eau-de-Nil drawing-room full of unexpected furniture from other rooms, and no one looked in the least bored, Mr. Campion felt that nothing very funda-

mental had changed when he and Peter Onyer walked in on
Johnny Carados's reassembled household. They were all there
except Eve, all a little older, all intensely anxious, but all
infinitely more competent to deal with any situation for being
once again together. It was a little before noon, and sherry
was in circulation.

But below the chatter the atmosphere of tension was very
noticeable. Johnny sat at the piano playing scraps of Scarlatti.
He was wearing the trousers of his uniform, but his torso was
covered by a remarkable, multi-coloured brocaded jacket,
with a quilted collar; a garment which belonged to a fashion
dead for thirty years. He sat with his chin thrust out, and his
eyes half closed. His short fingers were delicate on the notes,
but there was a surliness about him out of keeping with his
fancy dress. To all appearances he was unconscious to the rest
of the room.

In a corner on the floor and shut in by a sort of playpen of
chairs, sat Ricky Silva. His plump babyishness was encased in
the battle-dress of a private of the British Army, but his bare
feet were in sandals, and his gentle eyes were fixed on a box
of scraps of coloured silk which he was matching and contrast-
ing with earnest interest. As usual he was absorbed in himself
and completely unconscious of the picture he presented.

Gwenda Onyer, sandy and petitely graceful, like a whippet,
was talking to Captain Gold on the couch before the fire; her
fawn head was bent and she did not look up as the others
came in. Dolly Chivers, a picture of brisk usefulness, was
heartily busy with the glasses.

Onyer advanced purposefully. He was unhappy but determined, and he took the drink which Dolly thrust into his
hand without looking at it.

"I say," he said. "Just a moment, everybody. There's something I think you'd all better know."

Johnny brought his music to a sudden end.

"The Moppet was murdered," he said, "don't tell us again,
old boy. She was murdered and my dear mother can't quite
remember exactly where she found the corp. Don't repeat it,
we've got that far."

He began to play again, more vigorously this time, and
over in his corner Ricky laid a cerise ribbon across a piece of

rust-red satin and paused, his eyes half closed, to admire the clash. Onyer shrugged his shoulders and drank his sherry.

"As long as you know," he said. "We're waiting for the police, I suppose, or have they been?"

"We imagine they're on their way, Peter." Gwenda spoke quietly from the couch. She had a restrained, semi-tragic note in her voice which made Campion look at her sharply, wondering if she could possibly be enjoying the situation.

"Gwenda was at Number Twenty when Lady Carados came back with the Inspector," said Dolly, briefly making everything clear. "She found out a little of what had happened, and came back to tell us. It seems Lady Carados has altered her story a little since that A.R.P. man disappeared."

"She means well," said Captain Gold, revealing an unexpectedly deep voice for so small a man, "but then she always does."

"I say, Johnny, you must get some sense into her. It's serious, you know." Onyer's appeal was urgent and once again Carados took his hands from the piano.

"Don't be a mug, Pete," he said, lazily. "When did I ever have any control over Mother? She's decided how to save us and save us she will, no doubt. By the way, we've had other excitements. The wedding is postponed, the Admiral says so, he's full of good ideas. He's going to get everything shipshape, he and I are going to clear up the trouble, uncover the mystery, and get the whole thing straightened out. 'Pronto,' I think he said, Gwenda, didn't he?"

He turned as he spoke, and catching sight of Campion smiled with genuine welcome. "Hullo. Nice to see you, just the man we want. Got any ideas?"

"I collected him from Police Headquarters," Onyer remarked warningly.

"They picked you up, did they, Campion?" Johnny was not waiting for replies. "My poor chap, what trying friends you've got."

"Johnny dear." Gwenda's yellow eyes peered at him over the back of the couch. "Johnny, do be sensible, we don't know what to do, darling."

"If the Admiral is in this as well as your mother, we're in for hell's delight, leaving the police out of it," said Onyer seriously. "What line is he taking?"

"Action." Johnny's mouth curled, but his eyes remained gloomy. "Straight from the shoulder, go-in-and-win action. He's in the house now, you know."

" 'Strewth," said Major Onyer, "where?"

"Downstairs phoning 'someone with authority'—at the Admiralty, I suppose. He doesn't know it's murder yet. He came in just after Gwenda broke it to us and no one had the nerve to tell him. The suicide had got him down. He rushed over, postponed the marriage, leaving me here in Aunt Carados's wedding token, and is now getting his big guns on to the job. I think he'll get us all hanged. What do you think Campion?"

The thin man in the horn-rimmed spectacles sat down. He had bullied Onyer into letting him call in at his Club and was now comparatively neat and clean, but he was still weary. He looked at his host with interest.

"It's a wedding present, is it?" he enquired.

"The wrap?" Johnny jerked at the lapel of his brocaded coat. "Yes, from a thrifty aunt. Something my late uncle had by him and thought too precious to wear. I'm not sure he wasn't right."

"I should like to do a room for it," said Ricky, looking up from his corner. "Something Edwardian in green, and a rather hot red."

"Oh don't. Don't play the fool," Gwenda burst out wretchedly. "You're all so terrified you're just sitting about being silly."

"That's where you happen to be wrong, my dear girl." Ricky's full, childish lips narrowed spitefully and his soft eyes were near tears and annoyance. "I simply don't feel it's anything whatever to do with me̅, that's all."

There certainly was an irritating smugness in his voice, but no one was prepared for the irritation it produced in Gwenda.

"How dare you, Ricky," she said, leaning up on the couch, her cheeks flushing and her hair a little untidy. "You're just the same; always trying to shirk responsibilities. You who wept and howled in rage like a baby only last week because you were so afraid that when Johnny got married and the family split up there'd be no place for you any more."

"I didn't. You're a beast, Gwenda. My God, how I loathe you. I didn't. I didn't weep or—or howl." The man was on the verge of weeping now, and in any other circumstances must have made a supremely comic figure standing amid his coloured silks, every line in his plump body strained and his face crimson.

Johnny sat looking at him gloomy-eyed, but with the little muscles at the corners of his mouth twitching still.

"Oh, be quiet, Ricky," said Onyer, laughing.

"I shan't. You always take her part." His childishness was extraordinary, but there was no silencing him. "She's practically accusing me and I don't see why she should. If anybody really hated the idea of this marriage, she did, and you too, Peter. You both swore it would be the end of everything and you're both of you quite capable of staging this perfectly revolting thing to get your own way. In fact, everybody in this room is. Old Gee-gee Gold had as much to lose as anybody. Besides, what about Eve? She's been looking like death lately. If Johnny's decided to let us all down I don't see why you should decide that I was the one to do something about it."

"Ricky, shut up." Johnny spoke quietly, but there was tremendous authority in his voice.

"I shan't. I've been accused, and I shall have my way. Gwenda's always . . ."

Johnny got up and went over to him.

"I'll break your neck, Ricky," he said.

"Do," said Ricky recklessly. "You've got like everybody else since this blasted war. You're like the animals I have to spend my time with. I'm having hell, I tell you, absolute hell."

It dawned on Mr. Campion that he was probably speaking the truth. The life of a man like Ricky Silva as a conscript private in the British Army did not bear consideration. Something of the same idea had evidently occurred to Carados; he dropped his arms and his shoulders sagged a little. He looked old for his years, and weary, and once again Campion was aware of some far greater trouble than the one which appeared on the surface.

"Where are you lunching, Ricky?" said Johnny.

"I was going to old Carrie Larradine's. She's got some glorious dresses which belonged to her great-grandmother, and we were going to have them out and discuss them. She wants my advice. She promised me ages ago."

"I see. Well, would you like to go?"

Ricky looked at his wrist watch. He was trembling so violently that he could scarcely see the time, but his objection was as sulky as a child.

"I shall be fearfully early. Besides, I want to look at these scraps of mine. This is the only opportunity I have to study my own job. I don't care if you are all against me; I tell you I've got used to that. You've no idea what I have to put up with, but I've learnt to be cautious, I . . ."

"My dear chap, get out, will you?"

"All right, if you're in that mood. I think you're being very silly, Johnny. You think you can trust all these people, but you can't. Every single one of them was in London when this woman must have died. I know, because I saw them. Oh yes, I was here too, but I can prove what I was doing. They've all been on leave longer than you think."

He was moving as he talked, and the last words brought him to the doorway.

"This war's made people awfully reckless and—*coarse*," he said, and went out.

In the silence which followed his departure, Captain Gold began to laugh. He had a deep-throated chuckle like a very old dog beginning to growl.

"Poor Ricky," he said, "if this army is anything like the last he must be in purgatory."

Onyer, who appeared to feel some sort of responsibility for his Service, nodded. "Frightful," he said. "They keep him clerking, I suppose? He's a ghastly little cat, though. Gwenda and I have been in town since Friday, by the way, Johnny; I got leave earlier than I expected and we stayed at the Dorchester over the week-end. I didn't mention it because it didn't arise."

"I came up on Saturday myself," said Gold. "I'm not explaining where I've been. Does it matter?"

"And I've been here the whole time," said Dolly Chivers briskly. "I . . ." Her hearty voice ceased abruptly as the door opened. Ricky had come back. He wandered in with the studied nonchalance of the naughty child, a square parcel in his hands.

"I found this in the hall, Johnny," he said. "It's another

wedding present, I suppose. You'll have to send them all back. What a pity, isn't it?"

He spoke quite seriously and stepped back to await the unwrapping. His curiosity was so frank and innocent that Campion saw for the first time a reason why Carados had ever liked him sufficiently to allow him to live in the house. There was an honesty about his faults which was engaging.

The interruption was welcome; no one in the room was comfortable after his little confession, and Johnny plucked at the knots with nervous relief.

"Oh cut it," said Ricky, drawing a little penknife from his blouse. "I'll do it, shall I?"

As he watched the operation Mr. Campion was struck by something unexpected about the box and its wrapping, but he did not identify the impression immediately. Carados pulled off the brown paper, lifted the lid of the stout cardboard box within, and turned its contents on to the table.

"Mainly paper," he said, and paused. Something in the rigidity of his pose caught the general attention. As they watched the angry colour poured into his face. "What the hell's the meaning of this?" he said furiously.

Lying amid the crumpled tissue was a battered, artificial rose around the stem of which was wound a string of unconvincing pearls. It was a curious trophy, possibly in bad taste, but by far the most interesting thing about it was its effect upon Johnny Carados. The man was outraged, he was so angry that it occurred to Campion that he must be also startled.

"What a damn silly trick, Ricky," he said. "Who put you up to it?"

"Me? I haven't done anything. I only saw it in the hall and brought it in to you."

There was no mistaking the genuineness of the squeal of protest and Carados turned from him impatiently.

"Where did it come from?" he demanded. He was in command of himself again, but his eyes were wary and there was no longer any hint of a smile on his mouth. They all looked at him blankly. The Onyers appeared puzzled, Gold uncomfortable, and Dolly Chivers slightly amused.

"I found it in the hall," Ricky repeated.

Carados turned to Onyer. "Was it there when you came in?"

"I really don't remember, do you, Campion?"

"I didn't notice it. It may have been."

"Well, where did it come from?" Carados had raised his voice and for the first time he seemed aware of the unexpectedness of his own reaction. "I'd like to know," he said more normally. "Do you make anything of it, Campion?"

The man in the horn-rimmed spectacles turned over the wrapping. "It's old stuff," he said, "that's what struck me when Silva brought it in. It's a Welby & Smith parcel, the sort of thing they sent out before the war. There's no packing like this these days. This is out of someone's junk cupboard, I should think."

"I believe I've seen that rose before," said Gwenda. "I don't know why you're getting so excited, Johnny. Isn't it out of the dressing-up box, Dolly?"

"Yes, of course it is." Miss Chivers smiled to find a prosaic explanation. "There's any amount of rubbish in there, and the brown paper's kept there too. It's probably some sort of joke."

The big man took up the dilapidated yellow flower, and carried it over to Gwenda. "Are you sure you recognize it?" he said. "Come here, Dolly. Has this been in the house before?"

The two women glanced at each other.

"I think so," said Miss Chivers at last. "I'll go and look in a minute; there may be some more like it. We had a lot of this sort of thing for the musical comedy party in 'thirty-eight. Do you remember? I don't see the point of it though. Does it matter?"

Johnny hesitated. "It matters quite a bit if it came from outside," he said. "If it came from inside—well, I'm not particularly amused."

The threat was unmistakable, and once again they all looked at him. In the silence the door burst open, and Admiral Dickon came in.

7

UNTIL THAT MOMENT, Mr. Campion had stupidly supposed all great sailors to be uniformly small men, square and irascible, with shining skins and sky-blue eyes. The Admiral was a disappointment to him. Susan's father was a vast, red Drake of a man, with a head like a Saint Bernard and the same dog's air of rigidly controlled energy. Everything about him was large and the glance he gave the room was comprehensive and sweeping. Carados, who was a powerful figure himself, looked small beside him.

"I've got him," said the Admiral. "We're having lunch with him at the Saladin Club. I don't know if he can do much, but we've hooked him anyway."

He was clearly pleased, and stood waiting, expecting no doubt the lunching party to set out forthwith.

Meanwhile, Johnny was looking at Onyer and a silent argument was taking place between them. Finally Johnny shrugged his shoulders.

"Wait a bit, sir," he said slowly. "I'm afraid there's been a development. The unfortunate woman was murdered; at least, that seems to be the police idea."

The Admiral looked down at him for some time.

"Oh," he said.

An uncomfortable silence followed, during which it seemed to Campion that the full seriousness of the situation came home at last to everyone. Hitherto the little company had been considering its own personal positions, but this exuberant giant was essentially a normal man with normal reactions, and they saw the story for an instant as it must appear in his eyes. A woman had been killed, the unforgivable crime committed; somebody was going to be hanged.

"It puts a rather different colour on the tale," he said at last.

47

"I'm afraid so," Carados agreed.

His hands were behind his back and he twirled the battered yellow rose between his fingers.

The Admiral squared his shoulders. "Well, we've got to see the thing through, don't you know," he said. "This feller I've got hold of can only put a little gunpowder behind the police, and wake 'em up and spur 'em on. A thing like this mustn't be allowed to stand about. We want it cleared up and put right, and the criminal punished. That's a job for the police. This man can put them on their toes and keep them there. We'd better go and see him."

Mr. Campion thought of Oates and Superintendent Yeo, and sighed for them, and it occurred to him that if Yeo and the Admiral ever met on equal terms, which now seemed unlikely, they would certainly take an enormous fancy to each other. Meanwhile the old man was continuing.

"All the same," he was saying, "it's up to us to play scrupulously fair with this feller, naturally, so I'm going to ask you a direct question, Carados. I won't put it to you here, perhaps you'll come in another room with me."

There was nothing subtle about the Admiral; his meaning was obvious, and in that sophisticated company his naïveté and directness struck a slightly alarming note. Johnny appeared amazed.

"I didn't kill her, if that's what you're after, sir," he said.

The Admiral, who was already advancing upon the doorway, swung round again.

"That's what I wanted to know, and it's the answer I expected, my boy," he said. "You can give me your word on it, can you? It's all I want."

"I give you my word I did not kill her," repeated Johnny, looking as if he felt profoundly foolish.

"Good enough," said the Admiral. "Just one more thing. Do you know who did? No need to give names."

Johnny hesitated. It was the slightest pause imaginable, but it did occur.

"No," he said, a little too quickly. "No, I have no idea."

"On your word?"

"Yes. Yes, of course. On my word."

"Splendid. Well, if you'll change, we'll go."

The tension had slackened a little, but it was still in exis-

tence and the gathering split into little groups. Johnny went
off to get his tunic, and the Admiral, who, it transpired, had
known Mr. Campion's father, was graciously disposed to congratulate him both on that fact and on his recent work abroad.
The Onyers were talking together anxiously, and as soon as
Carados returned Gwenda appealed to him.

"Johnny, what about Edna and the police? Won't they be
coming here? I mean, oughtn't we to wait?"

Carados looked harassed.

"My mother was very definite when I saw her," he said.
"She never has liked interference, and if the police want us, I
imagine they'll find us."

"Good Lord, yes. We can't wait about for the police." The
Admiral was amused. "If they're not smartly on to their duty
now I think you'll find they'll pipe a different tune after this
evening. Come along, Carados, we can't keep this man
waiting."

"You see no reason why Gwenda and I shouldn't keep our
luncheon engagement?" said Onyer, following the warriors
into the hall. Apparently they reassured him, for he came
back relieved on that point, but still dubious. "I suppose
Johnny knows what he's doing," he observed to the room in
general. "He says carry on in a perfectly normal way. Perhaps
we ought to go over and see Edna first, Gwenda. What do
you say?"

"My dear, we must. I know she doesn't like interference,
but you know what she is. She may do anything."

"We'll go then," said Onyer, and glanced at Mr. Campion,
whose presence had become a responsibility to him. "I feel I
got you here on false pretences," he said uncomfortably, "I
didn't know they knew about it being so serious. Honestly, I
don't like the look of things now, do you? That old boy means
well, and will certainly stir up the police, but do we really
want that?"

He looked so serious that Campion smiled. "It will add to
the excitement," he suggested.

"I know." Onyer's gloom increased. "Not that anyone here
has much to fear, naturally, unless . . . Look here, Campion,
I don't know much about these things, but isn't there a very
good charge against Edna already? I mean, you can't go moving
bodies about like that, can you?"

"It could be thought over-enthusiastic," said Mr. Campion.

"You don't think they might have arrested her already?"

"My dear chap, don't ask me."

"Good heavens." Onyer was visibly paler. "What a hell of a family this is to look after," he said bitterly. "I'd better go over right away. You—er—you won't feel like coming, will you?"

As an invitation it was not pressing, and Mr. Campion declined gracefully. Ricky and Captain Gold had disappeared, and when the Onyers went off together he found himself alone with Miss Chivers, who was busy with a telephone directory.

"It's all got to be cancelled, you see," she said. "Would you believe it? I've been working on this wedding for three weeks and now I've got to undo everything at speed. Peter Onyer's right, it's a hell of a family to look after."

It was clear that she was very busy, but Campion did not move. He sat for a time watching her jot down telephone numbers, her big, well-modelled head bent over her work.

"Did that rose come from the house?" he enquired suddenly.

She closed the book, and looked at him across the small table at which she was working.

"The rose?" she repeated vaguely. "Oh, *that*. My dear man, don't take any notice of that. That's nothing."

"I thought it odd," said Mr. Campion.

"Did you?" She was laughing. "Hang around here for a bit, and you'll see odder things than that."

He did not move, and presently she seemed to take pity on him. Her broad, open face was alight with amusement.

"They're all cuckoo, always have been," she said indulgently. "Of course the rose came from the junk cupboard downstairs; Gwenda sent it, I should think."

"Mrs. Onyer? Why?"

"I don't know. Why does anyone do anything in this outfit? Perhaps she didn't. Perhaps she put Ricky up to it, or perhaps he thought it out himself. They're like that, don't take any notice of them. It didn't mean a thing."

Still he sat looking at her. She was so strong and intelligent-looking that her statements carried conviction in spite of their unexpectedness.

"It didn't look like a joke," he objected after a pause.

"Perhaps it wasn't one," said Dolly Chivers dryly.

"What would you say it was?" he persisted.

"I? I shouldn't mention it or even notice it." She glanced down at her work and then back at him, her fine, hard eyes suddenly determined. "You don't understand at all, do you?" she said, with a vehemence which surprised him. "I don't know if I can explain, or even if I ought to, but you can take it from me that when you get a clever, hypersensitive crowd like this all living together round one big personality, little jealousies and little affections do take on enormous proportions. No one liked Johnny marrying, you know. For some of them it must have seemed like the end of the world."

"Especially for Mrs. Onyer?"

"Yes, I suppose it hit her as much as anybody. She was always the mistress of the house here, you see."

"You think she sent the parcel?"

"I don't know anything about it, my dear," said Miss Chivers cheerfully. "All I say is, she probably did, and that therefore it meant exactly nothing. She stayed here last night and could have done it, but then Ricky's been prowling round the place since dawn, and Gee-gee Gold and I have had the same opportunity. Any of us might have done it, and it doesn't matter. I've told you, they're all nuts. They're always playing little dramatic tricks on each other. Let's hope they stick to roses."

"It must have meant something to Johnny."

"Probably it did," said Miss Chivers. "Possibly it reminded him of something nice and sentimental. Don't worry about it, leave that to him. Things like that happened every half-hour in the old days. Now, if you'll forgive me, I must get on. How does one address a bishop in a telegram?"

"You blow the extra pence," said Mr. Campion, "otherwise it goes to the Borough Council."

He waved her good-bye and went from the room and down the staircase, intending to let himself out. Since no one else appeared anxious to wait for the police he saw no earthly reason why he should. He was crossing the hall when a door on his right opened suddenly, and Susan Shering, looking prettier and if possible younger, peered out at him.

"Oh I'm sorry," she said. "I thought it might be my father. Has he gone?"

Mr. Campion paused. "I'm afraid he has," he said. "He went out with Johnny about fifteen minutes ago. They were going to lunch, I think."

"Oh, and he told me to wait in here for him. I suppose he forgot." She sounded more sad than surprised and Mr. Campion's respect for the Admiral increased. This was one way of managing women, of course; all the same, as a bride she was about the most forlorn and harassed person he had ever seen. He was feeling on the forlorn side himself.

"We're playthings of fate," he said. "Let's go and eat it off."

She hesitated. "I suppose you want to know where Lugg is?" she said. "I don't know, honestly I don't."

"I didn't think you did," he protested. "My mind was on food. We both seem a little redundant here, and neither of us has been fed. Let's see to that first. We should keep up our strength, we may need it. Where do people get food these days? I've been out of the country long enough for every restaurant I knew to get itself devastated, and for every chef in whom I had faith to get himself interned. Where shall we go?"

"I've been going to the Minoan lately," she said.

"The Minoan? I hope that doesn't meant aunties in white gym tunics?"

"No. It's nothing like that. It's in Frith Street."

"Oh," murmured Mr. Campion so darkly that for the first time she laughed, and he saw what she looked like when her eyes were dancing.

"It's awfully old-fashioned to be knowledgeable about food, except where to get some," she said. "Stavros has the best food in London at the moment, and very nearly the most, I should think."

Mr. Campion woke up. "Stavros? He's still about, is he? Good. Clever girl, how did you find him?"

"I went there to meet Eve Snow," said Susan unexpectedly, "and I've been there once or twice with Lieutenant Evers. That's where Miss Snow introduced us," she added naïvely, and blushed all over her face.

It was not until they were crossing the square to hunt for a taxi that he ventured to put the question.

"Known Miss Snow long?" he enquired.

"Not very," she admitted. "I like her, though, don't you? I

didn't realize she knew Johnny so well. I was astounded to see them come in together yesterday, and anyway I was too frightened and upset to welcome her, or anything. I'm afraid I behaved badly all round; I was so frightened. Lady Carados terrifies me to begin with, and then, then . . . I say, is there going to be a frightful row?"

"Not before lunch," said Mr. Campion. "Forget it. I'm trying to. You haven't known our Eve very long then. How did you meet her?"

"Through Gwenda, that's Mrs. Onyer, you know. Peter Onyer's a great friend of Johnny's and I met them both as soon as the engagement was announced. Gwenda said I must meet Miss Snow and she fixed it. Then Miss Snow introduced me to Don, I mean Lieutenant Evers."

"Gwenda put you on to Eve?"

"Yes. Everybody's been so terribly kind to me, that's why everything is so—so awful."

"Well, well," said Mr. Campion.

8

MR. CAMPION GLANCED round the Minoan Restaurant with interest. It was his first introduction to the era of elegant make-do. The glossy white walls, and the green-tinted table-linen were pleasant enough, but here was improvised grandeur, temporary tastefulness. In its not very distant past before Philip Stavros had transformed it, the building had been a pull-up for carmen, and even now the floors had a worn griminess and the woodwork a disgruntled air. However, the clientele, despite their uniforms and their new gravity, were recognizable. They sat taking their food seriously, and their wine with nostalgic sadness.

Stavros himself was standing near the doorway, and he came forward as the two appeared. He had altered considerably since Campion had last seen him, his famous stomach was now a mere drapery, and the dark smudges over his eyes were tinged with white, but he still walked with a roll and his manner was impressive as ever.

"For my friends, the lobster pilaf," he murmured, looking furtively about him as if he were imparting a state secret. "I bring you something to drink with it. Over there, behind the arch—a little table, kept for you."

It was his old approach to the unexpected guest for whom by some miracle there was yet room, and Campion, who had heard it many times before in the far-off days, was still amused.

"Of course I'm in disguise," he murmured foolishly.

The Greek raised his head sharply to look at him.

"But of course," he agreed smoothly, and then smiled suddenly, disclosing a whole treasure trove of gold and ivory. "Ah, now I know you," he said disarmingly. "Mr. Campion, how are you? Are you all right? I thought you were killed. Oh, my friend, my friend, the chaos, the disaster—we don't think of it."

"That's one way," observed Mr. Campion cheerfully. "How are you?"

"Terrible," said Stavros, with unexpected honesty. "My life has become catastrophic. Since this morning. I come and tell you about it later, maybe."

He sounded as if he meant it, and his small brown eyes with the yellow whites were naïve.

"How horrible," murmured Campion, as he manoeuvred Susan into a small, gilded kitchen chair. "Either I've grown a sympathetic face, or everyone I meet is having hell. An old lady with no manners cursed me in Beirut. Do you think I may have taken her too lightly?"

Even while he was speaking he realized the flippancy was misplaced. She shivered a little as she looked around. He watched her helplessly.

"What's up?" he demanded. "Memories, and all that?"

She blushed, and he saw to his horror that there were tears in her eyes, but she was game and nicely brought up, and her remark was formal.

"I've got a cold," she said. "It's very good of you to feed me like this."

"Not at all," he said gravely. "I only hope it cures it and that I don't catch it. Do we get real food? I see old Theo Bush over there; if he's drinking coloured water he's doing it very stoically. Study Theo, by the way, you may never see his like again. He's the greatest authority on the unfortified wines in the world, or was. Some old Hun with greater facilities may have caught up with him now, of course."

Susan glanced across the room obediently. "That rathe grim old man with the hideous child?"

"Child?"

"The girl about sixteen—white with spots."

Mr. Campion stared and was shocked. "Good heavens," he said. "I missed her. That must be Hebe, his niece—she sprang fully armed from a champagne bottle, I believe. We used to hear a great deal about her at one time; her parents were going to bring her up to have the perfect palate. I'm afraid the war must have ditched that. She was to have gone on a serious drinking tour of the world at fourteen, as far as I remember. Something like that."

He paused to watch his companion. She was not listening to him. Her young face was tragic, her eyes dark.

"I say," he said suddenly, "why on earth don't you cut the whole thing and go and tell Johnny? He's a good chap and really wasn't born yesterday. People have fallen out of love before, you know."

She raised her eyes and gave him the annihilating stare of the very young and very honest.

"You don't understand," she said. "You mean so well, but you don't understand at all."

Mr. Campion regarded her with his head on one side. "I've *been* young, though," he said at last, defensively.

For a moment he thought she was going to query it, but she was not as young as that and she smiled at him.

"It's not so easy for us now," she said, "there are so many different worlds, you see. We each have to live in two or three."

It was an echo of the remark Johnny had made when he had gone to find the taxi, and Campion remembered it with interest. "I'm living in two different worlds," he had said, "two utterly different worlds."

Susan was watching his expression across the table and her own face became very earnest.

"You think Don and I were saying good-bye yesterday, don't you?" she demanded.

It was exactly what he had thought and he felt it unfair to deny it.

"I know you did," she agreed, as he nodded, "but we weren't. We'd just decided we couldn't. That's why all this mess is even worse than it looks."

Campion sat looking at her. "You feel it unfair to announce your intention of jilting Johnny just when he appears to have become involved in a scandal," he said. "Well, that's all right by me. We used to get ideas like that in the twenties, and then someone set a fashion for passion being trumps and all was fair in love as well as war. It's turned the circle again now, has it?"

"It's got practical now," said the girl, "like everything else. You don't see the situation at all. In the first place I don't think Johnny's ever been in love with me, but I didn't know I'd never been in love with him until . . ." She hesitated.

"Until you did fall in love with someone else," said Campion. "Go on, I'm keeping up with you here and there."

"Yes. Well, there it is," she said. "I was going to explain it all to Johnny and he'd have got us both out of it. It wouldn't have been easy, but he'd have done it. Now it's going to look as if this beastly suicide is the cause of it, and it's going to be impossible."

Campion noticed that she still said suicide, but put that on one side. He was wondering how to put the question which had come into his mind, when she answered it.

"I think Johnny decided to marry me when my husband was killed," she said gravely. "You knew I'd been married before, didn't you? I knew Tom exactly six weeks. Five days after we were married he was killed. It's all part of the different world I was telling you about. Tom was one of Johnny's pilots and he asked Johnny to look after me. When he was killed, Johnny did. It sounds very young and peculiar in this sort of atmosphere, I know, but it wouldn't on an R.A.F. station, you know."

Mr. Campion looked up; the rare experience of surprise had come to him and he began to treat her confidences with a new respect. Of course she was right. A world in which everyone was young and everyone might die tomorrow was not the same world as the one mirrored in Stavros's new white paint. Johnny Carados belonged to both. It appeared to Mr. Campion that that fact might well account for quite a lot.

Susan smiled at him faintly, almost kindly, and he realized that for all her youth she probably knew more about the Great Absurdities than he did.

"Johnny is a hero, both there and here," she said. "Now do you understand?"

He nodded. "If Tom's girl gives the old man the bird because some damned tart wrote herself off on his doorstep, certain people will take a dim view, and they matter," he suggested.

"Yes," she said. "They matter terribly. That's it. But if Johnny had decided to pass the girl to some lad of whom he could approve, that would have been oke. No one in his home world liked him marrying me, they're quite as insular and all-for-one and one-for-all as Tom's crowd are. I realized that as soon as I saw them. I think Johnny saw it too as soon as he got back amongst them. That's the nicest thing about Johnny, he does so belong wherever he is."

He sat looking at her and thinking how right she was. Two different worlds, two utterly different worlds. Susan interrupted his reflections.

"I think that man you were talking about is coming over," she said. "He keeps looking at you."

"Theo Bush?" Campion turned his head to nod to the man who was waiting for his bill. "Yes, it looks like it," he agreed. "Let me see. His Temple got shaken up in the Blitz, didn't it? He was the moving spirit in the Museum of Wine, you know. Secretary Curator, and High Priest generally."

"Really?" She was politely interested. "Wasn't that the thing Johnny was mixed up in? It was all a bit precious, wasn't it?"

"Don't you believe it," said Mr. Campion feelingly. "The Museum of Wine was one of the more beautiful thoughts of the period you will always be told you were so lucky to have missed, and which you'll always regret never having seen. Johnny financed most of it and started it really with his father's wonderful collection of antique drinking vessels. In

fact, it was that collection which gave Theo the idea. He
found a little house in Jockey's Fields, near Barnabas the
publishers, and got himself put in charge." He shook his head
reminiscently. "It was a fascinating place; I went to the
opening. I hope it still exists."

Susan frowned. She was making a gallant effort to take a
proper interest.

"I'm afraid something did happen to it," she said. "I can't
quite remember what. Some cad drank it, perhaps. But it
was all books and cups and jewelled flasks and things, wasn't
it? There wasn't any actual wine there, was there?"

"No wine? My dear girl!" Mr. Campion was mildly
scandalized. "It was one of our most brilliant rules that certain approved connoisseurs, all subscribers of course, were
allowed to mature small quantities of their rarest vintages in
our ideal cellars under Theo's pontifical eye. No one was
permitted to take anything away, of course, until Theo pronounced it at its zenith, and at that psychological moment out
it had to go and Theo would come and help you drink it, if
pressed." He laughed. "Perhaps it was a bit precious and
luxurious by modern standards, but it was very nice old gentlemanly fun at the time."

"I bet it was," she said. "Did you keep anything there?"

"I think my heirloom half-bottle of Grandfather's Dream
was being used as a door-stop in one of the less sanctified
corridors," said Mr. Campion modestly. "I hope Theo isn't
coming over here to tell me he's lost it. Come to think of it,
he has that look, hasn't he?"

There was a small upheaval behind them, and Theodore
Bush came by. On his feet he appeared a smaller man than
he had done when sitting, but his presence was still impressive.
He had the head of a Victorian statesman and the skin of his
face was loose, giving him a structural appearance round the
skull, and much superfluous drapery about the chin; but his
eyes were bright and very intelligent and he had a way not so
much of smiling as of hinting that he was about to smile
which lent his face a pleasant uncertainty.

"I see you are back, Campion," he said, rather as if he
were imparting an interesting fact. "That's good, don't you
know, that's very good."

Mr. Campion made the prescribed happy noise, and the

older man nodded at him. "I shall hope to see something of you," he went on. "You heard about my little tragedy?"

"I was just wondering. Was the Museum destroyed?"

"Destroyed? Oh no." Bush brushed his wide-brimmed, black hat against the skirts of his enormous brown tweed overcoat. "No, nothing entirely catastrophic. We evacuated, you know. Unfortunately we left it rather late and were actually moving out in the very midst of the second of the big raids. Everything escaped except—"

"My half-bottle," murmured Mr. Campion.

Bush reproved him with a glance. "I saw no humour in it," he said coldly. "A whole lorry-load of utterly irreplaceable stuff was utterly destroyed. All those things in the cabinet under the south window in the big room went, all the Russian flasks, intrinsically some of the most valuable stuff in the whole collection; and there were ten cases of beautiful glass including all the modern Swedish exhibits."

"Any wine?"

"A little." Theo's small eyes rested for a moment on Mr. Campion's face. "A very little. One small parcel was put on at the last moment to make up the load. It was not entirely without interest, though, I'm afraid; it belonged to the Bishop of Devizes."

"My uncle," said Mr. Campion piously. "Good heavens."

"Oh, not the port, not the port, my dear fellow." Theo was reassuring. "That's safe. At the beginning of the war I made him take it home. Some of those cellars at the Palace are quite excellent; I told him so. Let me see, you're the only nephew now, aren't you? That sister of yours . . . ?"

"The port descends in the male line," said Mr. Campion so seriously that Susan was misled. Bush laughed.

"I have devoted my life to wine," he said, "and to me it is important and always will be. I shall hope to see you, Campion."

The faint emphasis on the final pronouncement made it sound like a command, and as he passed on, his coat brushing the tables on either side, Mr. Campion sat looking after him in astonishment, for as they had shaken hands a slip of paper had passed into his palm. He read the message now, under cover of the tablecloth. It was written on a leaf from a pocket diary and was brief and extraordinary:

"*I may need your help in near future. Stand by. Theodore Bush.*"

As a gesture it was so unlike the man as he remembered him that Campion blinked. He was still looking at the note when Susan spoke.

"Is he always like that?" she enquired. "Always portentous and mysterious?"

"Portentous, yes; mysterious, no," said Campion, rolling the message into a pill. "Dear me, what a jolly place this is. Do you come here much?"

"No, I don't, I'm afraid. Very seldom. I told you, Miss Snow introduced me to Don here; I believe she uses it a great deal, but she's not here today."

"Miss Evangeline Snow, miss?" The ancient waiter, whom Stavros had enticed from some country town hotel, cut into the conversation with the happy provincialism of his kind. "No, she's not here today, and I haven't seen her since the day before yesterday. She's often here, you know."

"That's nice for you," said Mr. Campion.

"Yes, it is, sir." The bleary eyes brightened. "She's very nice indeed. Such a *good* lady, if you know what I mean. She always comes to one of my tables. Last time I saw her here was on Sunday, dining over there with Lord Carados."

"With Johnny? But that's impossible. He didn't come home on leave until yesterday." Susan spoke involuntarily, and the old man's hand shook as he set down her plate.

"That's right, miss. I made a mistake," he said easily. "Now I come to think of it, it wasn't Lord Carados, it was another gentleman. It's very difficult to tell people in uniform, you know."

He wavered off, nervously, leaving an air of apology behind him.

"Wonderful to live to that age and still be indiscreet," observed Mr. Campion, glancing after him. "His life must have been one long fall downstairs, and still going strong, I see."

"But how extraordinary." Susan was unusually pale. "Johnny couldn't have been in London on Sunday night; that was the night that woman must have—died."

"Forget it," said Mr. Campion firmly. "Look, Susan, this is the first food I've had since I got home. So far we've had some lovely horse, and this looks like beautiful rice shape with raw medlars. Let's eat it, and forget our own and other people's troubles just for half an hour, shall we?"

Susan smiled. "Grand girl," said Mr. Campion, and raised his glass. He put it down again untasted, however; advancing down the room towards him, with a purposeful nonchalance which stamped "police" all over him, was Superintendent Yeo.

On the whole, Mr. Campion went quietly.

"I won't keep him a moment, miss," said Yeo to Susan. "I only want a word with him. I'll send him back in no time. Sorry, I'm sure, Mr. Campion."

"Gestapo!" said Campion, as they entered the passage behind the service door.

"No need to be abusive," said the Superintendent mildly. "You're going to be very interested in half a moment."

"That's nice," said Mr. Campion. "What'll you bet?"

Yeo did not reply immediately. He led the way to a small office whose single window looked over the yard behind the restaurant. It was deserted, but excitable sounds reached them faintly from an inner room.

"We've identified the body, sir." Yeo was wagging an imaginary tail. "Her name was Moppet Lewis once, but when she died she was Mrs. Philip Stavros, the wife of one of the partners of this restaurant. He says he hasn't seen much of her lately and he seems straight about it. But will you look out there, sir?"

Mr. Campion glanced out of the window and saw, in the yard, a uniformed constable keeping guard over an ancient taxi-cab. The near-side window had a hole through it, just such a hole might have been made in reinforced glass by the heel of a shoe.

"The handles have been filed off on the inside of the doors," remarked the Superintendent. "It makes you think, doesn't it?"

9

THE YARD WAS as gloomy and dirty as only a London crevice can be. It was both cold and unsavoury, homely and uninviting. As Mr. Campion climbed out of the taxi-cab after making an exhaustive examination, there was a hint of rain falling. Yeo's red face glistened above his magnificent overcoat.

"What hope?" he enquired.

"Of identifying it? Not a glimmer. Not in the witness-box. I had my little dust-up in the dark, you see. Besides, this damned thing looks like every cab there ever was; it's been cleaned, too, so there's not a hope of real proof. The suspicion is tremendous, of course."

Yeo sighed. "Suspicion doesn't count," he said. "Pity you can't remember something definite. Still, I don't blame you, you can't be too careful. I don't see where it fits in either; you said there was a connection between the two crimes and I admit it begins to look like it, but I don't see that helps us, it just makes it more difficult to my mind."

Mr. Campion turned up his coat collar. "What's their story?" he enquired.

"The restaurant's? Oh, they say they're minding the cab for a lad on active service. We can check that, but it's probably true."

The Superintendent began to move back to the house as he spoke. "They say it hasn't been out for a year," he went on, "and it's not licensed. So if it was on the road yesterday, the driver was taking a big risk."

"That's rather the kind of driver we're looking for," observed Mr. Campion as he followed him towards the house.

"Exactly," said Yeo irritably. "And so what? I tell you, Campion, I've had this case exactly twelve hours, and I'm tired of it; I've held this kind of baby before. It's going to be unlucky for policemen, I can smell it."

Recollecting the Admiral, Mr. Campion thought there well might be something in the prophecy, but tactfully forbore to say so, and the Superintendent went on. "Now we'll see Stavros," he said. "He'll have to identify the deceased formally this afternoon. We didn't realize there was a husband about at first, so we got her char to come along to the mortuary. That won't do, though, we must get the whole thing in order. There's a great deal to do and no daylight anywhere. Holly's with him now; a good officer, Holly, but hard, very hard, not like a London policeman, really."

All the time he was talking he was edging his companion towards the side door, and Campion, becoming aware of the manoeuvre, stopped abruptly.

"Do you need me?" he said.

"Yes, my lad, I do." Yeo took his arm. "You weren't surprised when I told you the dead woman was Stavros's wife. Why was that?"

Mr. Campion's pale eyes widened. "I hope you realize that I was safely on the high seas," he began.

"Yes, I do. And don't keep talking about it or I shall feel I've got to verify it. No, you're not a suspect, but you're friendly with people who may be. Also, you're missing your first home leave for three or four years, and once you've made certain your shady old chum, Lugg, is safely above ground, I shouldn't be at all surprised if you happened to forget any details which might keep you in London as a witness. That's how we stand, Campion. Have I made myself clear?"

"Horribly," said his companion. "It may surprise you to learn, Yeo, that you remind me vividly of my dear mother. She used to see things with the same clarity, and say them too, which is more serious."

The Superintendent grunted. "I don't feel like anybody's mother," he said. "How did you happen to be here, anyway? I don't have to have a suspicious nature to notice that, I suppose."

"I came here to eat," said Campion with dignity, "and I'm still hoping to do it. I met Mrs. Shering at the Caradoses' house and she brought me here because she often eats here, as do others of her circle. That is why I was here, and also why I was not surprised to learn the dead woman came from the place either. Until you told me that I could not imagine how the crowd who seem so determined to make a mystery of her death could ever have met her alive. When you came out with your little piece, I saw how it had happened, and therefore I was not surprised. Now, are you satisfied?"

Yeo sniffed. "You've covered yourself," he said maddeningly, "but you don't help. We got on to her through a laundry mark on her nightdress; our chap who specializes on them traced it to a firm in Notting Hill, and they gave us her address. The char did the rest. She didn't live with her husband, you see."

"She didn't live with Stavros? Didn't live here?" Mr. Campion, who was being forced up a narrow flight of stairs, paused in astonishment, and the Superintendent came up with his shoulder.

"That's right," he said. "She didn't live here. And if you can believe her husband's story she hasn't come here very often. She lived alone in a little art and crafty flat in Kensington High Street."

"When did they marry?"

"Beginning of the war. She was a widow then. The man Lewis appears to have been dead for years. According to Stavros he and she never did live together for more than a fortnight, yet he insists he was very fond of her."

Yeo was panting a little over the stairs, and had lowered his voice to an angry mumble. "You come and see him," he said. "He sounds almost on the level, which doesn't help, I tell you, Campion. I don't like the people in this case."

"Which people? Stavros, or Lady Carados and family?"

"All of them. They're all"—the Superintendent hesitated over the word—"they're all expense-and-talk-over-your-head," he said at last. "Class, that's what it is. It's all right in its proper place, no doubt."

"Where's that?" enquired Mr. Campion, side-tracked.

"On the stage," said Yeo stoutly. "I like it better than anywhere on the stage. But when I meet it in my business it gets round my feet. You come and hear this chap. He thinks he means something in a high-class foreign way, I don't doubt, but I can't say I follow him."

Mr. Campion gave up thinking about his meal, and did what he was told.

They found Stavros standing by a circular table in a small, dark room which was sometimes used for private dinner parties. A constable sat at the table taking notes, while Chief Inspector Holly stood on the hearthrug looking very neat and spare; his black hair receded sleekly from a pallid forehead that shone like china, and his eyes, which were remarkable for their coldness, looked large and blue and hard. On catching sight of Stavros, Mr. Campion's first impression was that he had changed, and only afterwards it occurred to him that he had become a private person. At the moment he had an entirely new dignity and a different courtesy in which there was nothing ingratiating; he stood easily, but quite still with his hands folded, and his head raised a little. His eyes flickered as Campion came in, but he did not speak.

Holly stepped across the room to meet Yeo. "He has nothing to add," he murmured, lowering his voice a tone or two, but making no real attempt to speak in confidence, "his story remains. The last time he saw the deceased was on Sunday when she looked in on him for ten minutes or so in the afternoon for a chat and a sherry. When she left, she did not tell him where she was going. He says he did not ask her."

Yeo turned and looked at Stavros with gloomy speculation. "Don't you want to add anything to that?" he said. "Nothing at all?"

The Greek grimaced nervously at Campion. "It is never easy to explain one's exact relations with a woman, is it?" he said.

Yeo's homely face cleared hopefully. "We're all men of the world here, Mr. Stavros," he said heartily, his fatherliness marred only by a gleam of policemanly embarrassment. "You won't find us narrow-minded. You just say what you want to."

Stavros coloured under his dark skin, and Campion felt profoundly sorry for him. "I loved my wife," said the man with an effort, "I loved her enough to marry her. Afterwards I still loved her, but not so much. She was not a woman to live with every day."

Holly's glass-cold eyes became contemptuous, while Yeo's were resigned. They were both married men, and Mrs. Yeo and Mrs. Holly were ladies who could be lived with every day or emphatically not at all. Stavros appeared aware of the impression he was making, but he floundered stoutly on.

"We lived very contentedly," he persisted, his round brown eyes fixed on Yeo's beseechingly. "Sometimes she came to see me, sometimes I visited her, but we did not live in the same house nor did we share the same friends. We were neither of us young, we were not unfaithful."

Holly's head was inclining more and more to one side, but Yeo had made up his mind to be sympathetic, and now did his best.

"Yes, I can see that," he said mendaciously, "but surely she'd tell you where she was going?"

"Why?" The other man seemed astonished, and Yeo was put out of his stride.

"I should have thought you'd have had a right to know," said Holly primly.

"But I did not want to know. I did not know where she came from that afternoon; where we each went, what we each did, was not the other's affair."

The constable wrote something in his notebook in a scholarly long-hand, and Campion glanced over his shoulder.

"Loveless marriage," he had written, and had drawn a curling line under the words.

Mr. Campion felt a trifle helpless. Yeo shook his head sadly. "You can't help us then," he said. "It's a great pity, Mr. Stavros. After all, a woman has been foully done to death, and she was your wife."

"Do you think I do not know that?"

The whole room was unprepared for the outburst. The man stood before them cracking visibly; his dignity and sophistication were gone, there were tears in his eyes and on his cheeks, and his mouth was ragged and hideous like the mouth of a tragedy mask.

"Do you think I don't know?" The words came in an ugly broken whisper, and he turned his back on them.

Yeo, who was by nature the kindest of men, was appalled; his red face became a little blue as he stepped away from his victim, and buttonholed Holly.

"Have you got the full description of the clothes she was

wearing when he last saw her?" he muttered, dropping his voice so low that it sounded like a growl.

"Yes. That's been done. I've got a note."

"Good. Well, I think I can leave this to you, Inspector." Yeo was retreating in bad order, and was not concealing the fact. "He'll have to identify her, you know, but give him time; don't hustle him, it's only a formality. Come on, Campion."

He hurried out of the room without a backward glance and paused in the passage to wipe his face.

"There you are," he said, "I told you, I don't understand these damned people. There was no fake about that, he's genuinely upset."

"Of course he is, poor chap. He was in love with her."

"Yet he only saw her now and again. Married her, and didn't live with her."

"That's probably why."

"Why what?"

"Why he was in love with her. I mean, perhaps that is how it was done. We haven't got much of a line on the sort of woman she actually was, you know."

Yeo regarded him with kindly regret. "Cynical," he said. "You may be right, but it's not nice."

"Not nice be blowed," said Campion stung to inelegance. "This man found he'd married a woman whom he loved sometimes, therefore he saw her sometimes. Eminently sensible. What you don't seem to have asked him is why she called."

The Superintendent appeared out of his depth. "Didn't she ever look up her husband?" he enquired innocently.

"I don't know, but I should think they usually met by appointment. I mean, that sort of relationship would require a certain amount of mutual tact, wouldn't it? Envisage it."

"I can't," said Yeo. "And if my missus heard you talking, she'd put you across her knee. Still, go on; I'm not too old to learn."

"Well, I don't know," said Campion again, "but it sounds to me as though either he phoned her or she him, and they had a week-end together occasionally. I don't swear it worked like this, but if she dropped in for ten minutes suddenly I should say it was to tell him something she'd rather not mention on the phone. That's the impression I get."

"Very French," commented the Superintendent.

"Not really," said Mr. Campion.

"Very well, I'll look into it." Yeo was grudging. "All the same it seems a funny thing for me to ask a man—why his wife went to see him." He shook his head darkly. "You don't know what we've got to contend with," he said. "Not all the evil in the world is on the Continent, and what have I got to do now? Trot along to see that terrifying woman."

"Lady Carados?"

"Yes. We've got to go over her place with a tooth-comb for the rest of Mrs. Stavros's clothes. She can't have come in out of the street in a nightdress. In the ordinary way I should leave that to someone else, but this is very special, and in police work the higher the rank of the bobby the thicker the kid gloves, or that's the theory. I doubt if it's true."

"Suppose you don't find the missing clothes at Lady Carados's house?" enquired Campion.

Yeo cocked an eye at him. "Then we shall make a bee-line for her son's place," he said. "Somebody smothered that woman knowing what he was doing. We shall get him, you know, Campion, and when we've got him we shall hang him."

Mr. Campion glanced at the powerful figure with sudden gravity.

"I back you," he said soberly.

Yeo grunted. "I'm glad to hear it," he observed. "We've got more on hand than you realize, my lad. Now you get back to your young lady, and don't forget I expect cooperation."

"You'll get it," said Campion. "See you at Philippi."

"It's called the 'Coach and Horses,'" murmured the Superintendent. "Up the wrong end of Early Street. Any time just before ten. So long."

Mr. Campion went back to the now practically deserted restaurant, and glancing across the room to his table saw as he had feared that all traces of the meal had been cleared away. Susan was still there, though, but she was not alone. A young man in green khaki was sitting beside her. Mr. Campion had only seen Don Evers once before, and then not in the happiest circumstances, but he had no difficulty in recognizing him; the youngster had a distinctive appearance and now, when he was paler than he had been on the doorstep of the flat in Bottle Street, his natural good looks had asserted themselves. He looked older than his years, and the strong lines which would one day lend character to his face showed faintly under his fair skin.

Susan was watching him with tragedy in her eyes. They were both unaware of their surroundings and were alone together.

Mr. Campion forbore to interrupt. He chose a table some distance away and sat down, and the old waiter, who could still talk too impulsively, came shambling up to him. Mr. Campion accepted his ultimatum that coffee alone or with a liqueur was the best that could be done for him, and was sniffing something which he trusted devoutly was not medicated paraffin before he ventured a casual question.

"Seen Mrs. Stavros lately?"

The watery eyes regarded him furtively. "Not since the quarrel, sir," said the old man. "That was some days ago. Sunday, I think."

10

MR. CAMPION REMAINED looking into those sunken and watery eyes for some little time. Then he set down his glass.

"Quarrels do occur," he said vaguely; "a plate or two smashed here and there, what does it matter?"

"Oh, it wasn't that sort of quarrel, sir." The old man hesitated. He seemed a little at sea, and Campion lit a cigarette with great care and concentration. The waiter drifted away, played with some crockery on a side table, came half-way back, changed his mind, and shambled to the entrance where, after a brief survey of the weather, he appeared to reach a decision. He came stumbling back to Campion.

"Perhaps I ought not to have mentioned it, sir," he said, fluttering before the table. "It was just a few high words. Not really high, either. Not high at all now I come to think of it."

"About a foot?" enquired Campion with apparent seriousness.

The other man stared at him, dawning suspicion on his crumpled face. "I'm old," he said, "things kind of slip out. They didn't ought to, but I'm not used to London, and well, you might say my old tongue, that runs away with me."

"Where do you come from?" said Campion. "Sudbury?"

The decrepit figure gaped at him. "I wasn't born far from there," he said. "Perhaps I've served you somewhere? Do you recognize me?"

"Only in a general way," murmured his guest. "You're never bored for long, are you?"

"Bored, sir?"

"Gravelled for lack of excitement. Things happen when you're around, and if they don't you help them on."

The old man looked at him steadily, and there was a glint of wicked amusement deep in the faded eyes. He picked up an empty glass and began to polish it.

"That weren't much of a quarrel," he said. "It was what she said to him when she left that made me wonder, especially when I heard she'd been found gorn."

"Gorn?"

"Dead, sir."

"Oh, I see. Well, what did she say when she left?"

The waiter hesitated, apparently not to waste any satisfaction there might be in the situation.

"I wouldn't like to go to the police because of my job, you see," he said.

"What do you think I am?"

The sinful old face cracked into a purely yokel smile.

"Not a policeman, sir," he said. "Quite likely you're as curious as what I am, but like me, you ain't a policeman. I'll tell you what she said. Up here people don't take the notice that we used to in the country; up here it's all mind your own business, and I dessay no one but me realized that when the lady and her husband was talking together on Sunday, they was riled, but I did. They went into his little office and had quite a noise together."

"Noise?"

"Well, a row, sir. At least I think so, because when they came out she was red in the face and nearly crying, and when she left she said: 'Good-bye, then, I can't promise nothing. You don't understand, I can't promise nothing.' Those were her actual words."

Mr. Campion doubted it, but he suspected the sense was correct.

"It made me think," said the waiter, "especially now she's gorn. *What* couldn't she promise? That's getting on my mind. I'd *like* to know that." He spoke with such genuine wistfulness that Mr. Campion smiled.

"What's your name?" he enquired.

"I couldn't go to no Court to give evidence."

"I doubt if you'd be asked to."

"I'd say I couldn't remember."

"I'm sure you would."

"Very well, then. Me name's Fred Parker."

"Really." Mr. Campion seemed delighted. "Any—er—nickname?"

Mr. Parker's old eyes narrowed. "No," he said. "No nickname; only Fred. Well, perhaps you'd like your bill, sir? You're paying for the young lady you came in with, are you?"

"It's the custom of the country," agreed Mr. Campion, glancing across the room to where Susan's fair head was drooping a little.

"Yes, so it is, sir," said the aged Fred idiotically. "Let's see; that's the young lady talking to the American officer over there, isn't it? Table Twelve, sir."

He spoke so innocently and with such a show of doddering inefficiency that despite his recent discovery Mr. Campion was almost taken in by the technique.

"That would be the young lady advertised to marry Lord Carados, wouldn't it? A very pretty young lady, if I may say so. I recognized her as soon as she came in; that's why I was so upset when I made the slip I did, sir." He raised his eyes and again the dreadful thirst for entertainment flickered in them.

"Yes. Well, you're a prize specimen," said Campion. "Tell me, do you ever get into serious trouble?"

Old Fred permitted himself an evil chuckle. It was soundless, and involved the display of a dreadful assortment of tooth stumps.

"You will have your joke, sir," he said. "I'm only an old man interested in what I see. I'm very careful who I talk to, very careful."

"I'm glad to hear it." Mr. Campion sounded sincere. "Otherwise even in times like these I should think Mr. Stavros might regret transporting you from the 'Eastern Lion,' or whatever it was."

"The 'Totham Sun,' sir; I was there for years. A very dull place it was compared to this one. No, it's not Mr. Stavros I have to watch out for." Fred was reflective. "No, it's that Mr. Pirri, the other partner. He ain't the person to come up against in a hurry."

Mr. Campion grinned. "Thank you for the tip," he said.

"No, thank you, sir," the old man said, and hurled himself off down the room laughing. When he returned and his client had done what was expected of him, Campion ventured a single question.

"Just to satisfy an academic curiosity, do you know who I am?" he enquired.

Old Fred paused, and the desire to score wrestled visibly with his native caution.

"I did ask about you, sir," he said at last. "As soon as the police gentleman came in I did ask who you was. They told me in the kitchen. The head waiter recognized you; he used to serve you before the war."

"I see. And so you thought I was the person to honour with a few confidences. Dear me, you don't miss much, do you?"

"No, I don't, sir." He took the observation as a tribute. "Very little. Very little indeed. By the way, sir, there's one thing I thought to have told you before; that American gentle-nan over there, sitting with your young lady guest, sir, he came in asking for you and I took him over to the young lady." The watery glance was fixed hopefully on Campion's face. "I thought it would be all right, sir, because he's been in here with her before, several times." He waited a moment to see the effect of this latest depth charge, and then sidled off with surprising speed.

Campion watched him pause before the two young people at the far table. They came back to earth reluctantly, and turned round. Don came over immediately, Susan following him; they were both apologetic, and both pathetically grateful.

"We had no idea you were back . . ."

"Have you been here long?"

"I don't know what you'll think of us . . ."

Susan's natural frankness suddenly asserted itself amid the polite chatter. "You're all right," she said, dropping her hand on his sleeve. "I like you. What have you been doing—digesting?"

"That's a pretty fantasy," said Campion with appreciation. "No, I've been talking to the aged Fred. He's a countryman."

"A hick, is he?" Don was interested. "I thought he couldn't be a natural part of the scenery. He's pretty terrible, in my opinion."

"Not a beautiful thing," Mr. Campion agreed. "Sees himself as the Hand of Fate. He says you were looking for me, Lieutenant."

"He is. He came looking for you but found me instead." Susan was still of an age to blush violently, Campion noticed with interest. "Now, I've got to go. I'm horribly late, I see. Thank you so much, Mr. Campion. I'm afraid I'm a rotten guest, but you're the nicest host I've ever met. I can't tell you how tremendously grateful I am to you."

She paused and stood looking at him, her eyes shining. "I wish I could help," she said impulsively. "There is one thing. Lugg is terribly fond of his pig, Mr. Campion, really terribly fond; I think he'd risk anything for it."

Campion, who had risen to take her hand, looked down at her sharply.

"Oh, would he?" he said. "Thank you, Susan. That's worth knowing."

Don escorted her to the doorway and when he came back he was frowning. "I owe you a debt of gratitude, sir," he said with that transatlantic formality so much more strict than anything in England. "I'm afraid I upset your luncheon party."

"Not at all," said Campion. "The police didn't help it, you know."

Don shook his young head. "It's very disturbing business," he said, "and I'm afraid you'll think the request I'm going to make rather flippant in the circumstances. As a matter of fact I hardly know how to approach you, but I just want to ask you to join me at a very special little party here tonight."

Mr. Campion, who had envisaged many requests, but not this one, appeared both gratified and surprised. Don forestalled his polite murmur.

"I guess I'd better explain," he said. "I believe we have a mutual friend in Mr. Theodore Bush."

Campion sighed. It was not his beaux yeux after all. "Yes," he said. "I saw him here as a matter of fact about an hour and a half ago."

"I know you did. He phoned me as soon as he left here and told me to come right along and not take no for an answer." Don was looking both gloomy and preoccupied. "I'm afraid the whole thing sounds crazy to you with so much serious business going on all around," he went on. "It does to me, but quite apart from the real business abroad a whole series of silly little things, some of them pretty serious and some of them pretty small, seem to be happening in this town at top speed."

Campion smiled at him from behind his spectacles. "I know," he said. "I've not been back for twenty-four hours yet, but already I've noticed a certain March-hare quality; a sinister March hare, if I may say so, about the old home. It's very odd. Rather alarming."

"Oh, so it's not always like this?" Don appeared relieved to hear it.

"Not at such speed," said Mr. Campion cautiously. "All the same, I'd like to come to the party. What is Theo up to? Not brewing his own, I hope?"

"No, I don't think it's come to that yet." Don was laughing. "Mr. Bush takes his liquor seriously," he said, "and that's how I come into the story. You see, my father is Richard Caxton Evers."

"Is he, by Jove." Mr. Campion's expression became intelligent. "He's Theo's only serious rival in the civilized world, I believe. They run neck and neck, don't they, for the ultimate arch-connoisseur stakes?"

"I don't know if Dad would concede that," said Don,

grinning. "He certainly has a healthy respect for Mr. Bush's opinions. I don't know a thing about wine myself; I imagine our lot feels it has something else to worry about, but I've gotten myself mixed up in it at the moment. I'll tell you. The man who keeps this place is a little guy called Stavros and he sold me a case of Burgundy; at least, he sold me a couple of bottles and told me he could get me three dozen if I wanted it. He wasn't actually exorbitant as things go over here now, yet it was clear that we were dealing in something pretty special."

Mr. Campion nodded to show intelligence, and the boy continued.

"It's a very ordinary story," he said, "so far. Here's where it takes a new turn. Although I'm the complete novice where wine is concerned I have been brought up by my old man, and I realized that if this bottle was half as good as Stavros said it was, then some sort of homage was due to it." He glanced up and his eyes were shy and amused. Campion began to like him. "I did what I thought I ought to," said the Lieutenant. "I took up an option on the three cases and I told Stavros to put the two bottles by for me, since I knew this spot of leave was due, and meanwhile I'd mentioned it in my letter home. It was something I could tell Dad which couldn't worry the censor."

"Was your father interested?"

"Interested? He sent me a cable. It was something like this: *'Contact Theodore Bush concerning bottle you hold stop if genuine which unlikely most remarkable stop Bush reliable judgment second to mine if he recommends expense immaterial and congratulations stop wish I were with you.'*" Don broke off laughing. "He's a grand old enthusiast," he said, "but he's not usually so excited. I got in touch with Bush at once and he was even more het up; in fact, he went off the deep end and set about making a little 'do' of it. I feel I've produced the elixir of life, or something. We're meeting in a room upstairs at half after seven."

"What fun," said Mr. Campion. "Dear me, this is the first remotely jolly story I've heard since I got home. What are the magic words on the label?"

"Ah, this is where it gets mysterious," said Don, "or at

least, I think so. It's a Vosne dated 1904, and it's called 'Les
Enfants Doux.' "

Mr. Campion looked blank. "I haven't my snob book by
me," he said, "but the year is classic. Frankly I've never
heard of the vineyard. Who are the shippers?"

"None mentioned." Don was apologetic. "And they may be
The Old Minoan Bathtub Company, so I warn you. I've
never heard of *Les Enfants* either; it's not in any of the books
and I asked a very decent firm of wine merchants about it and
they'd never heard of it. But Dad has, you see, and so has
Bush, and they ought to know."

"Oh Lord, yes, they know," said Campion, "and the great
moment is tonight, is it? I'm tremendously flattered and all
that, but with all due deference why do I get asked?"

Don looked at him helplessly. "Frankly, I don't know," he
said, "but I'll certainly be very glad to have you come."

"That's very handsome of you," said Campion sincerely.
"Who are the party? You, me, and Theo?"

"Well, no, unfortunately." Don was growing visibly more
and more embarrassed. "You see it began by Mr. Bush
arranging that he and I should investigate alone; then he felt
we ought to have another expert whose name I forget, and
just now he told me that he'd got hold of Carados, and that I
was to use every wile I could think of to get you to be present
also."

"My poor chap," said Mr. Campion with genuine sympathy.
"Do you want to entertain all these strangers?"

The young soldier passed his hand over his fair hair. "Well,
that's another awkward angle," he said. "In the beginning it
was definitely *my* party, but since then Mr. Bush has sort of
appropriated it. I protested, but he wouldn't take 'no' for an
answer; yet he insisted that I should ask you. It's all a little
peculiar, but since Dad put me on to him . . . you see?"

"Exactly," agreed Mr. Campion. "Odder and odder. This
isn't like Theo, you know. He's up to something."

"I wondered," the boy said. "He seemed a rather formal
person when I first met him. I wouldn't expect him to be so
unorthodox."

"No," said Campion, "nor would I. No, this is something
interesting. You can't remember who the other expert is, can

you? You see, neither Johnny nor myself could qualify as judges."

Don shook his head. "I'm sorry, I can't," he said. "He was some notability, but the name's gone clean out of my mind. You know Carados then?"

"Yes," said Mr. Campion, adding presently, "you'll find his inclusion a little awkward, won't you?"

"Awkward? You're telling me." The cry was heartfelt and the young man sat silent for some moments. "I don't know how great a friend of Susan's you are," he said at last, "I'm afraid we weren't talking about you just now."

"Er—no," murmured Mr. Campion. "No, I don't suppose you were."

The boy smiled at him briefly and hurried on. "I had a letter from her this morning written after I saw her yesterday and it knocked me endways. She said I wasn't to see her again; she'd made up her mind to go through with this marriage. I spent the morning fooling around wondering what I'd better do when old man Bush, whom I'd forgotten, telephoned me at the hotel and told me to come here to find you. He happened to mention that you were with Susan—I came."

The statement was in the nature of a confession and Mr. Campion acknowledged it gracefully. "I trust things are more satisfactory now," he ventured.

"I don't know." Don was dubious, but game. "The wedding is postponed anyway, which is something. I'm not lying down until I've got to. Susan has a darned good reason for her present attitude, unfortunately. I don't like it, naturally, but I do see what she means. She's a sweet kid, one in a million."

Mr. Campion liked his attitude and wished him luck. Aloud, he said casually:

"You met her through Eve Snow, didn't you?"

"Uh-huh. Only three weeks ago. Gwenda Onyer introduced me to Eve and Eve introduced me to Susan all in one evening. After that—well, you know how these things happen."

Mr. Campion did indeed, but he did not say so. He was frowning. "Eve didn't put you on to Gwenda?"

"No, the other way round. I got to know Mrs. Onyer when

I first came over here through some friends of my mother's. Do you know her?"

"Not well."

"She's a queer woman, or at least I thought so. She didn't take any notice of me when I first met her, and I thought she'd forgotten me. But quite three months after she suddenly hunted me up and carried me off to meet Eve Snow at the Royal Alexandra Theatre. I've never ceased to be grateful to her, because after that I got invited to the supper party here at which I met Susan."

"I see," said Mr. Campion slowly as he studied the tablecloth. "I see . . . Good Lord!"

The exclamation escaped him involuntarily, and both men sprang to their feet as the room was filled with angry noise. A service door had burst open and through it hurtled two shouting figures. The first was a stranger; he came backing in, his lanky figure, clad in disreputable grey trousers and a sweater, looking out of place in the elegant dining-room. Stavros followed him, apparently with intent to kill; his arm was raised, his face white with fury, and his small eyes blazing. They were bellowing at each other in several different languages, and the din was increased by the excited chatter of the staff in the passage behind them. Through the swinging doors, Campion caught a glimpse of blue uniforms as the police struggled to get by in the narrow way.

"Look out, he's got a knife," said Don, and plunged forward just as Stavros's victim turned to fly. In his alarm the man caught his foot in a tablecloth and brought down a mass of silver and glass across his path. He stumbled over the debris and fell sprawling. Stavros must have been upon him in a moment, had it not been for Don who caught him, and stripping the knife from his hand sent it spinning across the room.

Meanwhile Campion had collared the stranger, and, by the time a very angry Holly with a detective sergeant and constable behind him came striding up, the enemies were both on their feet facing one another, each held firmly by experienced captors. As soon as he was disarmed, the rage died out of Stavros. He stood drooping, his face grey and his shoulders limp.

"That settles it," said Holly to Stavros. "You're under arrest, and about time too."

"I don't charge him." The man in the sweater drew himself away from Campion and began hitching his clothes into position. "I don't charge him," he said. "We were having a friendly argument on our own premises; you can't do anything. I don't charge him."

He had an unexpected voice, very high and shrill, incongruous in one of his appearance; but there was nothing absurd in his argument, and Holly was discomfited.

"Do you always have your friendly arguments with knives?" he enquired.

"Sometimes we do," said the man in a sweater, in his high belligerent voice. "Why not? That's all right if we don't use them. There's no wound on me, is there? You can't touch him if I don't charge him, and I don't."

At this point it occurred to Mr. Campion that they must be dealing with the redoubtable Mr. Pirri.

"You must frighten each other occasionally, I suppose?" he suggested mildly.

Pirri swung round to look at him and saw him clearly for the first time during the incident. He stood staring, and his brown eyes widened visibly. Mr. Campion was taken aback himself. Although it is not possible to identify positively any man of whom one has seen no more than a single eye, and that reflected in the driving mirror of a taxi-cab, yet one may still entertain very powerful suspicions. The more he thought of it the more certain he was that here was his assailant of the evening before. He remained silent, and Pirri turned on Stavros.

"Who is this?" he demanded.

"An old customer," said Stavros dully, "a *good* old customer."

Pirri stared at Campion again, his expression frankly incredulous. Finally he shrugged his shoulders and walked back the way he had come. In the doorway he paused, and addressed Holly:

"I don't make any charge," he said firmly. "No charge whatever."

He went on in to the back of the house, and at a nod from Holly the detective sergeant closed on Stavros. "I'm afraid you'll have to come with me and do what we've got to do," he said. Stavros nodded; he looked broken and exhausted. "I'll come," he said.

Holly let the little procession pass out of the room before he went over to Campion and Don Evers. "These damned foreigners," he said. "We're trying to get this chap to go down and identify his wife, and on the way he suddenly sees his partner and makes a murderous assault on him. Then the partner won't prefer a charge. They're all alike; utterly unbalanced."

"Maybe he suspects his partner of having something to do with the death of his wife," said Don.

"Might be that." Holly was noncommittal. "He just saw him and rushed at him, and now the partner seems to suggest he often did it."

Mr. Campion nodded to Holly and took Don's arm.

"I think you know . . ." he murmured.

"I'm with you," agreed the young man promptly, and they went out into the cold sunshine together. "I suppose that all meant something to you," said Don diffidently, as they walked down the narrow road. "Being uninitiated I just get the impression that everyone's gone clean crazy around here."

"Not everyone," said Mr. Campion seriously. "Not everyone, but someone has, you know; someone has, and I'm open to bet it's not our friend Stavros."

11

IF MR. CAMPION had not been recognized as a valued friend by Taffy Warlock, the stage doorkeeper at the Alexandra Theatre, Shaftesbury Avenue, it is quite possible that the incident which first shocked him and then made him so angry would never have occurred. However, as soon as he presented himself in the concrete corridor at the seamy side of the footlights, Taffy put out his dusty head and greeted him with such unaffected joy that Campion (who had not after all so far received quite that welcome home to which every returning warrior has a right) was touched, albeit in every sense of the word.

Taffy was so certain that Miss Snow would be as delighted to see Mr. Campion as he was himself, that despite one of the strictest rules of the theatre, he sent him on down the staircase without bothering to announce him.

The matinée was well advanced into the second act, and from far away beyond the single bare bulb which marked a turn in the passage, came the first sound of the *Momma's Utility Baby Gets a Riveter's Lullaby* number, which was Eve's high spot in the middle of the show. Campion did not recognize it, although the rhythmic clanging interested him, and he did not realize that it was Miss Snow herself who was leading the chorus. He went along to the star's dressing-room, found her card upon the door, and knocked.

The door was opened abruptly and Stanislaus Oates looked out at him. The two old friends stared at each other with exactly the same degree of guarded casualness, and even then the situation might have been saved had not Johnny appeared behind Oates.

"Oh hello, Campion," he said blankly. "Come in." He was more transparent than they were and it was evident that he was put out; "caught out" was perhaps the more correct term, and Campion, whose first impression was that the Chief of the Criminal Investigation Department had for some reason or other decided to arrest the Marquess of Carados in person, began to understand that it was not nearly as easy as that.

Oates opened the door a little wider for him to enter. He was not at all pleased. Campion, who had known him well for close on seventeen years, was in no doubt about it. They were all three embarrassed and the newcomer did his best to withdraw.

"I dropped in to say hello to Eve," he said. "I didn't realize it was a party."

"It's not," said the Chief. "I'm just going. Miss Snow will forgive me if I don't wait for her. Say good-bye for me, Carados, will you?"

"All right." Johnny sounded dubious. "All right," he

repeated, adding suddenly, "you'd better take these, hadn't you?"

He gathered several papers from the settee in the corner where the two had apparently been sitting together, and handed them over. The Chief took them awkwardly, and his melancholy eyes met Mr. Campion's own for an instant. Mr. Campion had seen so many police memorandum slips in his time that he could hardly fail to recognize a bundle of them when they were passed under his nose, but he looked obligingly stupid. Oates was not deceived, and he nodded to him briefly as he thrust the packet into his breast pocket.

"I don't want you to leave London," he murmured. "Your train will wait."

It was said with belligerent jocularity, and Campion understood how ill at ease he was. The entire incident was very unlike Oates; for the life of him Campion could not help conveying his astonishment. The Chief's face darkened.

"Well, good-bye," he said, and hurried off.

It was a retreat, and Campion, the mildest of men, was first shocked and then made angry. This was too much like a secret rendezvous with a suspected person for it to pass without an explanation, if he was to consider himself in any way a party to the investigation. If he was not to be such a party, then why this infernal curtailing of his long overdue leave? His face grew hard and he eyed Carados, who was standing with his hands in his pockets, surveying him gloomily.

Johnny did not speak, and the silence went on for a long time until Campion broke it himself.

"I believe we're dining together tonight," he said.

"Are we?" Carados raised his big head at the words and a smile of sudden friendliness spread over his face. "I say, I am glad about that. Bush got hold of you, did he? What do you think of the story?"

"About the odd bottle of X, the mystery wine?"

"Yes, what do you make of it? Queer, eh?"

Campion was surprised. It had been an interesting little tale of a mild and gentlemanly kind, but when it was superimposed on a murder hunt and flanked by the most devastating conflict of all time, it seemed to him that it lost its piquancy. He was on the point of saying so when Carados forestalled him.

"It is extraordinary," he said. "I'm damned glad you're coming, Campion."

The thin man in the spectacles regarded his friend in astonishment. For a man who was a fair suspect for murder and had just had his wedding postponed on those grounds, he seemed to be engrossed in peculiar trivialities. Johnny walked up and down the room.

"Theo tells me the lad concerned is that youngster who's pinched my Susan," he said suddenly. He sounded cheerful if not particularly at ease, and Campion took off his spectacles the better to see him.

"I've just left Evers now," he said at last. "Nice, I thought."

"Is he?" Johnny seemed glad to hear it. "I must meet him. You think he's sound, do you? It matters to me quite a lot."

The enquiry was convincingly genuine and Campion did his best.

"I didn't look at his teeth or his bank balance," he said primly, "but I liked him."

"Good. Good." Johnny Carados rattled the coins in his pocket and began to whistle softly. "I hope to God he's a decent bloke," he went on presently. "I shan't part without a hell of a row if I don't approve, you know. She's got no people now except that old lion fish of a father; Tom always did say the old man needed a keeper, and my hat, how right he was. Tom was her husband, by the way, wrote himself off about a year ago. Best kid I ever knew."

"I had lunch with Mrs. Shering," said Campion.

"Did you?" Johnny paused in his walk and looked round. "Good chap. I was worrying about her. I haven't seen her since the wedding fizzle. She's a pet, isn't she?" He sighed. "I had lunch with papa, laying mines for the police. He's magnificent at sea, I believe; there's room there for his methods, no doubt. We lunched at Black's—not his element."

Campion said nothing at all, his face was expressionless, and for a while it seemed that Carados had forgotten him. But after a time he sat down opposite him on the dressing-table chair and faced him. He looked younger than Campion had ever seen him, and there was a startled expression in his grey-blue eyes. His question was unexpected.

"Campion," he said, "when you were out there on the Continent did you ever feel you were actively at war?"

After a long moment of self-control Mr. Campion said affably:

"You ring a faint bell."

Carados did not smile; his strong sensitive face remained anxious. "Well, then," he said, "in that case you know what a lot of people around here don't know, and that is, that when one is actively at war one simply does the most expedient thing. Ordinary peace-time considerations and institutions come to look a bit remote; pleasant and good and all that, but luxurious and impractical, don't they?"

Campion thought he understood him. He looked up nervously, wondering how far he was going. "Yes, I know," he said briefly.

"Well, there you are," said Johnny. "It's a relief to find someone informed. That's the devil of it over here just now. We're all mixed up in this country; the people who are actively fighting are living at home alongside the people who aren't. Out there you were at least all on the one job." He got up and grinned. "I've only seen all this in the last day or so," he said.

Campion sat looking at him. It was quite true, of course, it was a sidelight on the times which had not occurred to him before. He went on turning over the present situation in his mind.

"Johnny," he said suddenly, "do you think that woman was killed in your room because of this projected wedding?"

Carados met his eyes, and let his own drop before them. "What can I think?" he said. "I don't care why, it's who I'm worrying about."

He turned away to resume his tiger walk up and down the room. "When sophisticated people do crack, they crack to pieces," he said. "What's frightening me is this. I'm beginning to believe that one of us has gone mad. I've tried to make it mean something else, but it doesn't add up any other way."

Campion remained silent for some time. A little more light was filtering into the picture in his mind, but even so it was by no means clear while there was one great glaring unlikelihood in the story which he could not bring himself to swallow. He turned to an easier subject.

"What was she like?" he asked. "What sort of a woman?"

"Who? Moppet?" Johnny frowned. "Oh she was all right, you know," he said. "A jolly, vulgar little person with an interesting approach. You always felt she was just about to be terribly witty and yet she never was. She had an indescribable promise of romance, too, which turned out to be rather prim sentimentality; and yet you felt kindly towards her. The worst thing I remember about her was her energy, but I can't see anyone killing her for that. Besides, she was one of those people you like even when you can't stand them about any longer."

"That's what Stavros said," murmured Campion. "He said one couldn't live with her every day, but he only found that out after he'd married her."

"Married her?" Carados was staring at Campion in amazement. "Are you talking about Stavros at the Minoan?"

"Yes. She was his wife. He married her at the beginning of the war. Didn't you know?"

"No, I didn't know anything about her." A wave of pure relief passed over his face. "I say, are you sure about that?"

"Certain. The police know all about it."

"Oates didn't know." Johnny was frowning again and the dull wretchedness returned to his face. "He'd have told me."

Campion shrugged his shoulders. "The report may be waiting for him."

"Maybe. Maybe. I hope you're right, Campion. If this is true it's a break. It means there's a chance that the whole thing comes from outside." He broke off and stood looking at the other man. "Well, I'll see you tonight then," he said. "This is good news. I was in a flat spin, absolutely bags of panic, and now I do see there is just a chance I may have been mistaken . . . Oh, hello, Eve."

"Hello. I'm sorry but I must change. Albert, my dear, I didn't know you were here. How are you?" Miss Snow came in with a rush, followed by the consequential Mrs. Phipps, who had been her dresser for years. Her squeaky voice, so much beloved by her enormous public, expressed every shade of her surprise and pleasure, and Campion was warmed by it.

Eve was tired, but triumphant, and she made an absurd and attractive figure in a small, white boiler suit and a baby's bonnet; her face was painted like a doll's, and from her hand hung a little silver hammer trimmed with bells. She kissed Mr. Campion perfunctorily, and waved aside his excuses.

"No, darling, don't go," she said. "I want to talk to you. Phippy, you take these, and I'll do my face." She sat down at the mirror, while Mrs. Phipps, who reminded everybody of a hare in petticoats, moved around her in efficient bounds. When she was covered with a barber's cape Eve plunged her hands in the cold cream.

"You got rid of the policeman, Johnny?" she enquired. It was her first direct remark to him, and it came to Mr. Campion that a row was in progress.

"Yes," said Johnny.

"Well, is everything all right?"

"My dearest girl, I don't know." He looked down at her as she sat smearing the grease thickly over her mouth and eyebrows. "I don't know," he repeated. "Thank you for letting me see him here. Good-bye, Campion, see you tonight."

He was gone before either of them realized it, and the door snapped shut behind him. Eve did not speak, and Campion had re-seated himself on the couch a few feet away from her before he realized that she was crying. He got up and dropped a hand on her shoulder.

"I think I'd better clear off," he said awkwardly. "Lots to do, and all that."

"No, stay. Stay, Albert. I must talk to somebody with sense." The squeaky voice was urgent. "Darling, tell me, do you think the strain—the war strain, I mean, quite apart from this other awful thing—has got him *right* down?" The face she turned to him, multi-colored and shining, and tragic, was still miraculously attractive. Her big, honey-coloured eyes were devastatingly sincere.

Campion hesitated. "You mean, do I think the old lad's nuts?" he enquired bluntly.

"Yes, I've been wondering that."

Campion looked round but Mrs. Phipps had bounded off behind a screen in the corner and presumably considered herself absent.

"No," he said. "I think he's got the wind up at the moment, and I think he's worried. But he'll snap out of it. It's an alarming business, you know. Lady Carados tipped it over the edge into the frightful by heaving the body about like that. She's a little odd these days, I should say. It's very nerve-racking for Johnny."

"Of course it is," she agreed, wiping off the grease and her tears with it. "Of course it is, my dear, but I'm not thinking of the murder. Not only of that. It's all the other things I mean. It must have been coming on slowly for a long time, and I never knew."

"What other things?" enquired Campion.

Eve did not look at him. "Well, his marriage, for one thing," she said in a burst of frankness. "He's not in love with that child, Albert, and he never has been in love with her. I didn't believe it of course when he first told me. I thought she was young and lovely and that he had lost his head over her in a perfectly healthy way; I didn't blame him, you know, I didn't really. That sort of thing does happen, and that's all there is to it. But now I see he's been telling the truth. He doesn't love her, Albert, and he never has loved her."

"I don't see that proves him barmy." Mr. Campion realized he was floundering in delicate flower-beds, but saw no way of avoiding them.

"But he was going to marry her," the woman insisted. "He was going to marry her because he'd promised her young husband to look after her. That's insane, really insane. Mad, I mean. You can't imagine any modern man in his senses, anybody not in a book, doing that, can you? Not here in England, certainly not Johnny."

She began on her face again with swift, practised artistry, more than half her mind on the work.

"He broke my heart but it didn't frighten me when I thought he was in love," she said. "Now I really do see he's not and never has been, I'm terrified. He's unbalanced, what else can it mean?"

Mr. Campion regarded her helplessly. He saw her as she was; shrewd, kind and, above all, adult. He could appreciate her bewilderment but hesitated to point out that in a rapidly changing world she was just a little old-fashioned. All the same, he felt it his duty to attempt an explanation. It was a laborious business, and she let him speak uninterrupted for a minute or so. Suddenly he exasperated her.

"Two worlds," she repeated after him, her voice rising in her indignation. "You too! What's the matter with you all? If you tell me you're 'at war' I—I'll hit you, Albert. Good God, aren't we all at war?"

Mr. Campion sat quiet, and thought about his train, and the green meadows beyond its furthest journey. Eve laughed.

"Sorry, darling," she said. "It's all too—too near the heart, I'm afraid. I'm not reliable at the moment. I'll see what you mean in time." Presently she added pathetically:

"He's so angry with me, Albert."

"Is he?"

"Uh-huh. Furious. Furious with us all, it's so unlike him. Isn't it called 'persecution mania'? He thinks we're all in some conspiracy against him."

"To prevent the wedding?"

"Yes. That, and—oh, it must be only that. After all, that's enough."

Mr. Campion was frowning. "Did you think there might be something else?" he asked at last.

Eve was busy with an eyebrow pencil. "I wondered," she said without taking her eyes from the mirror.

"Why did you introduce Susan to young Evers?" said Campion suddenly.

"Me?" She put down the pencil and turned to face him. "I don't think I did, did I?"

"She says so. At a party, at the Minoan."

"So that's where I'd seen her before." Eve was relieved. "That's right. She came with a crowd Gwenda brought along. Gwenda's always bringing people. So I introduced them, did I? Quite likely. I was hostess."

"It wasn't part of a plot between you and Gwenda?"

"To get the girl interested in someone her own age? My dear boy!" Eve turned her back on him and went on with her dressing while Campion sat thinking. After nearly twenty-four hours of completely inconsequential happenings, he thought he was beginning to detect a faint, illusive, spider strand of sense in their history.

"Nobody," he said, "nobody ever killed anyone simply in order to provide an awkward corpse in someone else's house. I'm not sure of much, but I am of that. Nor do I believe that a deliberate murder is ever done for the sole purpose of providing evidence against a third person. There aren't many rules, but one of them is that the killer wishes the victim dead. Eve, my dear, do you know anything about an artificial rose and some Woolworth pearls?"

"A rose?"

He remembered she was an actress, but her surprise convinced him.

"An artificial rose, and a great rope of candlegrease peas."

"I don't know what you're talking about. What is this, some sort of trick? You're frightening me, Albert."

"I don't mean to, and there's nothing up my sleeve. Only one more question. What kind of woman is Gwenda?"

"Gwenda?" Eve began to laugh. "You're absurd. Gwenda is the silliest, woolliest little rabbit in the world. I've known her for years. Gwenda's always rushing about in a self-important panic trying to do something someone else has told her to do, and thinking she's blazing a trail."

Mrs. Phipps interrupted her with a reminder of the time, and she submitted to a cloud of net which was passed over her head. As she emerged into the light again and the dresser knelt before her pulling out the folds of her skirt, Campion looked into her face.

"You dined with Johnny at the Minoan on the night Moppet was killed," he said. "Did he stay with you all the evening?"

Eve returned his stare. Her face, which possessed so much more than beauty, was very serious. "I don't know how you know, but the answer is, every minute of the time," she said deliberately. "Every minute until morning."

He hesitated. "It may be rather awkward if you have to swear that," he murmured.

"I can't help it, I should swear it."

"However mad he is?" he ventured.

Eve closed her eyes. "Don't, darling," she said.

"All right, I won't. But think what you're doing."

"I do," she whispered, "all the time."

Mr. Campion left the theatre. So Johnny Carados had an alibi; if it was genuine or not, Eve was sufficiently in love with him to risk everything she considered important to give him it. It was very interesting, and all the more so because the longer he thought about it the more convinced he was that whoever had killed Moppet Stavros, it was not Johnny Carados.

Meanwhile, the trains went by.

12

WHEN MR. CAMPION walked into the Minoan that evening the first person he saw, sitting demurely at a table by himself, was his uncle, the Bishop of Devizes. Mr. Campion's mother, who had ever been a warrior, not to say a whole panzer division of the Church Militant, had used in her lifetime to speak resentfully of her brother-in-law. She said he was both timid and obstinate, yet in her own domain he was definitely known to be neither. He was a tiny person, soft-voiced and gentle, with the bluest eyes seen out of Scandinavia; but it was typical of him that at that moment it was not he, but the Minoan, which appeared a little out of place.

When Campion presented himself, he was delighted.

"My dear boy," he said, when the preliminary greetings were complete. "How very pleasant to see you here. I was afraid I was hardly going to see a face I knew this evening; it must be ten years since I ate outside my own Club when visiting London. This place looks very clean."

It was a most kindly meant observation, but Mr. Campion felt any debt the Minoan owed him was repaid.

"The Parnassus is still on its pillars, I hope, sir?" he enquired.

"The Club? Oh yes, I've just come from there. Yes, indeed, I wonder if I'm a little early." He consulted a very thin gold watch, and tucked it back in the folds of black silk. "Two minutes," he said, adding with a sudden mischievous glance, unexpected in one so patently innocent, "you wonder what I'm up to, don't you? I'll tell you something, my boy, so do I."

Inspiration came to Mr. Campion, and a large new section of the jig-saw slid neatly into place.

"You wouldn't be about to give your opinion on a bottle of wine by any chance?" he ventured.

The Bishop raised his fine eyebrows. "Ah, so you're in the party. I'm glad of that, very sensible of them. It's a most extraordinary business, don't you think?"

It was the second time that day that someone whom Mr. Campion would have supposed to have something better to excite him had professed the same enthusiasm for the mysterious bottle. This time, however, he was not quite so astonished.

"Yes," he said slowly, "I imagine it is."

The old man laughed his gentle little laugh which had made so many people his slaves in his long life.

"You're so much more used to this sort of thing than I am," he said. It was not exactly regret in his voice, but the hint of it was there. As an observation it was true; if his uncle meant what Campion thought it did. He felt mildly irritated with Bush for dragging the old man into such a business.

"I would come, you know," said the Bishop of Devizes, who appeared to add thought-reading to his other accomplishments. "Theodore Bush came to see me last week and I told him I insisted on being present. We must all do what we can in a case like this."

Mr. Campion gave it up. He could imagine Theo going to Devizes, or indeed to Durban on the Day of Judgment about a purloined case or so of wine, but that his uncle should come to the Minoan in war-time on the same business seemed incredible.

"I don't think I can have got the full story," he said.

"Then wait," said the Bishop. "Wait. Now, is that young man over there our host?"

Campion looked round to see Don Evers standing in the doorway leading to the private part of the building. He smiled at them, and came over. It was evident that he did not know the Bishop, and that he knew rather less than Mr. Campion of the matter in hand. However, there were no explanations. The Bishop was charming and amazingly adroit. He made it clear that he had come up from Devizes to dine with a young man he had never met, having been invited to do so by a third party not yet present, and he refused to see anything unusual in the proceeding. But he would not refer to the now tantalizing bottle, nor allow anyone else to do so. His small talk was masterly, and, to Campion's relief, Don appeared to like him after a certain initial bewilderment.

"We're eating upstairs," said the boy at last. "I thought Bush would be here, but I don't see him yet. Should we go up and let him follow us?"

"I really think we might. Young Carados is to come too, isn't he?"

Mr. Campion's uncle was already advancing down the room, his silver head bobbing against Don's shoulder.

"Do you know Carados, Lieutenant Evers? A most remarkable young man. Very strong in character. A little autocratic, perhaps, but a figure; definitely a figure of our times."

Campion who was following them saw the colour rise in Don's face, and was sorry for him. For a man whose only indiscretion appeared to be that he had told his father he had bought a bottle of Burgundy, his punishment seemed unduly severe.

The room they entered was the one in which Stavros had made his tragic statement that morning. It was brighter now, and warm; the lights were comforting and the silver shone. Campion was wondering what had happened to the man when he saw him. He was standing staring down at the table which had been set for five. His head was bowed and he seemed to have shrunk so that his clothes sagged a little. He did not notice Campion immediately. Don and the Bishop were in front of him and Stavros stepped back, bowing slightly. However, as he raised his head he came face to face with the thin man in the horn-rimmed spectacles. He was astounded and afterwards afraid. His professional calm deserted him, and colour appeared in patches in his grey face. For an instant he dithered, and then turned impulsively towards a corner of the room as if he were about to rush to it protectingly.

Campion followed his glance, and saw two bottles; two very ordinary black bottles with their corks as yet undrawn. As he looked, Don went over to him.

"I'm in a dilemma, sir," he said to the Bishop. "Mr. Bush gave me precise instructions that these corks should not be drawn until we were all present, but although I don't pretend to be an expert I do feel that if we're to drink the stuff tonight it ought to be decanted very soon. What do you think?"

Stavros hurried over and murmured something to him. Don took up one of the bottles very carefully and glanced at it.

"No," he said, "no. It's quite all right, Mr. Stavros, there's no mistake. This is it. *Les Enfants Doux*, nineteen hundred and four. I remember that ink scribble, too. Could you send me a corkscrew and a couple of decanters?"

Stavros still hesitated, and then, surprisingly, he shrugged his shoulders and went back to Campion, where he paused and looked him full in the eyes.

"What on earth does it matter?" he said, and went out.

He had not lowered his voice, and Don's incredulity would have been funny in any other circumstances. "It's got a kind of atmosphere, this place," he said dryly.

The Bishop laughed. "My dear boy," he said, "I really can't tell you how glad I am you are precisely the young man you are. Just let me look at that, will you?" He took the bottle reverently and brought it under the light, where the others joined him, Don doing his best not to look like the small boy who has picked up the rare fossil.

"Oh yes," said the Bishop of Devizes, "oh dear me, yes."

Producing a penknife, he attempted to raise a corner of the label. When he was satisfied this was impossible he turned his attention to the cork. For a long time he examined the black seal through a reading-glass.

"Yes," he said again. "Yes, I think so."

Mr. Campion avoided Don, but the Bishop had no shame. "Now," he said, "where's that corkscrew?"

Old Fred brought it, unholy interest in his bleary eyes, but was bundled out unceremoniously.

"That's right," said the Bishop. "We don't want anyone else here but ourselves. We ought to wait for the others, but I don't think we will, you know. I don't—think—so." He was at work as he spoke, his slender hands revealing practised skill. "No," he said, waving away his host's offer of assistance, "no, I'll do it myself, my dear fellow, if you don't mind. We must have the cork—we must have the cork intact."

Don laughed. "This is making me homesick," he said. "This is Dad's performance."

"Your father is a very sound judge," remarked Mr. Campion's uncle without looking up. "Very sound. I don't altogether agree with some of his theories, but that chapter on the Rhône is masterly . . . Ah!"

The cork had come out with a ghost of a pop; it was a beautiful sound, regretful, grateful, kind.

"There," said the old man, placing the bottle cautiously amid the napery. "Now, let us see."

Mr. Campion, who was quite prepared for a genie to come out of the bottle, by this time looked on with interest, as Don and the Bishop went over the cork with a reading-glass. At first they thought it was unmarked, but finally the old man sighed, as he laid a finger on a minute stamp low down on the red-stained side.

"Yes," he said. "Yes, I fear so."

He attended to the remainder of the ceremony himself, the deep bright wine ran into the crystal, caressing it, clinging to it, but the Bishop remained silent, and when he placed the full decanter on the side table, and brushed his hands with a napkin, he looked less happy than at any other time during the evening. Don suggested that they open the second bottle, but the Bishop objected.

"I think Mr. Bush will want to do that," he said, "but I couldn't resist the opportunity to satisfy my own curiosity. Where is Bush, by the way? And shouldn't Carados be here by this time?"

"He certainly should. I've been wondering. He was going to get here first." Don was still good-tempered, but he was puzzled. "Bush was very keen to be here before me; he was going to bring some sherry. He said it was the only thing we dare drink before this. I don't know him; is he likely to behave this way?"

"No," said the Bishop. "A most punctilious fellow. Dear me, I hope nothing has happened."

Campion had been trying to dismiss a faintly nagging anxiety for some time now, but he shook his head. "If it has it would hardly delay Carados too," he said. "Look, I don't want to appear unduly inquisitive but even I can hardly miss that there is something unusual about this party. Don't you think you might explain, sir? Quite apart from everything else, we seem to be behaving rather badly to our host."

"Don't worry about me. I'm taking it my father has a great hand in this, Mr. Campion." Don was at his best. "It seems to me that he must have got in touch with Mr. Bush without letting me know; the whole tone of the party has a kind of

parental flavour. He still feels I need a lot of protection from
the seamy side of life. Now I don't want to be suspicious in
any way, but I'm getting an idea that there's a distinct possibility that this wine has been pinched from somewhere. Am I
right?"

"My dear boy, I really must apologize." The Bishop's face
was as grieved as a mourning cherub's. "I wouldn't have had
this happen for worlds. We all did so hope it might never be
necessary to tell you. I did point out to Bush that we were
putting ourselves in a most invidious position by behaving
like this, but as he said, there are rather serious complica-
tions and strict secrecy is absolutely necessary in the circumstances. I had not met you, so I had no idea that we should
find a young man of your age so remarkably—er—tolerant
and courteous."

Don was rather startled by the compliment and Mr. Campion came to the rescue. "Is the suspect identified?" he
enquired.

"Oh yes, I think so." The Bishop took up the decanter and
sniffed it heartily. "I fear so. We must taste it, of course, but
even if one's palate were the scientifically exact instrument
which some of us are stupid enough to hope, even then the
other evidence must weigh very heavily. The cork, the seal,
and the bottle are all beyond question in my opinion. In fact
from those, and from the colour and the bouquet I think I can
commit myself and say definitely that this is the genuine *Les
Enfants Doux* of nineteen hundred and four."

Mr. Campion saw no reason to disagree with him, but
wondered, albeit respectfully, where precisely that conclu-
sion might be expected to lead them. Don was more practical.

"I think we'll have Mr. Stavros in right away," he said.

"Oh no. Don't do that, my dear boy, whatever you do."
The Bishop was firm. "There's a great deal more to it than
that. I promised Bush to leave any explanations we might
have to make entirely to him, but since you've asked me
directly I really do feel I must be allowed to tell you at least
the little I know."

Mr. Campion looked up. "You had three cases of *Les
Enfants Doux* in the lorry which got lost when the Museum of
Wine was evacuated, hadn't you?" he said.

"I had. You know the story then?"

"No, I don't. All I know is that there was such a lorry. Bush told me so this morning."

"Ah. And do you know of it, Lieutenant?"

"No. I never heard of the Museum even."

The Bishop was happy to explain. After some considerable preliminaries he got down to the main story.

"This lorry went out of London during the second big raid in September, nineteen forty," he said, his beautiful precise voice lingering on the words. "Poor Bush had left things dangerously late, silly fellow. He realizes that now. The lorry carried the most valuable exhibits in the entire Museum; the Gyrth Chalice was there and the Arthurian Vase, priceless things, both of them, as well as a great deal more, and also by way of make-weight, I suppose, the two cases of my *Les Enfants*. This lorry was last seen turning into Theobald's Road while the raid was actually in progress. Its path lay through that part of the City which was very badly damaged that night. It never reached its destination, and neither the driver nor his mate, both reputable men with wives and families, was ever seen again."

"Were the bodies found?" enquired Campion with entirely new interest.

"There's a great deal of uncertainty about it." The Bishop found the tale painful and his bright blue eyes were cold and angry. "The remains of many lorries were found in London after that night, several of them under buildings which had collapsed on them. Three were never claimed; one of these did contain two charred corpses, but complete scientific identification was never possible and there was no trace of any of the Museum's property. Finally it was assumed that this lorry had belonged to the Museum and all it contained was written off as a total loss. In other circumstances the enquiry might have been more thorough, but at that time, you may remember . . ." He shrugged his shoulders.

"Then I walked in on Mr. Bush with my story," said Don. "Well, I can understand his interest."

Mr. Campion, who had been sitting on the arm of a chair, looking at the crimson glow in the decanter, now stirred himself.

"Forgive me," he said diffidently, "but by what method

does one identify one particular bottle or set of bottles? I don't doubt that you can do it, sir, but I'd like to know how."

"Of course you would." At last the Bishop had extracted the question he was waiting for. "Now," he said. "This is the part of the story I always did mean to tell myself. I don't suppose either of you young men have ever heard of *Les Enfants Doux* before, have you?"

They shook their heads and he sighed, put crime behind him, and plunged happily into fairer country.

"Nearly all the vineyards of Vosne are small, and most of them are good," he began, lecturing them gently, one hand tucked under the tail of his coat and the other free for delicate emphasis. "Most of them are famous. There are, as you know, the three *Romanées* and the *Richebourg,* the *La Tache,* the lesser known *Les Malconsorts,* and others less important. But there is one little vineyard, I doubt if it extends to more than three-quarters of an acre, which is different, and in some opinions, in most years superior to them all. Its produce never reaches the market." He paused for his announcement to have the right effect. Nothing so forceful as a dramatic effect, but one in which just the right element of surprise and interest was as carefully blended as in, say, a very good Highland whisky.

"This little vineyard of *Les Enfants Doux* lies just beyond *La Tache.* It is hidden from the main road by a very gentle dip in the ground," he went on, his voice as mellow as the grapes of which he spoke. "The land has always belonged to a peasant family called Bigot, and at one time they had the honour of providing the great ladies of the House of Bragelonne with a wet nurse, whenever one was required." He paused, and smiled faintly. "I cannot tell you, I'm afraid, how this was arranged so felicitously, but that is the story, and on one occasion the twin sons of a certain Comte de Bragelonne were placed as infants in the care of Héloïse Bigot, the beautiful young wife of the owner of this little patch of land. About six months after their arrival an epidemic broke out in Burgundy, and the children died. The young nurse was fear-stricken and the mother heartbroken. The great lady, and the great ladies of France in those days were terrifyingly great, left the Court and drove down like a thundercloud upon the unfortunate Bigots. Her rage and grief, or perhaps it should have been the other way round, were formidable indeed, but when she came at last upon the woman she found her, so the story goes, dead of remorse (or of course it may have been the fever) lying across the tiny biers of her two charges.

"The Comtesse, touched by this devotion, for although heartbroken, you understand, she was nowhere near dying herself, suffered a most satisfactory change of heart, and instead of pressing home the punishment she had prepared for the wretched Papa Bigot, she made him what amends she could by providing a sum of money to be spent on planting his field with the Pinot, and undertaking that her family should purchase the entire output of the vineyard for ever."

"And they still do?" Don enquired.

"They still did until the beginning of this war," said the Bishop. "Heaven alone knows what tragedy may have occurred now, of course. The little place flourished, and the wine which grew there (some say from the very soil where the sweet children and their faithful foster-mother lie buried, but that is unlikely) certainly had a strange, gentle freshness to be found in no other vintage in the world. The Bragelonne family reserved the whole of the growth, about forty-five to fifty dozen a year, I suppose, and a superstition grew up among them decreeing that ill luck would befall the children of the house should the wine ever find its way off the estate."

"And yet you had three cases of it," ventured Mr. Campion.

"I had six cases once," said the Bishop of Devizes, "and I'll break my rule and tell you how I came by it. I never have told this story because it is both sentimental and romantic, and neither of those delightful things is the better for an airing, don't you know."

"If you'd rather not, sir," began Don hastily, and fumbled for the end of the sentence. "I guess we've got pretty positive proof by this time."

Mr. Campion knew his uncle well and was fond of him.

"I think I should like to hear it," he said.

"Over-ruled," murmured the Bishop, smiling at Don.

"Well, many years ago when I was a very young man, just after I came down from Oxford, I spent a holiday at Bragelonne tutoring the heir, who was a very delicate and rather stupid boy. He had an elder sister, her name was Elise; she was very beautiful and her birthday fell on the seventeenth of July. Now I would stress that there was no love affair. In those days we were circumspect, and in hopeless situations we may have formed attachments but we never had affairs."

He stood looking at them, his bright blue eyes alive with unconquerable youth. "For three years running I visited Bragelonne in the summer," he went on, "and on the last occasion I was able to congratulate my Elise on her betrothal to her cousin, Henri de Bragelonne, next in succession to her brother. I was present at the wedding and after that, although we never met, I used always to send her some trifle on her birthday and always in return she wrote to thank me and to give me an account of her fortunes. I suppose we corresponded in this way for twenty years. In the last war the little custom came to an abrupt end, but when at last the fighting was done and the German armies retreated I received a letter from a notary telling me Elise was dead. He enclosed a letter from her written very near her end, and also told me that six dozen of Burgundy was being forwarded to me at her order."

Mr. Campion gave up doubting, the old man had a very strong case. He was putting it very well, too, addressing himself mainly to Don to whom he had evidently taken a liking.

"Her letter was charming," he said, "but her news was bad. Her brother had died, her husband was killed almost immediately after succeeding to the estate, and a few months later her son had followed his father. She knew she was very ill and she feared that she would never write to me again, but as she said, she was still feminine and she did not want to be forgotten. Therefore (she was very practical, my dear Elise), she was sending me six dozen of *Les Enfants Doux* of the great year, and she begged that I would always drink a bottle of it on the seventeenth of July. Not the best time of year, you know, for a royal Burgundy, but how was she to know that, poor dear? Women were not connoisseurs in her day."

"You got the whole six dozen intact? That was a bit of a miracle in itself, wasn't it?" said Don curiously.

"It was. How she had managed to preserve anything so precious and yet so vulnerable during the whole of the Occupation, I cannot imagine, but she did. And as for the superstition, poor lady, I have no doubt that she felt no further ill luck could befall her family."

"It's very conclusive," murmured Mr. Campion, bringing the matter down to earth.

"Oh, it is. I'm afraid so." The Bishop picked up the empty bottle and pointed to a scribble in red ink on the lower right-hand corner of the label. "You see that?" he said. "That's J.D. They are the initials of the wine steward of the period. I remember him well, he was a great character called Jules Denise. You see, a certain percentage of the yield was put aside, always for the Comte's own table, as opposed to his chaplain's or his major-domo's or any of the other little establishments on the estate, and on each bottle of this little reserve Jules used to put his mark. All my six dozen had that scrawl; you mentioned it to Bush, Lieutenant, and when I heard of it I felt very sure. That is why I took the astonishing liberty of—er—'gate-crashing' your party."

"I should think so." Don was looking at the decanter with respect. "It seems criminal to drink it, this may be the last there is in the world. I don't think we need let Bush open that second bottle, do you? After all, a magnificent wine like that . . ."

"Needs no bush," said the Bishop shyly, laughing at the silly little joke which everybody made sooner or later. "Where is the man? I do hope nothing has happened. I'm afraid I've been talking for nearly an hour."

No one answered him, but in the silence which followed his remark, someone tapped at the door. It was old Fred, a gleam of anticipation in his watery eyes.

"Mr. Campion is wanted on the phone," he said. "The gentleman seemed upset, sir."

"Who is it?"

"He didn't say, sir, but he seemed very shaken. This way, it's in the passage just along here."

When Campion reached the telephone and before he had taken up the receiver he could hear someone shouting at the other end. "Hello. Hello. Hel-lo. Campion. Oh, there you are, are you? I say . . ."

It was Johnny Carados, sounding as nearly rattled as Campion had ever heard him.

"Yes?"

"Can you come round to Theodore Bush's house as soon as dammit? You know where it is, don't you? Forty-two Bedbridge Row. Come at once, will you?"

"I will."

"Good man. I need you. I say, Campion . . . ?"

"Yes?"

"I'm afraid I've killed the blighter. . . . Good-bye."

13

THE JOURNEY FROM the Minoan to Bedbridge Row in Holborn in a pitch-dark and taxi-less London proved to be more of an undertaking than the exile had expected, and it was nearly an hour later when at last he groped his way up the worn stone steps of the narrow Georgian house in the corner of the half-ruined cul-de-sac. During his stumbling journey he had plenty of time for thought, and the closer he came to this new development the less he liked it.

There were times, too, when he fancied he was being followed, but in these dark empty streets it was difficult to tell. In a crowded city square he could have been sure, but none of his past experience allowed for these vast open spaces wherein one set of footsteps rang out loudly in the silence. He was not alone at any rate. Someone else made that journey as well as himself.

The house when he reached it might have been empty for years. His small torch beam showed a worn door with dirty iron furnishings and brass numerals green with neglect, but when he pressed the bell-push a sound like a fire alarm echoed in the hall within.

To his surprise the door opened instantly, and in the darkness a woman seized his arm.

"Oh, there you are at last," she said. "Do go up to him, we

can't do anything with him, and he won't send for the police. Isn't it awful?"

Campion recognized Miss Chivers with surprise. He had not expected her. There was a faint blue light in the white-painted hall and her sensible face looked pallid in the gloom. She was still efficient, of course, and still preserved her confidential friendliness of manner, but alarm had intensified each characteristic so that she presented a caricature of herself.

"Don't stand there staring at me," she said. "I dare say you are surprised to see me here. I'm surprised to be here. But when he rang through I thought I'd better come. Gee-gee Gold is up there with Dion Robson, the doctor. Johnny rang me at Carados Square and told me to fetch him. I came along to see if I could do anything, but he won't speak to me. He's in the front room on the first floor. The others are all in the bathroom higher up; I'm keeping here to mind the door and to stop the old housekeeper coming up from the basement. My God, they are a lot."

"Doesn't the housekeeper know what's happened?"

"Nobody knows except us. It's madness, of course. They'll hang Johnny if he doesn't look out. He's gone out of his mind, Mr. Campion, the war's gone to his head."

"Is Bush actually dead?"

"He may be by this time. He wasn't half an hour ago—not quite. He will die, though, and then there will be an al-mighty row. For heaven's sake go upstairs, and get some sense into Johnny and make him send for the police."

She gave him a push which all but over-balanced him, and he started off down the passage obediently. At the foot of the stairs he paused, and looked back.

"Are you all right down here alone?"

"Me? My dear man, don't worry about *me*," she said, laughing irritably. "I'm only the secretary of the madhouse. It's the master you've got to look after."

Mr. Campion mounted the stairs and came into an elegant little hall with a grey-carpeted floor. If Theodore Bush did not bother about the outside of his house any more than he did about the outside of his bottles, like them the inside had considerable merit. The glossy door to the large living-room faced the stair head, and all was silent behind it. From

further up the stairs the sound of voices and restless movement floated down. Campion tapped on the door and waited.

"Hello, that you, Dion?" Johnny's voice was almost casual

"No. Campion here."

"Well, come in, you ape. I'm not waiting behind the door
with a club."

Campion entered a large and graceful yet entirely masculine room and looked about him. Carados was partially hidden in an enormous blue leather arm-chair, his legs stretched
out to the fire and his big chin resting on his breast. He did
not move as the other man came over to him, but raised his
eyes.

"This is a stinker," he said. "What do you know about this,
eh?"

"Almost nothing," said Campion. "I'm hoping to pick it up
as I go along. What have you done to him? Hit him on the
head with a bottle?"

"Oh no. No, I was much more subtle than that." The
grey-blue eyes rested on Campion's face with an expression
in them which he did not immediately recognize. Only gradually did it occur to him that Carados was afraid. "No, I
poisoned the poor old boy," he said at last. "I did, Campion.
I gave him God knows how much chloral hydrate and I saw
him mix it in a tooth-glass and knock it back at one go.
Dreadful, I shall never forget it. Poor old Theo. He was a bit
of a crank, of course. Believed in all the wrong things and was
heaven's own peculiar prize bore, but to kill him, Campion!
To kill him like that, all defenceless, in a neat little tucked
shirt and blue pants. No, I'll never forgive myself, never as
long as I live."

Campion sat down and crossed his long, thin legs.

"I hate to be vulgar, but that won't be long if this is the
story you're telling," he said affably.

Carados grunted. "I've got the wind up," he said. "Someone's
being horribly clever. I suspected it when I saw that wretched
woman lying dead in your flat. I thought then that someone
was going all out for me. Afterwards I wondered if perhaps I
was making myself too important in the story, but now I
know I was right. Someone is not only trying to get rid of me,
but they're trying to prove I'm ga-ga first. What about you?
Are you for me, or against me?"

"I'd take a drink from you," said Mr. Campion, considering it was a handsome offer in the circumstances.

"I wouldn't." Carados was bitter. "I wouldn't touch me or anything I had handled with a barge pole. I'm dangerous."

"Well, I don't know how long it's necessary to suffer to be interesting," said Campion with calculated brutality, "but I'll buy it. What did you think you were giving him?"

Johnny's face cleared and he felt in the breast pocket of his tunic. "The expert's calm is very important when you need it," he said. "Look. See this?" Campion took what appeared to be a small imitation-leather cigarette case from his outstretched hand. It was buttoned down, envelope fashion, and embossed on the grain in gilt script was the legend: "*Zo-zo. Pour l'ennui de l'estomac. Gilbert Frères. Paris. 15ième.*"

Mr. Campion raised the flap cautiously. Inside the case was divided into ten small partitions, each one of which normally contained a phial stoppered by a metal cap and sheathed in typical blue-and-green-striped metal paper. At the moment there were seven left.

"French bismuth type?" he enquired.

Carados nodded. "Yes. Only obtainable over there, and very expensive as those things go. About fifty francs, that lot, I suppose. There was a mild fashion for it over here just before the war, and when I saw Theo yesterday he was bewailing the fall of France, for all the wrong reasons as usual, and he mentioned the disappearance of these things as one of the minor evils which had come out of it. 'And to cap it all, you can't even get a Zo-zo,' he said, the silly old ape. He looked so miserable I told him I thought we probably had some about the house, and that I'd look them up for him if I could."

He spoke casually and Campion remembered this peculiarity of his. The incident was typical of him. In common with many big men of wide interests he had that side to him. He was a person who always did do little errands for people, not necessarily his closest friends. He was a man who remembered birthdays, and if a guest could not eat oysters, or always smoked Turkish cigarettes, and more than likely he would go out of his way to see such little desires were gratified. It was one of his most charming characteristics, but as an attribute it was rare enough to make his present story unconvincing to a jury.

"Go on," said Campion.

"Well, I did find them," said Carados, "and I brought them along when I called for the old man. He asked me to meet him here because there were one or two points in this business of *Les Enfants* turning up like this, which he felt we ought to discuss. He was certain the wine wasn't genuine and he wondered if we ought to make a statement. Good Lord, how small peace-time affectations seem these days, Campion. What fools we all were."

"It all depends on how you look at it," said Mr. Campion cautiously. "I don't know if our present occupation is very bright, fireworks and death. Still, get on with the story. You brought this stuff with you, did you?"

"Yes, I did. Theo was late and was changing. Apparently Theo can't give his opinion on a rare bottle if he isn't in virgin linen. It's against his religion, perhaps. Anyway he asked me to come up and talk while he dressed. I gave him that packet and he fell on it; from the way he behaved I thought he'd had chronic dyspepsia since nineteen thirty-nine. He said he'd take a dose at once if I didn't mind. I watched him take his tooth-glass, pour one of these things into it, stir it up in water, and gulp it down. Ten minutes afterwards he was in a coma. God knows how much chloral he's had."

"How do you know it's chloral?" Campion demanded.

"Because I recognized the stink of the stuff." Johnny told his appalling story in his usual casual way, apparently unaware of its weakness; only the new darkness in his eyes betrayed him.

"This is what happened," he said. "I noticed Theo getting a bit thick and wavery, but when he flopped it took me by surprise. He collapsed across the bed and began to breathe like a bomber. I didn't think it was heart and it sort of came to me—you know how it does—that he'd taken something. The only thing I knew he'd taken was this stuff I'd brought him. The empty phial was still on the dressing-table and I took it up and sniffed it; then I recognized it."

"You recognized chloral hydrate?"

Carados shook his head. For the first time he looked embarrassed. "Not exactly, I—I recognized *Bromot*."

"What's that?"

Carados sat forward in his chair and stubbed the fire.

"It's damned awkward," he said.

"I've heard worse, slightly," said Campion.

"You wait. There's bags to come. *Bromot* is a proprietary mixture sold to make you sleep. It's dangerous. Dion prescribed it for me years ago when I was going through a bad patch. You take about a fifth of the quantity which would go into one of those phials and it's got chloral hydrate in it, potassium bromide, and one or two other things, I forget what. The chief danger of it is the high specific gravity of the stuff makes it fall to the bottom, and you're always warned not to take the last dose in the bottle. I never did." He paused. "I bet there were a dozen bottles with one dose left in each kicking about the house just before the war," he said. "I remember them; they stood in a row at the back of the medicine cupboard. I always meant to tell someone to chuck them away, but I never did."

Campion said nothing, and Johnny nodded towards the case of phials.

"You sniff those," he said. "Five are *Zo-zo*, the other two, one at each end, are *Bromot*. The third which Theo took was *Bromot* too. Devilish, isn't it?"

"Didn't he notice the taste?"

"He must have done. The famous palate can't have been as bad as that, but he took it at a gulp, you see. They both looked vaguely alike, muddy and uninviting. He did say it was different, I remember, but it would never have occurred to him to doubt me. I mean, why should I kill him?"

"Yes," said Campion gravely. "Why should you kill him? Why should anybody kill him, for that matter?"

Johnny stirred. "It's all part of this other damned business," he began, and was silent.

Campion let him wait for a long time.

"I think I should tell it all," he ventured at last. "It's just an opinion, but I think I would. As the story stands there's not a Counsel in England who'd touch it."

Carados lay back in the chair. "I know it," he said. "I've been sitting here thinking it. It's frightful. You don't know the full strength of this business. The devil of it is that it keeps coming back to me. Whichever way one turns, what-

ever new line one takes, all paths lead back to me. To *me*,
mind you. Whenever I get a thread and follow it up and see a
vague figure disappearing at the end of it, and I press on until
I see his face, whom do you think it turns out to be? Me,
Campion. Myself. My God, it would almost be a relief to
think I was mad."

Behind his spectacles Mr. Campion blinked. There had
been times of late when he had thought that he was getting
old and that there were no more thrills, no more surprises in
the bag for him. But now, as he sat looking into those cold
steady eyes and heard the terrible confession, the half-forgotten
trickle ran down his spine again.

Johnny went on talking. "I don't think I'm permitted to tell
you anything," he said. "We'd better have Oates up here, I
suppose; but he's not sure of me, at least I don't think he is."

"No policeman is ever sure of anybody. That's the first
thing they learn at the college," said Campion. "Let me get
one part of the story clear in my own mind. Where did you
get this Zo-zo stuff today? My dear chap, you'll have to
explain that. Whatever else you choose to be chivalrous about
you can't leave that in the air."

Carados eyed him. "You're very shrewd, aren't you?" he
said savagely. "I'm not shielding anyone, at least not anyone
in particular, but I've got to be sure. You must see that. I got
that packet of Zo-zo off the table in the back hall of my own
house just before I went out with the Admiral this morning."

Campion's face remained blank.

"Just like that?" he enquired. "You just saw it and picked
it up?"

"No, not quite. Look here, Campion, if I tell you this
you've got to treat it as confidential until I give you the word.
I'll tell you exactly what happened. I was in London all day
yesterday; I came up on Sunday, as a matter of fact, and at
midday I looked in at the Junior Greys where I found about a
dozen enquiries for me from Bush. It seemed urgent and I
got hold of him. We had a chat and fixed up this gathering
this evening. It was then he mentioned the Zo-zo. Later on
in the afternoon I went to my own house, taking Eve with
me. No one was in at all, not a servant, not a soul. I made a
note of the Zo-zo so that I shouldn't forget it and left it on the
pad on that table in the back hall where I always did leave

notes. It was a custom of the house in the old days. I'd write down what I wanted and whoever knew something about it would see to it that the thing was got or done or seen to somehow."

"Things like 'Ink on the study carpet,' or 'Gone to Scotland' or 'Out of toothpaste,' " suggested Campion with interest.

"Yes. That sort of thing. Everybody did it, not only me. I suppose the butler used to dole out the jobs in the days when we had a butler. I never thought any more about it, I'm afraid. If it was on the pad no one could say they hadn't been told, it saved time and argument. That was the idea."

"I see. And yesterday you left a message there in the ordinary way. Is that message still in existence?"

"I expect so. I didn't notice, I just happened to see the stuff lying on the table when I went to get my coat and I pocketed it."

"I see. Can you remember the message you left?"

"Yes, I can. I just wrote: 'Please see if there is any Zo-zo in the house.' I think I probably added 'Burp mixture,' or something like that, to remind whoever it was what the stuff was like."

"Did you say it was for Bush?"

Carados raised his eyes and blushed. "I did, you know," he said. "I did, I know I did. It's so darned kiddish, isn't it, so silly? I didn't want anyone to think it was for me, I suppose. I know I added: 'Mr. Bush wants it,' like a school child. I've been sitting here remembering that and cursing."

"It's human enough," said Campion. "It'd pass, I think."

He sat quiet for some time, frowning. They were undisturbed, no sound reached them from the floor above and there was no traffic in the street outside. There was a blankness in the situation, a sense of frustration and defeat. At length he asked the inevitable question.

"Which one of them put it there?"

"I don't know." Carados spoke so softly that his voice scarcely reached across the hearthrug. "That's the hell of it. I have no idea whatever. I can't believe it of any one of them. There's only one really reckless damned fool in the whole gathering, I should have said, and that's—me."

Campion cocked an eye at him. "That way the loony bin lies," he said. "You have no idea when the stuff was left on

the table except that it must have been some time between
three or four yesterday afternoon and about twelve-thirty this
morning. Is that so?"

"Yes."

"And during that time all the old gang has been in the
place, not to mention the Admiral, myself, Susan, and, of
course, Eve?"

"Yes."

"Anyone who knew the house well could have got at your
Bromot dregs?"

"Anyone. They and the *Zo-zo* were probably on the same
shelf. It only needed the necessary filthy idea."

"I see." The scene of the morning with the odd incident of
the rose and the pearls returned vividly to Mr. Campion's
mind. That remarkable package also had been found upon a
hall table, as far as he remembered.

"Who knew you were going to have this bottle party with
Bush?" he enquired.

"Half London," said Carados wearily. "Bush made such a
set-out about getting hold of me that I should think everybody knew that he wanted my opinion on a bottle of wine.
He seems to have said everything except the actual name of
the stuff. How much do you know about it, Campion?"

"I know what the wine is and where it came from. I know
about the loss of the lorry and the two men in it."

"And that's all you know?"

"Practically all. Is there much more?"

Carados looked away. "Quite a bit," he said briefly. "Lives,
and treasure, and something rather more important. It's
Oates's pidgin. If he hasn't told you, I can't. Oh, Lord," he
said, "I wish this hadn't happened to Bush. I don't know what
they think they're doing upstairs. Gold is helping Dion, you
know. They wouldn't have me. They must have washed him
out by this time. They're trying artificial respiration, I suppose,
but it's no good, I saw what he took."

Mr. Campion got up. One of the principal mysteries of the
past twenty-four hours had been explained to him. His suspicions had been confirmed; whatever might be the precise
nature of the nightmare which had overtaken him so suddenly the previous evening, it was no simple story of theft
and murder. He felt like an actor who had stepped on to the

stage half-way through some considerable drama. He was far too experienced a performer to attempt to do any more just then than play his part blindly.

"I'll go up and see," he said. "Where are they? At the back of the house?"

"Yes. You'll see when you get up there. Tell them to come down. I'll have to do some explaining to Dion, I suppose. He's been dragged out here without ceremony."

With his hand on the latch, Campion turned and looked back. "One other thing, Johnny," he said. "Did your mother come to the house last night?"

As soon as he had spoken he saw the change in the man. His strong heavy body sagged. "I can't tell you," he said. "I don't know. She may have done, I can't tell you. Someone else may remember."

Mr. Campion was sorry for him. "If she was there, someone else will, you know," he said awkwardly, and opened the door.

The Dowager Lady Carados was standing outside.

14

MR. CAMPION KNEW just enough of the Dowager Marchioness not to be surprised by her. He felt he had had that. He stood looking at her with defensive vacancy, and she smiled at him frankly, as he thought she might.

"I heard you talking, and didn't like to disturb you," she said outrageously, "but I had to come and find Johnny. I telephoned the Minoan and they told me he was here."

"Mother, my dear girl!" Johnny appeared in the doorway behind Campion. He was very startled, and Campion, who had no wish to play Polonius to anybody's Hamlet, edged out of the way. "What on earth are you doing here, darling?"

"Oh, there you are at last. I'm so glad." She moved over to

him looking remarkably youthful and feminine in her blue fur
coat. "I felt somebody must warn you and it didn't seem wise
to talk on the phone. My dear, they've found that awful
woman's clothes."

"The police have?"

"Yes, and I'm afraid they're going to be very difficult.
They're so—so stodgy, aren't they? There's a little person
called Yeo, I think, who has no sense of humour whatever.
He's been following me about with a pair of corsets which
must have come out of the Ark. I told him they were probably Ricky Silva's and he took me quite seriously."

"Oh, God!" said Johnny, without impiety. "Look here,
dearest, where did they find these things? In your house?"

"No, darling, they didn't." She linked her arm through his
and stood looking up at him as once she must have looked at
his father who could refuse her nothing. "I have been foolish.
I do see that, so there's no use you or anybody else pointing
it out again. I've been very foolish and rather vulgar too, I'm
afraid. It's fashionable to be a go-getter and full of action, and
all that, but I don't think it really suits us older women. I'm
sorry I did it. I'm afraid I've got that man of yours into
trouble too, Mr. Campion, and it really is a pity because he's
an excellent old fellow and so faithful. What did you say?"

"I didn't," said Mr. Campion idiotically. "It didn't mean
anything, I was only muttering. Where did you say you'd
found the murdered woman's clothes?"

"Murdered? She wasn't murdered. She committed suicide,
poor beastly woman."

"The police . . ." Carados began.

"Oh, the police," she said with relief, "I don't take any
notice of the police. They're always so dramatic and gloomy,
and stodgy at the same time. Oh no, she committed suicide."

"Where did they find her clothes?" Johnny repeated very
slowly and distinctly.

"In your bedroom, dear," said his mother. "I couldn't see
them anywhere, but they found them. Apparently they were
on the window-seat, of all places, wrapped up in a shawl from
the chair. I must have seen the bundle and not noticed it. It's
all terribly awkward and difficult. Now, what we've got to do
is all to get together and make up our minds exactly what

we're going to do, and even more important, what we're going to say."

"Darling." Johnny took her elbow firmly and led her back into the room. Campion followed them and closed the door.

When she was safely in the fireside chair, her son released her and stood back on the hearthrug.

"Don't look like that, my pet. You're like your father," she said, "and he used to get enraged with me. I know I've been stupid and I've said I'm sorry. Can't we leave it like that? I only did it for you, dearest, only for you, silly. Now we must all act for the best."

"Now we must all tell the absolute truth, Mother."

"Yes, between ourselves, but not to everybody; that would be insane. No, we've got to be sensible."

"Of course we have, and that's why we're going to have a complete showdown." He spoke very gently, almost casually, and certainly reassuringly. Campion gave him full marks, but recognized the method by which Lady Carados had been able to survive so long; evidently this was the treatment to which she was used.

"What a dear you are, Johnny," she said, "so comforting. Give me a cigarette. We are in Theodore Bush's house, aren't we? He just isn't here, I suppose."

"That's right," said Carados, and the hand in which he held the match for her was perfectly steady. "Now, look here, darling, last night—my hat! was it only last night?—you told me that you'd been very silly and stupid and that you'd made a mistake when you first told me the story of Campion's flat. Last night, when we all got back, leaving that poor woman in the flat, you told me that you had found her dead in the basement of your own house and that was the story you told the police this morning, wasn't it?"

"Yes, I did." She was prettily businesslike, and emphasized her words with little stabs in the air with her cigarette. "I did, and I do reproach myself. Not for what I told the police, because I think they're blunted and warped, and no good anyway; but I do reproach myself for not telling you everything, darling. I wanted to spare you . . . Your leave and your wedding! Oh, it is insufferable, just when we were all going to be so happy."

Mr. Campion began to wonder if the sensation he felt

round the edge of his scalp really was the well-known beads of sweat appearing. His sympathy for Carados was tremendous, and in his mind's eye he could see the sturdy, Edwardian gentleman who had bequeathed this lovely spoilt darling to a more harassed generation. Johnny was experienced where his mother was concerned, however, and he patted her shoulder.

"Too bad, sweetheart," he said. "Now, let's just have the facts. The real, no-nonsense-about-it truth."

She looked at him with tolerant reproach. "I didn't mean it to be nonsense, Johnny: I was simply thinking of you."

"Of course you were, darling. Splendid of you. But just at this particular moment let's see what really has happened, and then . . ."

"Then we'll all go into a huddle and plan something."

"Yes, very well, if you like, but let us know where we are first. Now, is the original tale you told, the one you told me in Campion's flat, is that the literal truth?"

"Yes. Yes, Johnny. Substantially, I think it is." She had such poise and authority, even now when she was in her softest mood, that Campion could understand much which had hitherto puzzled him. The behavior of the police, for one thing, and Lugg's unaccountable obligingness, for another. Her potential dangerousness grew at every moment. She was like a beautiful, high-powered car driven by an engaging maniac.

Johnny was gentleness itself. "No, my dear," he said, " 'substantially' won't do. I want the whole truth just as it happened. At the flat you told me that you went to my house yesterday morning and found this woman dead in the bed which had been prepared for me. There was a medicine bottle by her side, and you assumed she had committed suicide; you made arrangements to remove her to an unoccupied flat. That was your first story. Then, later last night you told us you had a confession to make, and you then said that you had found her in a servant's bedroom in the basement of your own house. Now you say the first story is true. Is it?"

Lady Carados appeared to make a supreme effort.

"Yes, dear," she said. "You see, when I saw you all young and eager and happy on leave I felt I must protect you. You do understand, don't you?"

She believed what she was saying implicitly, and Campion

could see her acquitting herself nobly in the witness box.
Carados was beginning to look an old man; but he went on
steadily with his questions.

"I've got it right, have I? You did all this alone save for the
man Lugg?"

"Yes, I did." She was frank and proud. "When one's fighting for someone one loves, one gets incredible strength.
But, oh darling, it was terrible! Having to touch her, I
mean."

"Of course it was," he said hastily. "But you thought it out
all alone, did you?"

"Yes, it came to me that I could save us all a terrible
scandal. Because, you know, it did look frightful her being
found just there at this time. I mean, no one would believe
you hadn't broken her heart at least, would they? Perhaps
you did; I don't know. I don't want to, Johnny. I just love
you, you see."

"No one else knew except you and Lugg?"

"No one. I thought Miss Chivers might find out. She was
in another room when I found the terrible thing, so I sent her
away."

"On what excuse?"

She stared at him in astonishment. "My dear, I don't have
to make excuses to an employee."

"I see. You just said, 'Go away,' or words to that effect."

"Yes. I said 'I don't want you in this house, Miss Chivers,
until three o'clock this afternoon.' "

"Wasn't she surprised?"

"Johnny darling, how should I know? I know she's your
secretary, but I know nothing else about her. She's here now,
by the way, downstairs. She let me in."

"Yes, I sent for her," he said briefly. "Captain Gold is
here, too, upstairs. Now, darling, just to get the thing settled
once and for all, you're sure the only thing you did was to
move the body? And the medicine bottle, I suppose? Did you
take that along with you? I didn't notice it at the flat."

She was silent, and sat looking at the smoke rising unevenly
from her cigarette.

"Well, what about the bottle, dear?" The tremor in the
man's voice was barely impatient, but she frowned at him.

"My dearest, you mustn't bully me."

"Forgive me," he said. "I didn't mean to. Mustn't I ask about the bottle?"

"I'd rather you didn't," she said. "I don't want to make you unhappy."

The colour came into his face and he grinned. It was a brief flash of genuine entertainment, and Campion, who had begun to wonder about it, thought he saw at last where some of her tremendous charm for her menfolk lay.

"I'll bear it," said Johnny. "One can't be happy all the time. What about the bottle?"

"Well, I changed it," said Lady Carados.

There was a moment's complete silence, during which the men did not look at each other.

"Why?" Johnny's tone was deceptively conversational.

"I thought it best. Don't make me hurt you, darling. I've owned that I ought to have left everything alone, and I've said I'm sorry. Don't look at me like that, Johnny."

He sat down on the arm of her chair. "Tell us," he said.

"Oh, if I must I will, but I warn you, it's just annoying and it's horrible. The bottle that was by her side was yours, darling."

"Mine?"

"Yes, yours. You can see how bad it looked?"

"Yes, I can. But how do you mean it was mine?"

"Well, it had your name on it, dear. It was some of that stuff Doctor Robson prescribed for you long ago. Don't you remember? You had to take the prescription before you could buy it, and they'd never let you drink the last dose. I forget what it was called, but it had your name on it, and a prescription number."

"Do you mean *Bromot*?"

"Yes, that was it. I didn't know you had any left, but I remembered it as soon as I saw it. This must have been very old because it was all muddy and beastly-looking. There was about a quarter of a bottle left. Of course, I don't know how much she took."

"What did you do with it?"

"Oh, I put it back in the medicine cupboard outside your bathroom. I ought to have thrown it away because it had obviously gone bad, but I didn't think of it."

"And what bottle did you put by the cor . . . I mean, by the woman?"

"A little blue one I found. It had nothing but the chemist's name on it. I think it was some stuff they used to clean the bath with. Afterwards I remembered that they can tell what poison a person has died of, but this had 'Poison' on it clearly and I thought they might not go into it. It all sounds a little mad now, I know, but at the time I was so unnerved. It only seemed to me that I was making what *had* happened even more clear. Even now I don't think I did anything really wrong unless someone decides to get officious about it."

It was that last phrase which made Campion raise his eyes to look at her. She had spoken quite unconsciously, and even now, when the words were still hanging in the room, it was evident that she heard nothing odd in them. He wondered just how spoiled she was, just how far her notions of her private rights to do things which in more ordinary people were not permissible ranged into that abnormal which is politely called eccentricity. How far into, and how far beyond? He looked at Carados, and it occurred to him that he did not know either. Campion was very sorry for him.

"Well, what do we do now, darling?" said the lady bravely. "I'll do anything you want me to do. I'll even go and tell those over-stuffed policemen—why do they wear their collars so tight?—about the mistake I made if you tell me to. I don't want to, naturally, but we must all hang together, and if you think the first story is best . . ."

"My dearest girl!" Despite his efforts, Johnny's voice was rising. "It's not a question of 'Is it best?' Is it true?"

At once she was offended. She betrayed it very slightly, just enough to correct him, not enough to permit him to think for a moment that she was ungracious.

"Moralizing, Johnny?" she said. "I never thought I should hear that from you. Your father was always moralizing. It's not *quite* a simple question of right and wrong, is it? You see, it's not as if this dreadful thing was anything to do with us, dear. If it was our business, if we were actually concerned in it, if we were any of us to blame, even if *you* were, Johnny, then I think you know me well enough to realize that I should do just what I saw was right, whatever it cost us. But it's not like that. It's all so terribly *unfair*. This is just a wretched accident which happens to have occurred on our premises. We must protect ourselves, it's only sense. I told her so."

"You told her . . . ? Mother, whom did you tell?"

She blinked at him, undecided whether to disown the slip altogether, or to prevaricate.

"What, darling? Don't flare up like that. Your nerves are completely upset. Oh, this *is* annoying."

"Mother, tell me. Have you ever spoken to that woman who died?"

"No, darling, of course I haven't. Don't be so dramatic, dearest. You're making an awful fool of yourself."

"Of whom are you talking?" he said.

"When?"

"Just now. You said 'I told her so.' "

"Oh, that." She had had time to recover herself, and was laughing. "Why, I told Gwenda so this morning. I said, 'It's nothing to do with us and people are simply trying to drag us into it because we're wealthy and well known.' There are always people who do that. If one fights back, they squeal."

Campion glanced at Carados and saw that whether he was satisfied or not, and it hardly seemed possible that he should be, he would not press the point. Instead he said abruptly:

"What are the police doing now?"

"I don't know. They've taken the clothes away. One of them, the same stupid little person, told me he'd be obliged to me if I'd stay indoors until tomorrow morning, which seemed silly and officious."

"And yet you came down here?"

"Well, my dear, you don't suppose I intended—or he expected me to take him literally, do you?"

Johnny Carados said nothing. Both he and Campion were listening. Footsteps sounded on the floor above, and presently someone came down the stairs. Campion hurried out to meet Captain Gold, who was on the staircase. The man gaped at him.

"I was coming down to see if anyone could arrange some coffee," he said, his deep voice lowered. "Good, strong coffee. Robson says it's to be as black as they can get it."

"Gee-gee!" Johnny came out of the door as he spoke and

closed it firmly after him so that they were all huddled
together in the little hall. "Does that mean—?"

"Yes, I think so." Gold's teeth flashed in his beard. "It's
been a very near thing, but I believe Robson has pulled it off.
The old gentleman is made of tough material. I'm needed up
there, though, so if you could get some coffee made—. Robson will want you, Johnny. He's going to be a little sticky, I'm
afraid."

"Is he? Right. You go back, and we'll get the coffee."

Relief was shaking Carados as fear had never done. He
slurred his words a little and his hand shook on Campion's
arm.

"You'll see to it, won't you? I'll get back in here and try to
send her home. With luck no one need ever know about this.
Poor old boy, I'm glad. Oh God, I'm glad!"

Gee-gee Gold glanced at the door. "Mrs. Shering?" he
enquired.

"No, my mother."

"Oh, I see." It was evident he realized the gravity of the
situation. "I'll go back then. You get the coffee, Mr. Campion.
Very strong, and plenty of it."

He crept back up the stairs on fat, pointed feet, and
Carados turned to Campion again.

"Not a word to a soul," he said urgently. "With luck we'll
get clean away with it. I'll manage Bush and Dion; they'll see
reason. This is a heaven-sent break. I don't deserve it. I can
hardly believe it. I've been feeling like a murderer and it isn't
true."

As Mr. Campion went on down the stairs he wondered
about Johnny, and about his mother he wondered even more.
The one important and immediate problem, however, was
the coffee.

The house was quiet and cold, and when he found the front
hall empty he looked about for Miss Chivers with a certain
anxiety. There was no sign of her in the dark downstairs
room, but at last he found the entrance to a flight of service
stairs. Below in the basement it was still very quiet, but he
saw a crack of light beneath the centre doorway. He entered
without knocking and stepped into a vast, brightly lit, old-
fashioned kitchen with a stone floor, hooks in the ceiling, and

a huge table taking up nearly all the room. An old woman sat by the stove, her feet resting on a bright steel fender.

But it was not she who caught Mr. Campion's startled attention, for at the table, disconsolate as children kept in school, were two men each of whom appeared to be engaged in the melancholy business of sitting the other out. One was Superintendent Yeo, neat and clean in plain clothes, and the other, surprisingly clad in the uniform of a Civil Defence Warden, was a man Mr. Campion had seen twice before. Above the blue battle blouse lowered the narrow face and unforgettable eyes of Stavros's partner, the ubiquitous Mr. Pirri.

15

PRUDENTLY PLACING FIRST things first, Mr. Campion did not look at either of the visitors but concentrated on the housekeeper. She showed no surprise at his sudden appearance, but when he asked her for coffee she smiled and shook her head at him.

Yeo pushed a slate across the table at him. "You have to write it," he said briefly.

Mr. Pirri looked up sharply. It had been evident from the Superintendent's tone that he and Campion were acquainted. He got up at once, and with determined leisureliness strolled towards the door. On the threshold he looked back.

"Good night, all," he said.

"Good night," said Yeo, without turning to him, and sighed with relief when the area door closed behind him. "Thank the Lord for that," he said. "London is full of those chaps wandering into houses like regular constables getting cups of tea. People like 'em, but they cramp a professional's style." He was speaking absently, and Campion, who had by now established communication with the housekeeper, stepped back as she bustled from cupboard to stove.

"But not quite the style one would expect from a full-blown Superintendent," he said. It was an intentional blow below the belt, and Yeo flushed darkly.

"Special circumstances demand special tactics," he said defensively. "In the normal way when I put a person under house arrest and she breaks it, I pull her in. When I can't do that, I do the best I can." He hesitated, and smiled. "When I saw Her Ladyship enter the front door, I knocked at this one. This old dear opened it, and simply motioned me forward. I didn't realize she was deaf until I got inside and then I found that warden chap sitting here, and couldn't get any further. The next thing I know, you walk in. What's happening upstairs?"

Mr. Campion leaned across the table.

"Yeo," he said, "we must have known each other quite a time. During our association have you or have you not found me helpful, honest, tidy, clean, and modest in company?"

The Superintendent looked uncomfortable. "I don't know what you're playing at," he said stiffly.

"Exactly," said Campion. "And why? Because I'm not playing. While you people don't trust me I prefer not to know you. You've stopped my first home leave since the war broke out and what do you do with me? Nothing. You waste my time playing silly beggars in the dark. I have not the slightest glimmer of a night thought what you may think you're up to, and I take this opportunity of telling you I don't like the look of it, whatever it is. Good heavens, a Superintendent of the Special Branch breaking and entering; whatever next?"

It was very unfair. Yeo, who was a stickler for police etiquette, was stung to bitterness.

"Look here, my lad," he said. "I can't tell you anything. I'm working directly under the Chief and these are his orders. I know it's highly irregular, but then it's a—a highly irregular crime."

Mr. Campion took off his spectacles and looked at him coldly without speaking. Yeo turned away. Presently Campion took pity on him.

"You look like the original policeman's lot," he suggested.

The Superintendent swore softly. "It's a hell of a case," he began, adding more brightly, "I suppose I couldn't help you with that tray?"

"Thank you, no." Campion was polite but firm. "Since you have no reason to suspect that a felony is taking place upstairs, I really don't see how you can hope to get any further into the house."

"That's where you unofficial dicks have the advantage over us," said Yeo unpardonably, and Mr. Campion had no further compunction.

"I take it you're quite certain our hostess *is* deaf?" he enquired innocently.

Yeo laughed at him. "I like to see you being clever," he observed. "I'm not quite so senile as that. I tested her, she's deaf all right. Doesn't lip-read much, either."

"Smart work. And what about the warden?"

"The warden? The A.R.P. chap? No one suggested he was deaf. What are you getting at now? I saw nothing unusual about the warden."

"No, I gathered you didn't, but I did." Mr. Campion was already in the doorway. "His name is Pirri, and he's part owner of the Minoan; you must have missed him by about ten minutes or so this morning. Holly knows him. Last time I saw them together, Pirri was on the verge of being knifed by Stavros. Perhaps you heard about it."

As a revenge it was complete. The Superintendent sat gaping. "What the hell was he doing here?" he demanded.

"Imitating the new police methods, I shouldn't wonder," said Mr. Campion unpleasantly. "He followed me, though, not Lady Carados. Also, if it's of any interest to you, I'm fairly certain he was the man who drove my taxi last night. If you should see him, you might get it into his head that he's wasting his time on me. I've got nothing, tell him, not even the confidence of the police."

"I say, Mr. Campion . . ." But the thin man was already in the passage. He went upstairs with the coffee. Having begun on his small contribution towards the saving of Theodore's life, he saw no reason why he should not finish it; but he was more angry than he had been for years. There was still no sign of Miss Chivers in the hall, and as he passed the closed door on the first floor he could hear the gentle drone of Lady Carados's sweet, interminable voice behind it. He went on.

On the next landing there were other sounds, and he tapped at the most promising door. It was opened immediately by Gee-gee Gold, who seized the tray without a word, and turned back into the room with it. Mr. Campion followed him innocently.

The livid Theo, wretched and exhausted, and wrapped in blankets, was staggering about the room on the arm of a middle-aged doctor in shirt-sleeves. He stared ominously at Campion but did not speak to him.

Mr. Campion experienced a certain sympathy for Doctor Robson; it was evident he had not the temperament for adventures of this sort. Even now there was a hint of pompous importance in his manner, and his fiery eyes were outraged. Gee-gee was handling him cautiously but without making any real attempt to hide the fact. He bustled over with the coffee and stood holding out the pot, his head on one side and his beard cocked up enquiringly. The Doctor nodded irritably and took the cup while Gold poured out. It was all done in silence, and the moment the Doctor became preoccupied with his patient, Gold gripped Campion firmly by the arm and led him out on to the landing again.

"I know you don't mind," he said in a whisper which might well have carried through the door, "but better to leave them at this stage. Bush is coming round all right. It's an absolute miracle, but he is, thank God. Of course, he'll have to see reason, but it's going to be very difficult to persuade him."

"I don't see why he should if he feels that way about it," objected Mr. Campion.

Gold stared at him in amazement. "But he can make a most frightful row," he said.

"So I should imagine, but I don't see why he shouldn't, do you?"

"My dear man," said Gee-gee pityingly. "We can't have a row. After all, Johnny is who he is, isn't he? I know it's fashionable to pretend to ignore that, but one doesn't really, does one? No, we can't have Johnny involved in anything definitely unpleasant. That's absurd. Johnny's *sans reproche*. I'll get this chap to see reason, but it's not going to be a walkover. Doctors have got completely out of hand, these days. I'll have to concentrate on him if you don't mind. I'll see you downstairs, shall I?"

The last remark was not a question and he opened the door again. He spoke once more before he disappeared.

"Thanks for the coffee. Awfully good of you. There's not a lot of help in the kitchen, I'm afraid."

"You'd be surprised," said Mr. Campion briefly, and went downstairs.

He picked up his hat on the way and walked quietly out of the house. He met no one, and was thankful. The darkness swallowed him as he struck south-west purposefully. Having reached a decision he felt relieved; this was the end of them all, as far as he was concerned. There was just one more thing that must be done and then he'd wash his hands of them.

As he strode on through the misty darkness he tried to put the whole business out of his mind, but it was not so easy. After long years of practice he had developed a routine, and now, despite his inclinations, his brain persisted in carrying on quietly with the investigation. Every scrap of information which he had gathered in the twenty-four hours revolved before his inward eye, trying to slip into the pattern which was already forming. The discovery that Gold assumed automatically that Johnny was privileged beyond all the normal bounds of civilized behaviour was one of these. It had been odd coming from him and had reminded Mr. Campion of an incident of his own youth, when the nurse of the small friend who had just pushed him into the Round Pond had turned to his own avenging Nanny, and had said in exactly the same tone of startled protest:

"But he's a Duke."

At the age of four and a quarter, Mr. Campion had taken a poor view of the excuse and did so now, with the added advantage of knowing that ninety-nine per cent of the world agreed with him. All the same, he found it interesting to note that the remaining one per cent still existed, and was at large. Another little piece of the jig-saw slid into place.

It was at this point in his reflections that he realized that he was being followed again. His first reaction was exasperation. Of all the people who had presumed upon him in the past twenty hours, Pirri, he thought, had so far taken the prize. What on earth the wretched man thought he was doing was beyond Mr. Campion. He alone fitted nowhere into the picture which was slowly taking shape.

He was not certain his present trailer was Pirri, but it seemed reasonable to suppose so. He exerted himself. He quickened his pace, stepped swiftly into the next alley, and after waiting in the darkness until the footsteps passed came out again, crossed the road, and turned back the way he had come. The simple manoeuvre appeared to be successful, and after a while he continued on his way.

It was not quite so dark as it had been earlier in the evening; there was a moon somewhere behind the clouds, and a certain amount of greyish light shone through. He had reached the main road before he realized that the man was on his trail again. In the dusk Mr. Campion raised his eyebrows. His friend was not quite such a tyro after all. Still, there were many more tricks in the bag. He joined a bus queue for a vehicle going in the wrong direction and in the general scramble between those ascending and others alighting, slid round the bonnet and across the road again. He had gone some considerable way, when he heard the now familiar footsteps, and felt again that indefinable sensation which told him he was not alone. He revised his views of Mr. Pirri, and made for the first Underground station. Here he was lucky.

The central hall was crowded. He bought a ticket for a train going west, took his place on the escalator, and looked about him as he was carried slowly down. There was no sign of his man and he was slightly puzzled. He saw no face he knew, and took a chance on joining the outgoing stream on the staircase going up. He left the station by the second entrance, and once more headed straight for his objective. He was in the West End now, and among the crowds he felt surer of escape.

Just as he turned into Beak Street, however, his heart sank again. The footsteps had returned. They were slow and heavy, and there was always a little metallic ring as one foot struck the pavement. As he walked on it occurred to him that he'd been making a fool of himself; these were not the same feet which had trailed him to Bush's house. His mind had been playing tricks on him. Because Pirri had been following him on the first occasion, he had stupidly assumed that he would do it again. No, this was someone very different.

Orthodox methods having failed, he turned sharply and advanced towards the oncoming man. The steps retreated, and for a time Campion followed them. A crowd of soldiers surging out of a Service Club aided him; they bore down upon him in a stampede of army boots. He slackened his speed so that they came round and past him, and under cover of their noise, he turned swiftly, and ran. Another five minutes of doubling in and out of the narrow courts and passages found him free again.

He paused to listen. In the ghostly darkness London moved all round him; he could hear a thousand pairs of feet. The distant purr of petrol engines, voices, laughter, and, far away, the most characteristic of all sounds, the braying of tugs on the river. But of the one particular noise for which he waited, the slow, firm tread punctuated by the scrape of metal on stone, there was no trace at all. He sighed, he was very relieved. He wanted no companion upon the call he was about to make.

He waited listening for nearly five minutes and then set out for Carados Square.

It might be thought impossible for a stranger to locate in the dark a single pig-pen in the midst of a square covering five acres. But on this muggy London night there were means of detecting it.

All the railings were down, their slender grace long since sacrificed to salvage, and two strands of wire alone protected the oasis of dusty bushes and utilitarian tin huts. Mr. Campion circled the enclosure until his nose told him the time had come, then he slid through the wire and made his way to a little wooden court, lovingly contrived of the pillars from the staircase of a famous club, and the relics of the counter of a somewhat obscure bank.

As he approached, his spirits rose. He heard the sound of voices. To be exact, only one of these was making any intelligible communication; the other punctuated the remarks of the first with a series of acquiescing snorts.

"You're goin' on nicely, old dear. You're a picture now; real class about you. Did they give you a bit o' grub teatime?" The murmur, tender and solicitous as a lover's, reached Mr. Campion happily through the gloom. " 'Oo give it to yer?" it continued. "Old Warty Warden? You like 'im, don't yer, old lady? 'E's all right in 'is way. I like 'im too, but 'e'll never be the pal I've bin to yer. Never go runnin' away wiv that idea.

Don't you go trying anything funny. I'll come and see yer nights. I'm wiv yer, though you can't see me, see? You are a fat old devil. Wot yer got round yer chops? Wrinkles? Fat, that is; fat and crackling. You've got 'air on yer ears, d'you know that?"

In the darkness Campion edged nearer to the barrier. He could see nothing whatever in the evil-smelling pit below him, but the black hillock which he had hitherto mistaken for a shed roof now heaved itself and disappeared further into the shade.

"Call that a neck?" said the voice, now considerably nearer ground level.

Mr. Campion could bear it no longer. "Has she got your eyes?" he enquired.

The hillock changed shape abruptly, and Mr. Lugg swore in the dark.

"You might 'ave startled 'er," he said reproachfully, adding in a tone of studious casualness, "so you're back in town, are yer? Couldn't leave trouble alone, I suppose?"

"Not quite the way I should have put it myself," said Campion. "What do you think you've been doing?"

A gleam from a truculent eye reached him through the dusk. "Ever 'eard of tactics?" enquired the pig-keeper. "I've been 'aving a slice of them. This is a strategic withdrawal, a gettin' out quick, and if I were you, I'd do the same."

"I couldn't agree with you more, but you seem to be better at it than I am. You rang up the police and reported the corpse, giving my name, did you?"

"You couldn't leave it there, cock." Lugg was on the defensive. "It'd 'ave to be moved sooner or later, and as I was supposed to be caretaking, I thought the rozzers 'ad better get on with it. I did give them your name; if it's been awkward, I'm sorry. No one could say more."

"Couldn't they? I could astound you. I suppose you realize that you're an accessory after the fact."

There was a long silence. Lugg was so quiet he might have died. When at last he spoke his voice was thin.

"So the old girl did 'er in, did she? I did wonder, and kicked myself for letting it come in me 'ead? Gawd! That shows yer, doesn't it? This is a treat, this is. What do I do now?"

He sat down as he spoke on something that sounded like a pail. "Lumme!" he said.

Campion was sorry for him but not heartbroken.

"Who suggested you should fade away?" he demanded.

"Wot? Yesterday?"

"Naturally. Don't fool about. Who put you up to it?"

"She did. 'Er Dowager Whatnot did, of course, but I'd thought of it meself by that time. 'There's no use of you 'anging around 'ere any more, Mr. Lugg,' she said, 'is there? You git away and forget it,' she says. 'I'm afraid we've stirred up a bit of trouble for ourselves, and we must face it. There's no need to involve you,' she says." He sniffed. "I fell for it, there's no 'iding that. I took it in like a goldfish. I might 'ave known, I know that, so don't you go sayin' it, but it cast a spell over me; it always does, these days. I can't 'elp it."

"What does?" enquired Mr. Campion, taken aback.

"Ler Hote Mond," said the deep voice from the darkness. "That's Pole for the article, if you don't know. A nice little bloke in a pub told me that. I've been learnin' a few things while you've been away."

"So it would appear, but not enough," agreed Mr. Campion brutally. "What are you going to do now?"

"Ah." The voice was considering. "Now you're askin', cock. Wot 'ave they got on me so far, d'you know?"

Mr. Campion told him, and again there was silence.

"Changed 'er tale," said Lugg at last. "Changed 'er curly, and the first wasn't so 'ot neither, was it? *And* it was true."

"Well, was it? Suppose you clear your mind. Where did you get the body?"

"Where from?"

"Yes, that's the point at issue."

"Out of 'is RAF's 'ouse. That big 'un over there wiv the top orf."

"You're sure of that?"

Mr. Lugg arose from his pail. "I'm not in the dock yet," he said, "nor I ain't in the bin, and you're a pal, or used to be. I know I've bin a mug, but I 'ad a respeck for 'er Ladyship's manner, which was matey, and 'er title, which was not. Now I've bin let down. You've got slightly common out at the war, 'aven't yer? Where's yer feeling?"

"Feeling?"

"Yus. For my feelings. I wish I'd never set eyes on that bit of uplift. She's a wonderful woman. I didn't think she 'ad it in 'er to do anybody in. Not right in. It's upset me."

"I'm sorry," said Campion, inadequately, he felt.

"That's all right." Lugg was magnanimous. "We'll forget it. Wot about you? Are you on the run too?"

"Well, I'm trying to get down to Nidd."

"Are yer? I'll come wiv yer. I wish I could take my old gel in the pen 'ere. She's a beauty when you see 'er. Skin like alpaca."

"That's out of the question."

"I know it is. Don't rub it in. They'll feed 'er 'ere, but she won't get on without me." He turned back to the sty. "Pore old lady," he said, "I'm goin' to leave yer, ducks."

"Perhaps you'd like me to wait in the square," suggested Campion.

"I 'ate yer in this mood." Lugg was embarrassed. "I've got fond of 'er, that's all. I'm coming. We'll 'ave to nip back to my place first—now wot's up?"

Mr. Campion had gripped his arm. Footsteps were advancing down the quiet road to meet them. They were distinctive footsteps, heavy and assured, and at every other stroke there came the little click of metal against stone.

They came closer and closer, and before the pig court's distinctive presence they paused and advanced towards the wire.

It was not until that moment that Campion recognized their owner, and understood why he had met his match. He laughed softly in the darkness.

"Oates, you old sinner," he said aloud, "what are you doing here?"

16

THE CHIEF OF the Criminal Investigation Department crawled through the wire, grumbling a little.

"Hello," he said, "that's Lugg you've got with you, isn't it? I say, what an infernal stink! Don't you C.D. fellows ever get complaints about this?"

At Mr. Campion's side his friend and his friend's friend both breathed deeply.

"I can't smell nothin'," said Lugg evilly.

"Good Lord, can't you? It's frightful. I've been looking for you, Campion; you thought you'd shaken me off, didn't you?" His drooping figure surged towards them in the gloom; he sounded privately pleased with himself.

"A fair cop," agreed Mr. Campion. "I didn't realize it was a battle of giants. What have you done? Demoted yourself? I thought you got other ranks to do this sort of thing. Just the labour shortage, I suppose?"

Oates linked an arm through his. "That will be quite enough from you," he said. "This is a private call on an old friend. You and I must have a chat. I'm very pleased to see I can still do my stuff, though. Strewth, Lugg, isn't there somewhere round here where we can talk that's a bit more salubrious?"

"Do we understand Lugg is under arrest?" murmured Campion.

"No." The pressure on his arm increased. "Come off it, Campion. I need you and it's important. Faugh! Have you been standing here long?"

Lugg could bear the insult no longer. "Since a little 'ooman nature upsets yer," he began, ominously, but thought better of it and changed his tune. "Perhaps you'd like to come along to my place. You'd be comfortable there."

"Is it far?"

"No. Just over 'ere."

"Right. We'll follow you. You may thrive in this, but I think it's unhealthy." The Chief was quite unconscious of giving offence and he urged Campion towards the wire. "You thought you'd shed me in that Tube Station, didn't you?" he said.

Campion grinned in the darkness. "I did. You stayed in the booking hall, I suppose, banking on me not taking a train. I got away from you in Beak Street, though."

"Ah," said Oates, "but by that time I knew where you were going. It's more than I do now, though. Where are you taking us, Lugg?"

"Mind yer step," said their prospective host. "It's acrost this bit of no-man's land."

They had reached the other side of the square by this time and the dark figure ahead of them plunged down an alley between two ruined buildings. They came out into an area the size of a football pitch, which had been razed to the ground, and already demolition squads had tidied the road into little mounds of assorted rubble. Lugg pushed on, and paused at last before what appeared at first to be a heap of debris, but which proved to be a scullery with a single chimney, the only relic of a small mews cottage which had once stood there.

" 'Ere we are." Their guide produced a key and solemnly unlocked his domain. "It's bijou," he said with sly pride, "but it does for me. I've been using it for a smoke ever since they uncovered it. But I've only slep' 'ere since the bit of trouble last night."

He disappeared and they heard him find a box of matches. The light from a single candle revealed a minute room containing two chairs, a table, a sink, and three bottles of beer. Lugg indicated the stove, bright but unlit.

"I don't use it because of the smoke," he said frankly. "I don't want to 'ave to pay rent."

There were still traces of former habitation in the room; an ancient rag mat lay on the floor and there was a bowl and scrubbing brush under the sink. Over the mantel-shelf hung a mirror, and tucked into it a photograph cut from *The Farmers' Weekly* showing a mighty middle-white with a prize litter. Mr. Campion took the candle to look at this more clearly.

"Charming pin-up," he remarked. "Is this she?"

"No, that's 'er granny, but she takes after 'er. How's that for a treat?"

The Chief looked over their shoulders without enthusiasm. Presently he sat down. "This'll do," he said.

"I'll wait outside," said their host obligingly. "Or I might nip back and give 'er 'er afters. I'll be about when you want me. Our trip is still on, is it?"

Oates glanced at Campion. "You were going to Nidd?"

"We thought of it."

"I see."

He took out his pipe and began to fill it. Lugg went out quietly, and Campion stood with his back to the cold stove and surveyed his friend, who at that moment looked so surprisingly little different from the Chief Inspector Stanislaus Oates of the old days.

"I don't understand it," he said.

"I don't blame you." The Chief made the observation mildly, as he pressed the tobacco carefully into the bowl. "I don't blame you at all, but it's a nasty business. Thirty-two killings, or presumed killings, so far, and God knows how much irreplaceable stuff in the wrong hands. But that's not the real trouble."

"It sounds a good beginning."

"Oh, it's plenty. I've known the time when we'd have considered it a plateful. No, looked at in one way—the *right* way, mind you, Campion—that's quite enough. I don't suppose you remember the old McSweeney gang? They were about in nineteen ten and the whole police force of the country was buzzing like a first-night vestibule. And what did it amount to? Half a dozen old ladies bumped off and fifty thousand quids' worth of coloured stones shipped off to Amsterdam. We thought it plenty in those days, but times have changed. Today the world crooks have got to work on a grand scale. Today they murder them in thousands and pinch valuables in train-loads. I don't say I've got blasé, but when I hear of a sailor getting tight and putting his girl out for seven-and-six, I don't feel the same·about him as I did once. I know he's the villain he always was and I proceed according to the rules, but I don't *feel* the same way towards him."

Mr. Campion sat down on the edge of the sink, and his face wore its old expression of vacant bewilderment. "You're shocking me rather," he said.

"I dare say I am." Oates got his pipe alight at last. "But I'm talking to you like this because I want you to be useful if you can. Now as I see it, just at this moment in the history of the present civilization, the crime of murder for gain is not quite what it was; it's not at the top of the list any more. There's a worse one than that because it's more dangerous to the community."

Mr. Campion did not speak.

"Double-crossing," said Oates.

"Double-crossing?"

He looked up gravely. "That's what I call it. As I get older I hear people talking about this ism and that ism and war and the causes of war, and it makes me tired. God bless my soul, this present affair isn't a war!"

"Eh?" said Mr. Campion.

"No." The Chief was as nearly vehement as he ever was. "There are rules in war but in crime there are none. This is crime on a colossal scale and the view I take of it is professional, naturally. In my opinion the most dangerous aspect of the whole thing, when seen broadly, is this element of double-crossing—running with the hare and hunting with the hounds, if you prefer it. That's something which has got to be hunted down and torn right out if we're not going to have the whole thing over again. And as I see it, it's a police job."

"Catching spies?" enquired Mr. Campion stupidly.

"No, no. Spies are all right. They're regulation." Oates was impatient. "We catch theirs, and they catch ours. Spies are almost clean. No, the men I'm after are the Judases. The men who kiss and serve and sell; the lads who sit snug in one way of life and still serve the other. The men who don't know what's important. We've still got them here, and when we've won we'll still have them waiting to do it again. They're the chaps I'm after. My hands are on a whole bunch of them and I'll get the lot if it's the last thing I do. This is personal, Campion; I hate those blokes."

He was speaking with more passion than his friend had

ever suspected he possessed. Campion was enlightened; the picture in his mind was taking a larger, darker shape, and the spectacle of high-ranking police officials scuttling about like constables no longer astonished him, but there was still much he found bewildering.

"Are you suggesting this treasure lorry's disappearance was an enemy-inspired job?" he enquired blankly.

"That and the rest."

"The rest?"

Oates leant back in his chair. "In the January of 'forty," he said, "a railway truck containing the more important items in Lord Croker's collection, including five Vandykes—one of them the *Head of a Soldier*—Vermeer's *Anna and the Virgin*, and that thing, *The Maltsters*—whose is that?"

"Franz Hals."

"Is it? Yes. Well, that and one or two more, was dismantled at a siding; the guard was murdered. In March the same year three private cars carrying the National Museum's collection of Cellinis were held up in Wales and robbed. Three men lost their lives that time. In March also—there was a great deal of treasure evacuation going on at that time, you may remember—a small motor van with a police motorcycle escort disappeared with all the personnel concerned. When it left London it carried the Stephen tapestries—lovely things. I've seen the photographs—eight hundred years old. We recovered two bodies. Do you want me to go on?"

"Is there much more?"

"Forty-one separate instances," said the old man calmly. "Some of the stuff I can't bring myself to name. I can't think of it without going cold. Where do you imagine the *White Sun of India* is now?"

Campion stared at him. "But that's in the . . ." he began, and was silent. "I don't believe it," he said presently.

"I feel like that about a great many things which have happened these last five years," remarked Oates dryly. "You've only got to look about you to write off incredulity as old-fashioned, and the sooner you realize it the less likely you are to lose your reason."

"Yes, I know," said Campion, "but are you trying to tell me that at the beginning of the war, during the evacuation of the treasures from the big cities, there was systematic enemy-inspired—"

"Looting," put in Oates briefly. "Pre-victory looting, that's what it was. Well organized, damned thorough, and impudently previous. Just like Jerry. He just wanted to make quite certain that the best things were somewhere where he couldn't possibly hit them before he arrived and were waiting for him when he did. So he made arrangements."

Campion remained staring at his old friend in uneasy amazement. "I take your word for it," he said with unconvincing slowness, "but how did he get away with it? What were your people doing?"

"At the beginning of the war the police were fairly occupied," said Oates reminiscently. "You may remember it."

Glancing backward, Mr. Campion did, and he apologized.

"You didn't spot what was happening at first, either," he ventured.

"No. And when we did, we didn't believe it. Our reaction was just like yours is now. I hate to admit it, but we had seven of these treasure hold-ups before we saw the obvious. Even then the owners, the State Departments concerned, the Museum Boards and Art Curators didn't believe us. Look at that chap Bush. He waited until the raids were actually on before he moved his stuff, and then pitched it all into a lorry with a couple of old faithfuls in charge and bunged it out into the Blitz. We were fools, God knows, but we didn't compare with some people."

"Dear me," said Mr. Campion. "All the same, though, I don't see how you managed to miss them every time."

"We didn't, of course we didn't." Oates was indignant. "Out of the whole forty-one, we frustrated twenty-three. We saved the Cassiobury Apollo, for one thing, and we got back a whole crockery shop of exquisite Chinese pottery (Ming, is it?) which the William and Mary Museum was trotting up to Scotland in a furniture van. Of course we did something; we were bad, but not criminally so."

"Did you get any of the men concerned?"

"Oh Lord, yes. At one period we pulled them in in shoals. They always worked very full-handed; no expense spared, good equipment and all the rest of it, and they were all professional crooks. That's what foxed us in the beginning.

They never used the same men twice, and each bunch thought their own particular job was unique. It was brilliantly organized, you had to take your hat off to them for that."

"You never got to the higher-ups?"

Oates looked down at his pipe and prodded it again. "I haven't got him yet," he said. "Not quite."

17

THERE WAS A long silence while Campion fitted these new and staggering data into the story as he knew it. Gradually the full significance of the facts became clear to him, and a dozen questions with one horrifying possibility shot into his mind.

"It wasn't a matter of making them squeal," Oates said suddenly. "Most of them talked, and not one had any idea he was working for the enemy. Some of them were almost funny on that subject. Do you remember a dreadful little man called Knapp—Thos Knapp, he called himself—we caught him when we frustrated the Cassiobury business; he was appalled at the suggestion he was working for Jerry, he thought it was a respectable job, he said; and he honestly did think he was working for Kuyper, the big shot in the silver racket. He went down for eighteen months and is now out in Italy, pulling his weight, I believe. He's a crook, but not a traitor."

"Was Kuyper in it?"

"No. He cleared out just before the war, he's in South America—resting. No, these chaps used his name on this occasion, that was all. The man who did the actual organizing was that fellow Whitey Smith."

Campion grimaced. "He was smooth," he said. "Where is he now?"

"In the bag. We got him to talk in the end only to find that he didn't know much. He was merely employed to organize the underworld and he certainly did his stuff. His immediate boss was a queer little cuss called King. He'd never been on our books before and had had a solicitor's office in London for some years before the war. Until this business there was nothing very much against him, but he had some rum contacts and in 'thirty-seven he was in serious need of money. Some time at the end of that year he got plenty. He won't speak; he's much more frightened of someone else than he is of our gentlemanly police force. And, of course, he knows all the tricks. We've got him inside, but only on a three years' sentence; he prefers to serve that rather than open his mouth."

"Is this as far as you've got?"

Oates looked at the younger man steadily. Campion remembered that cold appraisal of old and it had always made him feel slightly uncomfortable. "No, there's a bit more," said the Chief at last, "and that's where we come up against something interesting. How long have you known Carados?"

"Johnny?" Mr. Campion felt cold. All through the latter part of the Chief's revelation he had been trying to avoid this horrifying suspicion. "Oh no," he said, "no. That's out of the question. Think of his record."

"Exactly. That's how we all feel. That's how the R.A.F. feels; that's how the Home Office feels. Think of his record, think of his background, think of the man he is."

The Chief sighed, and stirred himself.

"That's why we're muffling ourselves up in kid gloves and doing our best to disbelieve our own eyes. It's a damnable business."

Campion remained obstinately blank. "You don't think," he began at last, "you don't think the size of the thing might have—well, have magnified the probable size of the—er—perpetrator, so that your people have naturally tended to, to—"

"Go a bit nutty," said Oates dryly. "No, I don't. Nor do I think that the fact that the crimes have been inspired by Fascists has deluded the poor, silly Police Force into thinking they must be the work of the upper classes. No, I wish you were wrong. I don't like the idea any more than you do. Or than he does, poor blighter. I don't believe he's sure, you know."

Mr. Campion felt his eyes flicker. "Who, Johnny?"

"I wish you wouldn't keep calling him 'Johnny'; his name's 'Carados.'"

"I'm sorry; he was called Johnny at school."

Oates smothered an exclamation of an un-police-chief-like nature. "There you are. 'At school.' Half the influential people in the country seem to have been at school with him."

"I wasn't. I only played cricket against him once or twice."

"It's the same thing. You've known of him for a lifetime, therefore he can't be a crook. I hear it on all sides, everybody says it. I admit I like him myself and I say that the fellow doesn't know if he's guilty or if he isn't."

Mr. Campion sat thinking of Johnny Carados, and the last conversation he had with him. Some of the remarks which had then sounded so fantastic were now being echoed by Oates, who was of all things not fantastical.

"Dual personality and what not?" he ventured dubiously.

Oates shrugged his shoulders. "I'm only an old copper, raised to my present eminence by a flash of intelligence in the head of some higher official," he said, "but in my opinion much of this mental disease we hear about is mainly moral. I know that man well, and I don't think he's mad. I also think he's a good chap, fundamentally; he's brave, he's original and he's used to thinking nothing's too big for him."

"Well then . . . ?"

"Well then." Oates was not to be interrupted. "Consider the circumstances. It was a very funny time just before the war. Here's a chap who's devoted his life and his money to the care and fostering of beautiful things. Isn't there something about Art knowing no frontiers?"

"No. That's Science."

"Same thing. Anyway, there he was, all ready for some clever chap from the other side to work on."

"Yes, I know, but I can't see him dealing with the underworld."

"He wouldn't have to, King would see to that. He wouldn't even handle the cash; he'd just lend his name and make the original contacts."

"You think he might not have realized how it was going to be run?"

"I think he might not have cared," said Oates grimly.

"Don't you read your newspapers? There's a lot of cultured people who believe a life or two is well spent protecting the right kind of picture or pot. He doesn't mind risking his own life, we know that. Very few people do, funnily enough. They only differ about the things they die for. Suppose he doesn't think he's ever been working for Germany; suppose he's certain he's simply been working for Art; suppose he settles his conscience this way?"

"Then he's mad."

"Is he? I don't think the best counsel in the world could prove it in court."

Campion turned this new possibility over in his mind. Everything but his reason revolted against it.

"I don't like it," he said. "I don't want to believe it possible."

"That's everybody's reaction," said Oates. "I told you, yet all the evidence leads straight to him."

"Circumstantial evidence?"

"Naturally, or we'd have had to arrest him." The Chief put both hands on his knees to rub them thoughtfully. "I'm not trying to make a case against the chap," he complained, "I'm trying not to. We all are. It's these damnable instructions; they still come to him from time to time."

"From the other side?"

"Yes." The Chief took the pipe out of his mouth and began to use it to point his story. "We hadn't a ghost of a line on anybody until just about ten months ago, when one of the neutral governments put in a query to my office about a naturalized Rumanian living in Streatham. I suppose you know how the friendly neutrals do these things? They don't lay information, they just ask a shy little question, and that's all there is to it. When the opportunity occurs, we return the compliment."

Mr. Campion had known it, but wasted no time in saying so.

"We nabbed the bloke just at the right moment," said Oates. "Caught him with a house full of incriminating stuff. He was untidy, that was the thing which damned him. He was the only agent I've ever known who wasn't meticulous. He left papers in his collar drawer, even under the bed; I suppose he thought he was safe. He'd been over here thirty-five years, and had a house and a little block-making business in the City, and he'd changed his name to something good and Scots and all his dear old pals of the eight-fifteen swore he was as loyal as a Trafalgar Square lion. But he hadn't a hope, of course. He died in the Tower, very bravely, really. He had some deep emotional dream about castles and counts and kings and mountains and what not, but all in Rumania, unfortunately."

The Chief paused and shook his head. "What a world," he said. "Well, among this chap's activities was the usual one of forwarding letters. He used to get them via some six or seven accommodation addresses near where he worked. They get into the country in various ways. A refugee smuggles in what looks like a straight love-letter from a chance acquaintance, and nearly always he acts in complete innocence. He posts it in the ordinary way. Some of the others I honestly believe are dropped.

"Suppose a country chap finds a sealed letter lying in the road. It is stamped and addressed; sometimes he opens it, and its contents mean very little to him. More often than not he just sticks it in a letter-box. Our Rumanian decoded those he received, typed out the message neatly on his little machine and sent them off as ordinary business letters. When he was caught, he was actually doing one. We got the message both in the code and the clear; it was addressed to Carados."

"I see. And when you showed it to Johnny?"

"He said he'd be damned," said the Chief. "He convinced me completely. He was so interested, so keen to help and so naturally angry. No innocent man could have behaved more normally. He let it get him for a bit, and kept turning up with suggestions; he gave us every facility and we went over all his papers. We turned his houses out, we talked to all his associates, and we watched his mail, and there wasn't a thing to pin on him. Yeo was in charge of the enquiry, and you know him. He was like an old woman looking for a postal order she thought she had somewhere; he went on and on and over and over, never tired, and always remembering just one more place to look. Finally he gave it up and said he would as soon suspect himself. Meanwhile the instructions kept coming in to Carados."

"How? Oh I see. You kept the Rumanian's establishment open. What about the address?"

"Ah, that was the snag. The Rumanian insisted he used Carados's private address and nothing could shift him on that point. But when we decoded the next message to come in and sent it along there, there was hell to pay. Carados opened it and came roaring round to us with it at once. He swore it was the first he had received, and I must say he convinced me."

Campion shrugged his shoulders. "That's probably it," he said. "Someone was using his name. Possibly even the enemy was deceived. Jerry is extraordinary in that way."

"That's what we thought," Oates agreed placidly, "until we heard from Gonfalon."

"Lord Gonfalon? Loopy Clarence?"

Oates sniffed. "You know that, do you? That's the snag, of course."

"I know Gonfalon is the prize crank of all time," said Mr. Campion. "Eight hundred years of solid loafing are behind him, and considered purely as the result, he's logical. After that, the word doesn't apply."

"We found that out, of course." The Chief's gloom deepened. "He has a remarkable wife, though; she's a French woman, a burning patriot. I understand his family considered it a *mésalliance*, but good Lord, without her he'd be penniless, certifiable and probably dead. She lets him do what he likes up to a certain point, but when it begins to look dangerous, she lays about him. Do you know her?"

"Sweet Hortense? Only from the song," said Campion flippantly. "No, really, any evidence connected with that pair can't be taken seriously."

"There again you take the conventional view." Oates was injured rather than annoyed. "Now I'll tell you what happened. One day, soon after we'd decided Carados wasn't implicated, this old fellow Gonfalon walked in to see me, and he told me an absurd story about rare peonies and Siamese cats and I don't know what else, and finally announced in so many words that just before the war he'd been in communication with the enemy government concerning the preservation of these and other treasures in event of danger. He was quite open about it; he said his wife had now discovered the whole business and had sent him up to see me to make a clean breast of it."

"Was there any truth in it at all?"

"Oh yes. We went into it, of course, and Holly went down there and brought back all the correspondence he could find and the cats and the greenhouses, not to mention about five acres of mounted armour of all periods, as well as any quantity of valuable or semi-valuable junk. We read the letters, and I must say he seemed to me to have completely fooled the enemy as to his importance in the country. They certainly had the idea that he was one of our hereditary rulers, and while I don't know what his own letters to them were like, having had one or two from him myself, I can well imagine they were impressive and mysterious to a foreigner.

"To do them justice they didn't trust him with much, but they gave him painstaking details concerning the best way to preserve his valuables, and when war did break out he got a communication, probably via the Rumanian, instructing him to communicate with Carados if anything important occurred, and he should need advice or assistance."

"Wasn't that to be expected?" said Campion quickly. "I mean, once we've accepted the fact that someone was using Johnny's name, then . . ."

"Yes, yes, I know." Oates was impatient. "But you see he had a reply."

"From Johnny?"

"Yes, we've got it."

Mr. Campion stared at him briefly. "I should have thought that was the finish," he said.

"No, it wasn't. That was the unsatisfactory part about it. It wasn't." Oates considered a moment before he went on. "The whole incident was crazy and the explanation we had from Carados was just feasible, yet it left an unpleasant taste. Gonfalon is definitely sub, you see."

"Oh yes, definitely. Hardly human."

"No, I wouldn't say that; he's a crank. What happened was that one day one of our planes accidentally dropped a practice bomb in the field next door to one of Gonfalon's largest greenhouses. The whole thing came down and he lost two or three of his rarest plants. In his excitement at what he took to be a direct attack, he wrote at once to Carados reporting the occurrence, mentioning their secret brotherhood, and saying, in effect, what about it? Carados replied in the same vein, and promised 'to attend to it.' "

"Did you *see* Gonfalon's original letter?"

The Chief's sallow face grew a shade darker. He looked uncomfortable.

"Well, yes, I did, as a matter of fact," he admitted. "We got it from Carados. He had had it framed for his Mess."

Campion laughed. "That's what I should have expected," he said. "Did it actually mention an association with the enemy?"

"No. Gonfalon said he was trying to be cautious, and the actual phrase was 'the august body whom we both serve.' Carados said he thought he was talking about the Royal Horticultural Society."

"I should say that was fair." Campion was still mildly amused. "Everybody knows of Gonfalon, you see; he's good for a laugh before he does anything. No, I don't think you'll get much by barking up that tree."

"I don't know." Oates remained grave. "After he got the letter and framed it and had everybody laughing at it, Carados did go to extraordinary lengths to try to prevent training aircraft flying anywhere near the Gonfalon estate. He has influence, you see, and he did make a point of it. Now that doesn't sound quite like a joke to me."

Campion made no comment, and the Chief went on:

"He told a wonderful story, and on the face of it we had to believe it, but he admits he's no personal friend of Gonfalon. He knows the man is sub-normal and yet he goes out of his way like this. Why? It's not too satisfactory, is it?"

Campion sat very still. He was thinking of Johnny and that other story which he had told less than a couple of hours before; the story of the poisoning of Theodore Bush. That, too, had been a wonderful story and one which, on the face of it, had had to be believed. He did not forget Johnny's peculiarity, however; his passion for going out of his way to do little things to assist people he knew but slightly.

"It's very difficult," said Oates. "We've locked Gonfalon up on his estate, of course, but you don't know what to believe quite, do you?"

Campion did not care to comment. Instead he said abruptly:

"What about this bottle of wine?"

"Oh," said Oates, "you're in on that too, are you? I did wonder. I saw Yeo just now; in fact I went down to Bedbridge Row with him, and he told me you said you had been followed from the Minoan. It's funny, I saw Carados on this very subject in Eve Snow's dressing-room this afternoon, and he didn't tell me you were to be one of the party."

A question which had been bothering Mr. Campion for some time was answered, and instead of replying directly he raised his eyebrows.

"You've been allowing Johnny 'to collaborate' on the side, I take it?" he enquired. "That's a dirty old police trick, Stanis; I'm embarrassed by you."

"That's why you'll never make a policeman," said Oates seriously. "You don't see it as I do; you see a man, I see a menace. I wouldn't put it past you to feel that if a man has a kink it doesn't matter so much what he does, but I never feel like that. If Carados is the man I'm beginning to believe he must be, then from my point of view he's an evil thing and I'll treat him as I'd treat a typhus germ. I know we've just about won this war but we haven't won the next, nor the one after it, and while men like this are free and in power we're in danger. When it's a case of freedom versus slavery the lad who hasn't got his mind quite clear is against you. I don't care what I do to catch him and crush him and the others with him."

He broke off abruptly and laughed at himself.

"So far, I admit, he's either been honest enough or clever enough to appear remarkably straight," he conceded. "He came to me with this story about the wine as soon as Bush approached him, even though it brought him right back into the business again, which is suspicious in itself at this stage. Once again I was forced to believe him. He didn't tell me that you were going to be one of the tasting party, though. Now why was that?"

"Possibly because he didn't know," said Mr. Campion. "Don Evers invited me and I told Johnny I was coming when I saw him at the theatre."

"How did he take it?"

"He seemed unexpectedly pleased."

"Over-effusive?"

"No, I don't think so. He did seem very pleased."

"Why?"

Campion did not reply. The full weight of the evidence against Johnny Carados was piling up upon the scales before him. The dreadful possibility was now a probability and tragedy imminent. He stole a glance at Oates, sitting grey and impartial by the empty stove, and remembering all he knew of him reflected that here was the most nearly just intelligence he had ever met. Clearly the time had come when he must be forced to make his own contribution to the facts as known to the police. Yet it was a very distasteful duty. He began abruptly.

"Theodore Bush nearly died tonight," he said. "Someone intended to kill him. This is the story as I had it from Carados, but I warn you that in spite of all you've told me since I still believe it."

Oates did not speak until the whole story of the evening had been laid before him. He had a gift for listening, never interrupting, never missing a point.

"So I left them," said Campion finally. "Bush will recover, and I shall be astounded if he prefers a charge against Carados. The doctor may be more difficult, but I doubt it."

Oates rose to his feet. He looked tired. "There you are," he said, "it's always the same. Every lead takes us straight to him; whatever turns up has him slap in the middle of it and he always has an explanation which is so daft that you can't believe it can be anything but the truth. However, this time he's worked a bit too fast. That woman we found in your flat had enough chloral in her to kill her if she hadn't been smothered first."

"So I gathered."

"Did you? How?" Oates pounced on him suspiciously. "That's a piece of information we haven't released. How did you know, did he tell you?"

"No, he didn't. Lady Carados conveyed it. She said she changed the bottles."

The Chief made no coherent sound, but he ran a finger round the inside of his collar.

"Something will have to be done with that woman," he said. "She's loose without a keeper for the first time in her life. Don't you think so?"

Campion stood wondering about the woman who had talked

so long and so terrifyingly in Theodore Bush's mannered room, and a new and startling idea occurred to him. Here was a person who had a curious outlook on life if ever there was one; here was a person with an imperious will, who believed in astonishing privileges for certain people; here was somebody whom Johnny would shield.

"I say, Oates," he began diffidently, but got not further. Someone was tapping discreetly on the flame-scarred scullery door.

18

WHEN CAMPION PULLED open the door it was not the familiar figure in blue battle-dress who stepped briskly into the room, but a slender pink-faced young man in a neat office suit.

"Mr. Campion, I presume?" he said innocently. "Mr. Oates? Oh, there you are, sir. I hope I've done the right thing, but in the circumstances I thought I ought to find you."

The Chief turned to Campion, who was looking at the newcomer as if he did not believe in him, and made the introductions.

"This is my secretary," he said. "How did you get here, Tovey?"

The young man stood up stiffly and made his report as if he were in court.

"I heard from Superintendent Yeo that you, sir, had followed Mr. Campion who was presumed to be searching for his employee, Lugg. Recollecting that you had told me that the man Lugg was reputed to be strongly attached to a pet animal which he kept in Carados Square, I set out there assuming that you, sir, would by that time have attained your quarry. I found the man and with some difficulty persuaded him to direct me here. If I might suggest it, sir, your presence in your office now would be advisable."

"He talks like a good book, doesn't he?" said Oates to Campion. "But he's got here, which is the answer, if you're interested."

Tovey grew pinker with pleasure but remained at attention when invited to proceed.

"In your absence, sir," he began, "Chief Inspector Holly has interviewed a person by the name of Angus Sloane, who came to lay evidence concerning the alleged discovery of several items listed in the files of missing articles. In consequence of this interview Chief Inspector Holly despatched Sergeant Dacre to bring in Lieutenant Don Evers of the U.S. Army, and there is some doubt in my mind about the legality of this step. At any rate, I thought you should know of it, because when the young man arrived he had someone with him, sir."

"Someone with him? What are you talking about, Tovey? You're so damned exact I can't follow you. Whom did he have with him?"

Tovey swallowed. "He had a Bishop with him, sir," he said. "When I saw that I thought I'd better find you."

Reflecting that it was hard luck on his uncle that on his first night out for ten years he should end up at Scotland Yard, Mr. Campion cut in to the somewhat startled silence.

"Is that Angus Sloane, the Bond Street man?" he enquired.

"Yes, sir. He's a very reputable art dealer, I believe."

"Yes," said Mr. Campion. "I suppose that covers it."

"He's *the* man, isn't he?" murmured Oates. "What's he got hold of?"

Tovey looked uncomfortable. "I think he said he knew where the Croker Venus was, sir."

Both men were staring at him.

"And in consequence of this Inspector Holly called in Don Evers?" demanded Campion.

"Yes, sir."

Oates took Campion's arm. "We'll go at once," he said.

Tovey beamed. "The car is against the kerb, sir. This way."

As he sat beside Oates in the back of the sedan, while the efficient young man drove them through the dark streets, Mr. Campion permitted himself a brief deviation from the matter in hand.

"Hardly a success as a fugitive, our Lugg?" he suggested.

"The searching cops just cover their eyes with their hands when they see him coming, I suppose?"

The Chief stirred irritably. "He's safer there than anywhere. There are more chains than clank, as we used to say when I was a boy. Yeo has him when he wants him, and hasn't when he doesn't, which is more to the point. No one wants his evidence at the moment; no one wants to lose the big fish in a row over a silly society woman."

Mr. Campion reflected that the peccadilloes of the breed had pepped up considerably while he had been away, but he did not say so, and presently the Chief spoke again.

"Would Sloane know the Croker Venus if he saw it? Know if it was genuine, I mean."

"Oh, I think so. He makes his living giving that kind of opinion."

"Does he?" Oates groaned. "I wish I did," he said seriously. He was still unsmiling some ten minutes later when he was questioning Holly rather more closely than a Chief Inspector expects to be questioned as to the precise nature of the invitation which had brought Lieutenant Evers to the Yard. Holly was nettled, his eyes were arctic, but he remained smooth.

"There was never any question of arrest; he came as a favour to us, Mr. Oates," he explained. "We put it to him and he came at once, bringing with him the friend with whom he was dining."

"With the Bishop of Devizes," supplemented Oates grimly. "It will sound good on an official chit from the U.S. Army authorities."

Holly's chill began to pervade the room. "No one could have expected him to be dining with a Bishop," he protested, unreasonably Mr. Campion thought. "However, it's all right, Mr. Oates. At least, I think it is. They were both very nice about it as far as they went. I said I was very sorry, of course, and up to a point the young man was cooperative, except that . . ."

"Has there been a row?"

"No, Mr. Oates, not exactly. No unpleasantness, you know, but . . ."

"Good Lord, Holly, you didn't detain them?"

"No, Mr. Oates. I know my limitations. I did ask them if they'd wait a bit."

Oates consulted his watch. "Are they here now?"

'Yes, they are as a matter of fact. They're very comfortable in my office . . ."

The Chief groaned.

"What authority have you over your uncle, Campion?" he enquired.

"Let's call it influence," said Campion. "I'll go down, shall I?"

Inspector Holly cleared his throat. He was excited, and it was evident that although he appreciated the danger of his tactics, he felt he could afford them. "This statement of Mr. Sloane's ought to be considered, Mr. Oates," he said. "It'll only take you five minutes to read, or I can give you the gist of it in two. I think when you hear it you'll feel I've been justified."

Oates leant back in his chair. "What is it? I hope it's good."

"I think it's what we've been waiting for." For a moment Holly became the eager young plain-clothes man whose tenacity had earned his promotion. "This fellow Sloane came here this afternoon and when he found I was out said he'd wait. He didn't want to talk to anyone except the Inspector who had sent out that confidential list we put round to the art dealers in March. I didn't get back till eight, but he was still waiting. When I saw him he told me straight that he'd got an irregularity to report and I told him not to worry but to go ahead."

Oates nodded encouragingly.

"He said he knew where the Croker Venus was," Holly continued, "and he convinced me that he knew what he was talking about. It appears he had an enquiry from a client who told him that he had heard that the picture was in private hands, and gave him the address of a woman living in the Home Counties. The client evidently did not realize that the picture had been stolen; it's not one of the well-known things on the list, is it? This chap imagined some purchase must have been made, and he asked Sloane if he'd enquire if it would be sold again. That was where Sloane went wrong."

"In not coming to you at once?"

"Yes, that was what he ought to have done, and he knows

it." Holly sounded aggrieved but tolerant. "No, he thought
he'd be clever and trot down to the address he'd been given.
It turned out to be a quiet house in the country and he asked
to see the lady." He took a deep breath. "I wish you had seen
Sloane," he said. "He's a fattish, self-important little fellow,
and he looked positively scared when he told me this.

"The old servant took him into the drawing-room to wait
for her mistress and he says as he walked in he practically
dropped. The whole room was plastered with missing stuff. It
was like a dealer's daydream by the sound of it; priceless
treasures cheek by jowl with Victorian junk. The little Venus
was there, he said he'd know it anywhere, hanging over a
desk in the corner as if it had been done by somebody's aunt,
and *Dedham Pightle* was over the fireplace. It's the Lauderdale House lot, by the sound of it. That was the second lot
that went, if you remember, Mr. Oates."

"I do." The Chief waved him on.

"Well, he says there was a Cellini bronze on the whatnot,
and the Scribe collection of miniatures in a glass-topped
table, all mixed up with paper-knives and crested china."

Excitement was raising the Inspector's voice, and his colour was growing.

"The whole place was alive with stuff, and he stood gasping.
He does know what he's saying, too. He's one of the very big
men in his line. What about that for a story? If I've forgotten
one or two points of procedure, I'm sorry, but it's knocked
the breath out of me."

Triumph and truculence had robbed him both of years and
dignity. He looked like a boy. The others sat staring at him;
then Oates laughed suddenly. Campion remained serious.

"I know Sloane," he said. "He's not an over-enthusiastic
bird. Rather cautious as a rule. He hasn't gone mad, Inspector,
by any chance?"

"He's had a shock," said Holly, revealing a flash of unexpectedly handsome teeth, "but he's all right; he knows what
he's doing."

"Did he see the woman?" Oates demanded.

"Oh yes. He behaved very sensibly. She seems to have
been a surprise to him too. I don't know what he expected,
but she wasn't it. He says she was elderly and unmarried,

and very strong-minded, and he didn't believe she had the faintest idea what she'd got hold of."

"What line did he take?" enquired Campion, fascinated.

Holly shrugged his shoulders. "I've only got his story, but he says he was most careful. If you ask me, he was thunder-struck and stood there goggling at her, but he says he'd given his name to the maid, and not being able to think of any other story on the spur of the moment he just told her he was representing his firm and had heard she might be willing to sell some pictures."

"Yes?"

"Then she threw him out."

"Did she?"

"Yes. But in a perfectly genteel way. She just said No, she hadn't any need to sell her treasures, and would he go, please."

"And that's all he got?"

"No." Holly's voice was rising to a squeak. "He said he apologized, and admired the Venus in passing. And she said Yes, it was very pretty, and she was minding it for a friend. Sloane didn't ask her outright for a name, but just as he was going she couldn't help mentioning that her friend was a nobleman and that she had agreed to help him out when a hall in the village which had been hired by a storage firm to house evacuated furniture had suddenly been commandeered by the military. So he went down and found the hall . . ."

"Did he, by Jove. Good man. He didn't get the name of the firm, I suppose?"

"He did," said Holly reverently. "It seems like a miracle when you think of all we've done without results, but Sloane is energetic. He found the hall was owned by the local parish council; and he looked up the parish clerk who had the name in his ledger. Here it is: 'Peters and Jack, Ledbury Street, Clerkenwell.' I've put Sergeant Pelly on to it. He'll get it all out of them before they know they're talking, and then if the name of the nobleman is the one I expect, most of our work will be done."

Campion remained hunched up in his chair. He was very weary, but his eyes behind his big spectacles were alive and thoughtful.

"I wonder," he said. "They may not have any books; in fact, neither Peter nor Jack may be in, don't you think?"

Holly grimaced. "You think the whole thing may be phoney," he said. "That's an idea."

"It would be one way of doing it, don't you think?" ventured Mr. Campion. "Ever since I've heard this story I've been wondering about their chief problem, which obviously is where to keep what must be now rather embarrassing possessions. All this stolen stuff is the kind which has to be taken care of, you see. Even at the time, it couldn't have been easy, when they only expected to hang on to it for a few months. But now when their bosses certainly aren't going to come for it, it must be a nightmare to them. A bogus haulage and storage firm is probably the answer."

"In that case we'll get the lot," said Holly flatly. "I hope you're right. Pelly is a terrier on things like this, he'll worry his way through anything. He'll get them if they're there at all. Now I hope you'll feel I've done right, Mr. Oates."

"Eh?" The Chief looked at him gloomily. After the first shock his reaction to the news had been steadily more and more depressed. "What?" he said. "Yes. Oh yes. Very good work. Very good luck. But I still don't see why you wanted to pull that American boy in. What has he got to do with it?"

Holly burst out laughing. "Why, I am a fool," he said, in what appeared to be delighted surprise, "I've left out what I was trying to tell you. The client who put Mr. Sloane on to the woman in the first place was an American, Mr. Oates, a Mr. Evers of New York. This young man's father. And in his letter to Sloane he says distinctly that he had heard the Venus was there from his son, who was in the army over here. I had to see the youngster, didn't I?"

Oates breathed heavily through his nose. "Yes, of course," he said. "And is his explanation satisfactory?"

Holly did not answer immediately. "Up to a point," he said, "but he knows more than he's saying . . . Which is very funny, when you come to think of it."

19

THE BISHOP OF Devizes was not amused. He knew he had no business to be there for one thing, and moreover, he expected better manners in officials than Sergeant Dacre in his excitement had displayed. But he stuck to his determination to stand by the persecuted young foreigner, to whom he had taken a liking.

He sat in the visitor's chair, looking graceful and out of place in the Chief's office, and regarded Holly without enthusiasm. It was evident that Don was unhappy. He had refused a chair and now stood, young and splendid before the desk, while Oates and Holly watched him and Mr. Campion hung about unobtrusively in the background.

"I've told the Inspector," he was saying, "I don't want to obstruct you people in any way, and I don't know why you're interested, but I had an idea that if I said anything out of place in my letters home the censor would have taken note of it."

"It's not a question for the censor," Holly began, and Oates suddenly took over.

"The fact is," he said, in his old country bobby voice, "we want help. We can write to America and invite your father to explain, if he will, what you told him in a letter. I have no doubt he'd oblige us, and very likely we will do just that, but if you'd tell us, it'd save a lot of time, you know. Don't you do it if you don't want to, though."

He sounded plaintive as country constables often do, and Don, who expected something a little more impressive from the Chief of the Criminal Investigation Department, looked at him in astonishment.

"I told the Inspector what happened," he said at last. "It's not my tale at all. My father is a man who expects a letter every week; he likes plenty of news and he likes it often. I guess I sometimes get a little short of stories for him."

"So you tell him all the gossip," said Oates. "That's right. That's what I like from my boy. Can you remember what you told him about this lady down in the country?"

"Yes, as I told your Inspector, I came into it through a friend of mine—a guy who's over here in the U.S. Army, too—he was stationed down at this little town—village, you'd call it—named Chessing and he got an introduction to a lady there. You know how it is, you meet someone in town who says, 'Oh, you're stationed at so-and-so, are you? You must go and see my aunt or my cousin or whoever it is, she lives there.' You know how that happens." He was making very heavy weather of it and Campion saw why Holly had queried him. Don was not good at subterfuge.

"Well, this friend of mine," he continued, adding with sudden relief, "you may as well have his name; it's Mark Elder, he's a major in the Artillery. He's a cultured man who used to teach in college before it occurred to him that there was a modern war he might take a little notice of before he got wrapped up with the ancient ones. He and I came over at the same time, and when I saw him last he told me this story in detail. He mentioned the lady's name, and I remember it for the same reason that he did. She was called Miss Dorothy Pork, and that kind of improved the story. He didn't take up the introduction, but she found him when she was helping at a canteen they had in the Town Hall, and he mentioned it then, and she insisted he come up to the house and have tea with her some time. Apparently it was a great honour, for she never had folk to tea, but he said she was everything he'd ever read about in England. She had very thick shoes, and a white underskirt showing under her tweeds at the back, and altogether he wasn't too excited about it to begin with. But he didn't want to hurt her feelings, and after the third time she asked him, he went up there."

His audience was listening to him with sympathy, and a smile curled Oates's thin lips. "This is fine," he said. "This is what we want to know."

"Well," said Don again, "Mark reported the house was just what he'd read about too, until he was taken into the drawing-room, and there he said he'd never seen such fine pictures in his life. He recognized one of them from reproductions, and he thought this must be a copy until he looked at it carefully and realized he was seeing the real thing. He said the old lady had no taste at all, herself, and he mentioned it to me as one of the minor mysteries of this island. I was short of a story to tell Dad in my letter, and I just wrote down what he told me. The picture was a Venus of some sort, I forget what, but I'd made a note of it, and I put it in the letter. There, that's all, sir, that's the best I can do, I'm afraid."

Oates remained looking at him, and his smile was genuine. "We're very grateful to you," he said. "It's a coincidence, an extraordinary coincidence, unless—Lieutenant Evers, do you know who gave Major Elder the introduction to Miss Pork?"

Don shut his mouth, and to his chagrin blushed violently. The colour rushed up over his face and his eyes grew very fierce. "I'm afraid that's all I can tell you."

Holly would have spoken, but Oates was before him.

"All right," he said easily, "we can't force you, and we don't want to. We'll have to contact the Major, though. Perhaps he won't want to oblige us, and then we'll have to try the lady."

Mr. Campion ventured to interfere. "I take it there's no blame attached to the introduction?" he said to Oates. "I mean, no one who had any special reason for wishing Miss Pork's drawing-room to remain unseen would give anyone on earth an introduction to her, would they? I may be wrong, but the whole thing sounds a little careless to me. Did Mrs. Susan Shering tell your friend to call on Miss Pork, Lieutenant?"

Don's expression betrayed him, and Campion was genuinely regretful. "I'm sorry," he said, "but I couldn't think of anyone else over here whom you would feel in duty bound to protect. She can't be involved in this, you know. This isn't her kind of party at all."

"I think my nephew is right, you know, Lieutenant. Innocence is a remarkably apparent thing." The Bishop, who had been temporarily forgotten, made the remark rather like a judge from the Olympic seclusion of the Bench, and Don threw in his chivalrous hand.

"Very well," he said. "I'm relying on you though, Mr. Campion. I know Mrs. Shering can't have anything serious to hide and I didn't want her to be bothered. It was she who told Mark to look up the lady." He paused and looked round him. "It was the most casual thing you can imagine," he said. "She and I were having dinner together at the Berkeley, and Mark came in. He stood chatting with us for a bit and she asked him where he was stationed, and he said it was a very picturesque but remarkably uncomfortable little hole called Chessing. She said, 'Oh dear, I know it is, but if you need a bath or a glass of gooseberry wine at any time, you ought to call on Dorothy Pork.' " He paused, and a faint smile passed over his worried young face. "She didn't see anything amusing in the name until we laughed, and we said we didn't think there was anybody called 'Dorothy Pork' anyway, and we started fooling, and—well, that's what happened."

It was so obviously exactly what *had* happened that even Holly was silent. It was the Bishop who asked the question which had come into all their minds.

"Do I understand Miss Pork was a relative of Mrs. Shering?" he enquired.

"Oh no." Don seemed horrified at this suggestion. "No. She said she was a friend of the aunt who brought Susan, I mean Mrs. Shering, up. She just said she was a character."

"The English rose of yesteryear, no doubt," said Mr. Campion absently. "Dear me, yes, that's very clear, isn't it, Mr. Oates?"

The Chief said it was indeed, and with many apologies and expressions of goodwill on the one side, and reserved friendliness on the other, the visitors were escorted downstairs by Tovey and Mr. Campion. As they shook hands Don smiled shyly at Campion.

"What a wine you missed!" he said.

Campion laughed. "Did you drink it?"

"We did," said the Bishop primly. "A very pleasant evening."

As they came back into the Chief's office, Oates looked across the room at Campion. "It's getting very close to Carados," he said.

"It certainly is," said Holly, "there's no getting away from it. It's always just one step away from him every time."

Mr. Campion thrust his hands in his pockets and walked up and down the room.

"Nobleman gives the friend of the aunt of his affianced

bride a hundred thousand quids' worth of stolen art treasures, all so well known that the first intelligent visitor spots them," he said. "What a chap, eh?"

Oates frowned. "It sounds absurd when you put it like that," he admitted, but Holly was annoyed.

"It's highly suspicious, Mr. Campion," he said. "I know it sounds an amazing story, but the whole thing is out of the ordinary. We're getting on, though. Do you think we ought to see Mrs. Shering now, Mr. Oates, or . . . ?"

"No." The Chief got up. "No," he said again, "I think the next person we see is Miss Pork. I tell you what, Holly, we'll *all* go."

"I'm rising forty-four," said Mr. Campion suddenly, "and unless you count the bang on the head I had last night, I've not slept for forty-eight hours."

"Then you can do it in the car. Come on, Holly."

"Now, sir?" The Chief Inspector was startled by this sudden display of youthful zeal. Oates was shaking himself gently like an elderly dog; he felt for his pipe, his money and his matches, settled his coat, and reached for his hat on the desk.

"We'll go now," he said. "We'll go before we've got the report from Pelly, we'll go before Yeo comes back. We'll go before either that man Sloane of yours or this pleasant soldier-boy and his clerical friend have time to breathe a word to a soul. Tovey," he added, "get me a car and a revolver."

Campion began to laugh. "You've forgotten the cigar," he said, "otherwise it's an excellent impersonation. Come on, Holly, now we're going to see how they used to do it in the old days."

The Inspector looked scandalized, but whether at the *lèse-majesté* or the unprecedented interference of his Chief was not apparent. Oates was smiling faintly.

"We'll take a sergeant," he said, "just for the look of the thing."

20

IT WAS AN angry-coloured house, puce rather than red, and it skulked at the end of a narrow drive flanked with too many shrubs; an essay in Victorian Gothic at its worst. They were early, but not indecently so. Mr. Campion had insisted on eating, and Holly had pressed to be allowed to make certain checks on Angus Sloane's story before they acted upon it. But all the same, it was only just after nine when Tovey, in his capacity as the necessary sergeant, brought the car up to the porch with the stained-glass windows.

Miss Pork kept them waiting in a hall which to searchers after beauty was discouraging. Despite the Chief's card, she sent word that she was at breakfast and would see Mr. Oates when she had finished, and Holly, who took a suspicious view of the excuse, was startled by the discovery that this was indeed a fact. Through panels of iron-work and glass in the door immediately on their right, a dim figure could be seen at a meal.

Oates grunted amiably at the elderly maid who brought the message, and seated himself on a hard, wooden chair which had a heart cut out in its waisted back. He looked both patient and immovable. Holly was more fidgety. He stood very near the dreadful door, and peered through it at times, his face set in disapproval. Tovey, imitating his Chief, took another wooden chair, but Mr. Campion wandered.

It had occurred to him that he had seen houses like this before; he looked for the door of a room which would have a southern view, and having located it, he drifted towards it casually.

Presently, when he was forgotten, he opened it gently, popped his head inside, and came out looking amazed. After that, his impatience to see Miss Pork was almost unbearable.

157

She came at last, bustling through the baroquerie, a surprise to everybody. Miss Pork had never been an English rose, nor any other flower; she was made of different stuff. She was very small, a fact which she countered by holding herself bolt upright, and she was scarlet. Mr. Campion thought he never had seen a redder human being; red face, red hands, she even had limp reddish hair, which escaped its moorings and hung fiercely round a protuberant red forehead. Her clothes were utilitarian and drooped backwards, and on her feet were large upturned, patriotically wooden shoes. She had a wide mouth and a voice with a quack in it, and, as she said herself, she was usually talking. Bright round eyes peered at them each in turn, and flickered as Oates rose to meet her.

"Well," she said, "what have you come for, eh?"

It was a direct attack of flame-thrower effect, and Campion thought how fitting it was that just such a castle should contain such a dragon.

Oates was not disconcerted. He remained sadly contemplative. "Are you Miss Dorothy Pork, ma'am?"

"I am. And you're Mr. Oates, Chief of the C.I.D. Well, state your business. If you've got something to say, say it; we can't waste time, there's a lot to be done. My goodness, if I stood about all the morning I don't know where we'd be. These are busy times; I've got work to do, you know."

"I dare say you have, ma'am." Oates was mild as ever. "We're none of us idle. I've come down from London to have a word or two with you about some goods which you took over from the Peters and Jack storage company. You have got them, haven't you?"

Miss Pork grew darker in colour, a surprising and even alarming sight. "This is the limit," she said, dating herself. "Really the outside edge. I suppose you sent that commercial traveller who gave himself such airs. You're doing this under one of those disgraceful new laws, are you? Or haven't you any authority at all? I shouldn't be surprised; I shall ring up my solicitor."

"Now, that would be a good idea," said Oates, with sudden enthusiasm. "Very sensible. Does he live near here? Could you get him over?"

Taken out of her stride, a little grunting laugh escaped Miss Pork. "No, don't be silly," she said unexpectedly. "He's a dreadful old fool. What is it you want? Only don't keep me standing about."

It was not that she melted so much as that she cooled a little. She smiled, too, widely, transforming herself into a slightly merry old dragon, in a way which was disarming. Oates smiled back at her.

"Have you got the stuff here, ma'am?" he enquired.

"Well, I've got a few pictures," she said, her good humour persisting, "and a few little ornaments. But I know whom they belong to, and I'm only doing it as a favour to him. I made that very clear at the time. Some of them are in here. Wipe your feet, won't you? I've just had the carpet cleaned; my mother made it many years ago and it's ra-ther precious. This way."

They trooped after her into the room that Mr. Campion had found and stood transfixed. Even Holly, who did not set up to have rigid views on the art of interior decoration, was silenced. It was a large room with huge, narrow windows and vast, thick curtains, but even so the effect was cramping. Mr. Campion had seen furniture like it before, but not in use. Two large corner-seats with trellised backs which turned into shelves for pottery dominated the far end of the apartment, and strange, many-seated stuffed contraptions sprawled in the foreground. Chandeliers in coloured beads, and one very lovely old candelabrum hung from the ceiling, and the wool carpet on which they trod bore evidence that Miss Pork's taste was hereditary.

The Croker Venus smiled wantonly from the wall just above a sensible office desk, and a truly magnificent bronze horse rose like a flame from a rosewood bracket hung with alternate ebony and ivory beads.

The Constable was nearly hidden by a pair of Benares candlesticks, a couple of very charming Chelsea figures, and a marble clock in the shape, roughly, of the Parthenon.

"Of course," said Miss Pork, cheerfully, "many of these treasures are my own. Now that," she went on, pointing to a small print framed in loops of brass wire which flanked the Venus, "that little Scottie with his baby mistress. I know it's only a Christmas card, but I've kept it for years because I like it. It may be sentimental, but it's very well done. That girl in the chemise next to it is a picture I'm minding. One or two people have admired it, but I was in two minds about having it up; it was only because the cellar was damp and I didn't want to get it injured. It's not everybody's meat and some years ago I should have hesitated to hang it in any downstairs room. But times have changed, haven't they? And a good thing too. I like to see these Land Girls in their knickers; so sensible and healthy."

She paused for breath and re-grouping, but no one seized the opportunity. Oates was looking round him very carefully. Holly was nervous, aware of ignorance, and Mr. Campion appeared lost in wonder and delight.

"Now, you don't just want to see pretty things," said Miss Pork, taking in hand a situation to which she was doubtless used. "You want to talk and you want to know what is mine and what is not. Isn't that so?"

"Is this all?" enquired Campion, suddenly emerging from his enchantment. "I mean, is it all here?"

Miss Pork's gooseberry eyes were turned upon him in astonishment. "All that came up from the hall? Oh, dear me, no, of course not. I didn't move the cases which were in the *dry* end of the cellar. I only peeped into those. I really haven't had time. There's a lot to do in a house like this. You'd be surprised, being a man."

"A lot to dust," ventured Tovey brightly.

"And wash," said Miss Pork. "I wash everything. I like things clean. Curtains, covers, carpets, tweeds—I wash them all. Now, these pictures could all do with a scrub. Good white soap and water never hurt anything. But of course," she added, seeing their expressions, "I shouldn't wash *his* things without asking."

"When you say 'his,' " said Oates, more for form's sake than anything else, "whom do you mean?"

"Oh, nonsense!" objected Miss Pork roundly. "None of that sort of rubbish, if you please. You must know whose the things are, or you wouldn't come looking for them, would you? I can see exactly what has happened. I only brought these things up to my drawing-room about six weeks ago. I did it solely to save them from damp, but people have admired them, and they must have talked. What of course they don't know, and I dare say you don't either, is that I'm a very old friend of the girl the Marquess of Carados is going to marry. I don't see her often, and I don't write to her because I don't write; I never write, if I can help it, and I don't read either. I believe in action. When I saw these things were in danger of spoiling, I said to my maid Jones, 'We must protect these, and the best place for them is in the drawing-room.' She agreed with me and we unpacked them. I didn't tell anybody this, why should I? Does it really matter where in the house the things are as long as they're looked after? Of course it doesn't. Now, you've come running down here all for nothing because I've seen to it now. Everything is quite in order now."

Her exertions and her triumph brought her to boiling-point again, and she glowed at them.

"What have you done, ma'am?" Holly's voice was commendably quiet.

"I've written to him, of course," she said.

"To Carados?"

"Yes. As soon as that little man, the commercial traveller, was his name Sloane? Yes, well, as soon as he came I realized that if word of my little change in the arrangements reached the Marquess without an explanation, he might well wonder what I was doing, for some of his things are quite nice, you know. So I sat down over there at once, and I wrote to him. I introduced myself, I told him I was the person who was housing his things, and I explained quite frankly about the damp. I also put in a postscript telling him to tell Susan that the jardinière I sent her for a present *was* from me. I haven't heard from her, and I remember I couldn't have put my name in; I never have a card handy when I want one. So there you are, you see, it's all settled now."

The visitors exchanged glances. "I should think it might be," said Mr. Campion. "When did you send this letter, Miss Pork, do you remember?"

"Perfectly. The day before yesterday. Directly after the commercial traveller left. It took me some time because as I say I don't write much and I had to find everything; clean notepaper and a good pen, you know. But I caught the post, I think, although I might have been a minute or two late, not enough to matter though, and he should have got it yesterday afternoon. At any rate you can be sure he's got it now, so if you go back and ask him I think you'll find there's nothing more to worry about."

She smiled at them again, and relented.

"I'm sorry you've had all this journey for nothing. Let me get you a glass of wine—beetroot. Home-made, but before the war. Very nice, rather like a very sweet port with a taste of cloves."

"No, thank you, ma'am. We won't trouble you." The Chief's bleak old eyes were laughing, despite his disappointment. "There's just a little formality before we go. We'll have to know exactly what you've got here, and how it came here, and where from."

At first it looked as if Miss Pork was about to protest, but whether she had taken a fancy to Oates, or whether she was enjoying the excitement, the fact remained that she decided to give them a few more minutes.

"Very well," she conceded, "but we must hurry. I've got to run down to the church and do the flowers before lunch, and they're always a bother. People do criticize so. Personally I like a lot of flowers in a vase, especially on an altar, there's nothing so cheerful. Well, you've seen these things up here; now we'll go down to the cellar and I can tell you all about it there. This way. You'll have to mind your heads, for you are all tall, I see."

She was out of the room before she had finished speaking, steaming along like a little red train, her wooden shoes clattering rhythmically on the coloured tiles. A low door in the varnished panelling led them to a flight of steep stairs up which rose a strong odour of decay and onions.

"I hang my shallots down here," said Miss Pork. "They're good for the moth as well as being so useful in stews and illness; so they serve two purposes, you see. Be careful of the third step from the bottom, there's only half of it there."

Since they were descending from the top, of course this last injunction took everybody's attention, and they arrived in a low-ceilinged chamber in silence. Vast packing cases filled all one half of it, and Holly was regretting that he had not brought two sergeants and a working constable when Miss Pork spoke again.

"There, you see," she said. "There is the damp."

And there it was indeed. It ran in green rivers from iron

gratings high in the wall, and lay in iridescent pools on the mouldering floor.

"You couldn't keep pictures there," she said. "Not even furniture, although it's wonderful what good furniture will stand. So I took the contents of three packing cases upstairs. There are some little figurines which I put in the spare bedroom, by the way; ugly little things in some sort of ivory, but the rest you've seen in the drawing-room. Now, do you really want to undo all these boxes?"

"I'm very much afraid we shall have to, ma'am." Holly spoke from his heart. He was shining his torch on to one box less professional-looking than the rest, and the Chief glanced over his shoulder. An old label upon it, carelessly chalked across, announced that Messrs. Bull & Butler, wine merchants of Old Jewry, had at one time delivered the case to the Marquess of Carados. The newer label was still hidden against the side of the package next it.

"There's only some cardboard in there," cut in Miss Pork brightly. "I took a peep. It looks like scenery for a toy theatre. But there's some gilt ware in this big one; very elaborate pieces. One of them looks like a water pitcher for a bedroom, but it's covered with little figures and flowers, far too elaborate for use, but beautifully packed, so I hardly disturbed it. Now, where would you like to begin?"

"Just a moment, ma'am, if you please." Oates was polite but authoritative. "Before I have a complete inventory taken, I want to put one or two questions. When exactly did you take possession of all this?"

"Oh, a long while ago." Miss Pork was definite. "I've been so busy I've not had a moment to think about it; it was only the damp which reminded me it was here at all. Quite six or eight months, I should think, or was it this time last year? I'll ask Jones. She remembers what I forget, that's how we get along. I organize my life. It must have been quite a time, though, or I should never have thought of opening it. If one's known a parcel a year, one feels one can take liberties, don't you know."

The Chief seemed a little bewildered by this reasoning, but he rallied.

"You gave a receipt, of course, ma'am," he began cannily. "Didn't you have a memorandum at the same time? A document? Something written down to remind you what you'd got?"

"Oh yes, I understand you. I'm not mentally defective." Miss Pork's ruby face betrayed ferocious amusement. "I had a copy of the inventory on the firm's paper, of course, and I had some money. They paid me a sum for housing it all. That was why I felt I had an obligation in the matter. If one takes money, and one does nowadays, one must fulfil one's commitments. Mind you, I wouldn't have done it for anyone, but when I understood who owned it all, then I said to the woman that I felt I should do what I could. The aristocracy is dying, I know, but they mustn't be hurried, I said."

"The woman?" cried Holly, unable to play the Chief's more patient game.

"Certainly." Miss Pork turned her blazing glance upward. "The representative of the storage firm was a woman. I've entirely forgotten her name if I ever knew it, but she certainly was a woman. I don't see anything unusual in that, do you? Women do many things beside representing storage firms."

Having finished with Holly she turned to Oates. "Now, as I was just going to tell you, I received a sum of money for one year's rent on my cellar in advance, and as I have not yet received any more I deduce the year is not yet up. I hope you don't expect me to tell you how much money I received; I'll tell you if you like, but surely you don't expect me to."

"I'd like to have seen the cheque, ma'am."

"Oh, there was no cheque. As it was a small sum I accepted two five-pound notes. It suited me. I like to have a little money in the house; certain things are always paid in cash, the oil man, for instance, and . . ."

"But you kept the inventory, ma'am?" Oates managed to divert rather than to check the flow.

"Of course I did," she said. "In my desk. I kept it right up to a few months ago, and I've got a bit of it now, which I'll show you."

"A bit of it?" murmured Oates, his head on one side.

"Yes, the end quarter. It just says 'Sealed Case twenty-nine' or something like that. I know, because I've been looking at it lately. A young American officer came to tea and admired one of the pictures in the drawing-room; he asked what it was called, and I said I'd find out because I must say I like a boy to be interested in the home. So I went to my desk, and then I found out."

"The name of the picture?" demanded Holly in excitement.

"No." Miss Pork laughed at herself. "No. I was so annoyed. I found I'd only got this end bit of the inventory. As soon as I laid eyes on it I remembered what I must have done. I don't know if things like that come back to you, but they do to me. As soon as I saw it I knew what had happened. I came in here late one night in the winter and I couldn't find any matches; I didn't like to turn on the lights because the black-out wasn't done, but I never think a single flame counts, do you? There was a little fire in the grate left, so I went to my desk in the dark and took out something to make a spill to light a candle. I tore it in half, I remember that, for one mustn't waste paper, and I thrust one half back in the drawer, and of course that must have been the inventory. I've kept the end half, though, and I'll get it for you now."

She was off before they could stop her, her limp skirt flapping almost to her ankles as she clattered up the steps.

The Chief looked at Campion, and the younger man nodded. "Oh yes, God made her," he said, "no one else would have the nerve. They grow like that in the corners of rural England. I wonder what she's got in the spare bedroom. The Waterlow Ivories, or something like that?"

Holly, who was sitting on a packing case, studying some typewritten pages which he had taken from his pocket, glanced up. "It's the Lauderdale House stuff here," he said huskily; "that ewer she mentioned, that's the Lauderdale Treasure by the sound of it. There's a basin and a chalice made by an Italian called Mattioti; it's very valuable according to the owners. Solid, blessed gold for one thing, and she's keeping it down here." He looked round the cellar, his eyes protruding slightly. "It's wonderful, isn't it?" he said.

Oates sniffed. He had been considering the packing cases and now came to a decision. "If I were you, Holly, I'd get the local cops in on this, d'you know," he said. "There's a lot of work here, and it must be done carefully. Old Colonel Rufus is the C.C., and he's a very decent old stick. When our good lady comes back I'd slip up to the phone and have a word with him."

"Just what I had in mind, Mr. Oates." Holly spoke with relief. "It'll take care of this end and leave me free to go straight after Carados. I think we've got him now. All this will have to be checked, of course, but I think the evidence is here if we look for it."

Oates was not so sure. "There's her word and that old label on the box over there so far," he objected. "Neither is exactly concrete, I should like something better than that. But perhaps you're right. I'd like to see that inventory. I suppose she is coming back."

Holly looked up blankly. "Why, I never thought," he began, but got no further.

A woman was coming down the stairs. It was not Miss Pork, but the maidservant who had admitted them. She held a scrap of paper on a tray and thrust it out towards the group.

"Madam asked me to give this to Mr. Oates," she said. "She hopes you'll excuse her coming down for a minute or two, but she's just had a visitor come. She said I was to tell you who it was as she thought you'd like to know."

"Oh yes?" said Oates, stretching out his hand to take what was left of the inventory.

The woman dropped her glance, and spoke in a respectful murmur. "It's the Marquess of Carados upstairs," she said. "Him and a lady. The one who came here before."

21

NO ONE MOVED until the old woman had gone, lifting herself painfully up the dangerous stairs. When the sound of her feet died on the tiles above, Oates took Campion's elbow.

No word was spoken, but they all four went up quietly into the hall, which was dark, yet dappled with many coloured patches of sunlight streaming in through the stained glass in the porch.

The drawing-room door was closed, but one beside it stood open, and Campion, who had not wasted his time during the original interview, led the way into a small anteroom in which there was another of the glass-and-iron doors like that through which they had first observed Miss Pork at breakfast. It led into an alcove in the drawing-room as he had noticed, and it was ajar.

Miss Pork's voice was audible to them now, although she was out of their sight hidden by a pedestal supporting a brass pot which had pampas grass sprouting from it, but they could see Johnny and the woman beside him. He was standing a little in front of his companion with his hands in his pockets, his strong, good-natured face strangely expressionless.

The little crowd in the ante-room concentrated on the woman, and Campion, as he looked at her, felt a thrill of disappointment and dismay. She was the one woman who could make no difference to the evidence, the one woman whose appearance in the matter did not alter Johnny's position in it. It was Miss Chivers.

She was standing solidly on her heels, her hands folded across her bag, and her cheerful face raised enquiringly. As usual, she conveyed that she was tolerant but quite above the difficulty whatever it might be; yet Campion suspected that she was rattled, for there was a suppressed urgency about her which he had not noticed before.

Miss Pork's voice, the quack in it more pronounced than ever, continued at speed. Obviously so far the visitors had had very little opportunity to speak at all, and even now their chances of doing so did not seem high.

"Oh, you mustn't think I mind," she was saying. "It's no trouble at all, and I knew you'd understand about the damp. Pretty things need air, everything needs air, we do ourselves; look at the flowers. So I just brought them up here and treated them exactly like my own treasures. Some of them are charming, you know, well worth taking care of, but I expect you know that. Where would you like me to send them and when? There's a very good lorry in the village which often needs a second load and—"

"Wait," said Johnny suddenly. He had spoken more loudly

than he intended and the word thundered in the room. "I'm sorry," he went on hastily, "I didn't mean to shout at you, but—"

"Of course you didn't," put in Miss Pork indefatigably. "People often do, though, I find. It's nervousness, I expect. You don't look it, but were you nervous as a child?"

She made the question an important one, but he was not to be side-tracked.

"There has been a mistake," he said doggedly. "I'm afraid most of the things you have here are not mine. I've been trying to tell you. There is only one box which—"

"Not yours? Oh, but I understood they were. I don't think I should have taken them in if I hadn't been sure of that, you know, and you made it clear to me, didn't you, my dear?" she added, turning no doubt on Miss Chivers. "You're the secretary, are you? I didn't realize that at the time, you know, I thought you were the representative of the storage firm. I may have been a little muddled, but I don't think you said secretary; I should have remembered that."

At Mr. Campion's side Oates stirred as he noted the point.

"Oh yes, I'm sure I should have remembered that." Miss Pork did not laugh aloud, but the quack had a snigger in it. "I don't store things for ordinary people; why should I?"

"No, I don't think you would, and I do thank you for it." Johnny was talking resolutely, the words advancing steadily under her fire. "But there's been a mistake. Only one case of mine was sent down here and that contained a puppet theatre . . ."

"A puppet theatre—cardboard? Oh yes. I've got that, I . . ."

"Which," said Johnny Carados firmly, "belongs to a friend of mine called Ricky Silva. He made it himself and values it highly, and to please him my secretary sent it down to the country. She tells me she did this in the ordinary way, and when the storage firm had to give up the premises they had hired in Chessing they notified her, and she, rather than have the thing sent back to London, took the liberty of asking you to mind it."

"Why did she choose me?" said Miss Pork very reasonably.

"She had heard of you from Susan Shering. Susan and her first husband, who was a great friend of mine, spent a week in town with me about a year ago. Miss Chivers heard Mrs.

Shering speak of you then, and she remembered your name and the name of the village, probably because she knew Ricky's theatre was stored down here. When she had made an arrangement with you she told the firm what she was doing, and they seem to have sent all their goods to you. That is so, isn't it, Dolly?"

"Yes, that's what happened." Miss Chivers sounded sorry for the woolly-mindedness of all the rest of the human race. "They were unreliable, stupid people who took on more than they could chew, I imagine."

"Oh," said Miss Pork, advancing into the line of vision from the alcove door, intense disappointment in every blush. "Then, if much of what I have here is not yours, whose is it? You must have been very surprised when you got my letter."

"I was," Johnny said. He was still expressionless, still un- usually quiet. "I found it waiting for me when I got home last night. You had marked it 'Personal' and it hadn't been opened. I couldn't understand it at all, so I phoned Miss Chivers at her flat although it was very late, and when she came round and explained I decided we'd come down here at once."

Miss Pork stood looking at him with her head on one side, her embarrassingly shrewd eyes fixed on his own. "To see if the toy theatre was safe, no doubt," she said dryly.

In his corner the Chief grimaced, but Campion did not see him, his attention was fixed on something else. Johnny did not answer, Miss Pork gave him no opportunity.

With a sudden gesture, which in almost any other woman would have been wholly charming, she stepped a little closer and peered up into his face.

"Cards on the table," she said. "There's something very wrong, isn't there? What have I got? A lot of stolen property?" Again she gave him no chance to speak. "I'm not quite a fool," she said, "and I know something like that must have happened. The police are in the cellar, you know."

"The police?"

"Yes, nice conscientious men, working very hard. They didn't say so outright, but I knew they must have some very good reason for calling, and they have, haven't they, Miss Secretary?"

The speed with which she swung round on Miss Chivers

was extraordinary, and the girl, who was in the act of taking her handkerchief out of her bag, paused to stare at her.

"Have they?" she said dully.

"Yes, of course they have." Miss Pork's aggressiveness was startling. "Don't you treat me like a silly old woman. That's one of the few things I'm not. I've got my wits about me. When you came to see me last year you represented yourself as an employee of the storage company, and you arranged that I should look after all these boxes, not only the one with the toy theatre in it. No, don't speak. I know what I'm saying. You told me they all belonged to the Marquess because you thought I was an old snob, as I am, you're quite right, and you thought that would keep me quiet and loyal, as it did. You arranged it all, and you gave me the inventory."

Miss Chivers did not change colour; she had moved up to Johnny and now stood close to his elbow. She towered above Miss Pork.

"The firm sent you the inventory three days after I called," she said.

"Ah!" There was triumph in Miss Pork's cracked voice. "How do you know? How do you know, my girl?"

There was a moment of terrifying revelation, and then Mr. Campion moved with the speed of long practice. He snatched the brass bowl from the ebony pedestal and sent it, pampas grass and all, hurling across the room just as the shot rang out.

Miss Pork made a thin sound, and one of the chandeliers burst, sending a shower of glass beads all over the room. It was a big room, full of obstacles, and as Holly pitched himself across it towards the woman with the revolver there were many man-traps in his way.

Dolly Chivers escaped him. The gun with the handkerchief still round it dropped to the floor, and she turned from side to side like a cornered animal. Oates barred her way to one door, and Johnny, his face blank with incredulity, was between her and the other. She leaped for the low window half obscured by its decoration of drapery, flower-baskets and bird-cages, and threw herself at it as if it were no more than an opening, an avenue to freedom.

They saw her. They all saw her face. In one dreadful moment, which, as such moments do, spread itself into a long nightmare of understanding, they saw the reckless terror there. They saw her strong, cheerful efficiency blotted out by fear; they saw also the madness of the fear, the stark terror in which reason had no longer any part. It blazed from her as from a demon in possession and the glass splintered and tore and crashed as her heavy shoulder hit it squarely.

"The area!" screamed Miss Pork. "The area!"

Dolly Chivers did not scream. For a long time afterwards Mr. Campion could remember that silence of hers, and it shook him more than any sound he had ever heard. There was not a whimper, not a sigh, not a strangled breath. There were other noises. The thin harsh sound of the glass, the dreadful soft thud and ring of bone on stone, and the scraping. And then only the silence.

They saw the area afterwards. It was one of those narrow, damp shafts built like a grave, and designed to give grudging light to kitchens which any architect might well have preferred to keep obscure. It lay out only a few feet from the house and was protected from the garden by a narrow railing of cast iron. From above it had no protection, but gaped upward greedily like the mouth of a heraldic fish.

While they awaited the local police, the doctor and the Chief Constable, Oates and Campion stood under a copper beech on a lawn cut into as many shapes as a sheet of pastry before baking. Johnny was still in the house in grim conference with Holly, and Tovey was doing his best to settle both Miss Pork's nerves and her curiosity.

The Chief of the Criminal Investigation Department was rooting up a daisy with the toe of his shoe. "I didn't see it happening," he said. "It riles me and it frightens me. I'm getting old, Campion. If you hadn't been so quick, we'd have had the wrong corpse on our hands. All the same, I can't believe him now. You may be right, but I can't see it yet. She might have held the gun in her handkerchief simply so that it shouldn't be seen."

Campion took his arm. They were both shaken without realizing it, and when he spoke his quiet voice was unusually tense. "She might," he agreed, "but she didn't. She held it like that for the good old-fashioned reason that she had no intention of allowing it to show fingerprints. I've looked at it, it's perfectly clean, unnaturally clean. There's only one thing that can mean. No, I'm sure I'm right. It all hangs together at last. It's Johnny's gun, that's the important thing."

"Oh, I see what you mean. I understand you, but I don't accept it yet." Oates was still dubious. "He certainly identified it at once. Said he'd left it in his desk for his leave, didn't he? I don't like it, Campion. It's the same as all the other incidents. He comes right up to the point of exposure and then side-steps. At the moment he seems stupefied, but is that genuine? I don't understand the chap and I don't see how he's doing it."

"Look," said Mr. Campion imploringly, "just for a moment take it that he isn't doing it and hasn't been doing it. Let us consider what we've seen with our own eyes. We saw that girl sidle up to him so that she stood in a position as near his own as dammit. She fired with his gun, holding it with a handkerchief at a woman who was exposing her. Those are the facts, aren't they?"

"Yes."

"You agree?"

"Yes."

"Well then, my dear chap, suppose you hadn't seen them, suppose you had still been down in the cellar where she thought you were, suppose you had heard the shot and come beetling in and found Miss Pork dead and Johnny with a gun in his hand and no fingerprints but his own on it; what then, whose story would you believe then? His, or Dolly Chivers?"

Oates was impressed, but not convinced. "Why should he be holding the gun?"

"Because as soon as she fired the girl intended to give it to him."

"How on earth can you deduce that?"

"I think it likely, because that's what she always did, figuratively speaking. She always handed the baby to him. She left Mrs. Stavros in his bed, poisoned with his chloral, she left the capsule for him to take to Theodore Bush, she told Miss Pork that the packing cases belong to him. Now at last we've actually seen her doing it, and we know it was done."

Oates shook his grey head. "It's not quite right," he said. "You've got something there, but it's not quite right yet. I think I almost grant you those mechanics, there can't be two killers, and we know for a fact that she was one. But you know she didn't do this thing alone."

Mr. Campion was silent for a while, facing the dreadful possibility which had leapt into his mind in the beginning. "No," he said at last, "no, she can't have done it alone, not all of it. She was a lieutenant, not the principal. I rather think, you know, Oates, that she was a lieutenant who lost her head and tried to shoot her way out. She was out of her mind with terror, that girl. She started to kill and couldn't stop."

"Oh yes, she was afraid." Oates spoke softly. "That was the thing which startled me. She went through that window like a lunatic. Even if that damned death-trap hadn't been outside the window how could she ever have hoped to escape? She wasn't thinking; her mind wasn't working." He paused and sighed. "Yes, it's very consistent. The murders were like that, wilder and more reckless as they went on. I think that's about the size of that, Campion. I think so, and I hope so, but—why did she keep on involving Carados unless he was the principal himself?"

Now that the thought was out, put into unrelenting words, Mr. Campion stared at him fascinated. Oates walked on, skirting the beds shaped like crescents and the beds shaped like stars.

"Now I'll do some supposing," he said. "Supposing she did most of the donkey-work, got herself thoroughly involved and then saw, as they must all have seen, that it wasn't going to work out, in fact that the war wasn't going to end that way. That must have left her with a pile of worry." He paused, feeling round in his mind for the truth of it. Then he said: "Then she must have done something that gave her away. Something careless."

"Something to do with the wine," said Mr. Campion. "I see there's one case of *Les Enfants Doux* downstairs in the cellar. The other must have been broken into, possibly, even, the bottles were loose in their straw, anything might have happened in that hurry. She took them thinking they were valueless, and Stavros and his missus got to her and black-mailed her, perhaps. Anyway, at some point she must have lost her head and decided to kill the woman."

"That's it," said Oates, his grey eyes dark as they always were when the chase ran close, "that's it. And because she realized that if ever it did come to a show-down all the proof lay against her and not her principal, she did her best to put the blame on him. How's that?"

Mr. Campion thrust his hands deep in his pockets and his chin sank into his collar. "There's no proof whatever against him," he said.

"There never is against a big man in this sort of business." Oates spoke bitterly. "But I'll get him," he added grimly. "In the end."

Campion glanced towards the drive. There was still no sign of police cars. The gardener on duty by the arch had his back towards the dreadful sight within it, and was rubbing his neck with a coloured handkerchief. Neither Holly nor his quarry had yet appeared. It was all very sunny and ugly and comfortable.

"You can't hold him," said Campion at last. "Not on present evidence?"

"No, of course I can't." For Oates the voice was harsh. "But on the other hand I can't lose him."

"How do you mean?"

Oates laughed savagely. "A man in his position with a name like his and a job like his can't hide himself in a country this size in its present restricted state," he said. "That's the one break I've got. All England is a cage for him until I get the proof I want. There's no way out for him, none at all."

Campion could think of one, but he did not mention it. The emotional effect upon him of the new developments went deeper than he cared to admit. It was not so much that Johnny Carados was an old acquaintance as that he was a figure long admired. Treachery from him was more than treachery; there was insult in it and betrayal. As the reflection spread through his mind, others followed it, and he remembered those other well-loved figures whom the war had revealed unworthy of the general pride. Was Johnny Carados to join that dismal parade? The question so shook him that it was with relief that he saw Holly striding across the grass towards them. The Inspector was excited, and the essential policeman in him was very evident.

"Two things, Mr. Oates," he said. "First I've been on to the Yard and spoken to Superintendent Yeo. Then I've had it out with Carados. He sticks to his story, by the way; it's straightforward and I can't shake him. He seems genuinely upset about the girl—sort of stunned. Also he says he's got to get back to his duty."

"Well, he can't at the moment, that's certain."

"I've told him so, but he says he must be back on his station by tonight. He says it's vital."

The Chief allowed his lips to form several words before he chose the one he wanted. "Do you see any way we can hold him, Holly?"

"No, sir. Seeing who he is we can't step over the line anywhere. He swears he'll be back for the inquest if it's any time after noon tomorrow."

Oates shrugged his shoulders. "There's nothing for it, is there?"

"I don't think so, sir." Holly was as gloomy as his superior officer. "I don't think he can get away though. He thinks he's safe and he can't make a run for it. Anyway, we've got nothing on him as far as the killing is concerned. We saw it happen. If we hadn't been there . . ."

"Ah, but we were," said Oates. "We were, and we weren't quick enough or that poor girl could have told us something."

"Poor girl, sir?" Holly was startled at this commiseration for the first cold-blooded murderer he had ever been privileged to witness in action.

Oates noticed it and was unimpressed. "I'm always a little sorry for anyone who completely loses his nerve," he said, adding irrelevantly, "especially if they're as valuable as that poor woman could have been to us. No, we'll have to let him go again, but it's the last time, Holly, the very last time. What about Yeo? He's not too pleased with us, I expect."

"I think he felt we might have waited for him, sir."

"So we ought to have done. I could give myself the sack for that." The Chief spoke complacently. "But we've justified ourselves. We got here just at the right time. You told him?"

"Yes, Mr. Oates, I did. And he's got something. They've been busy, and they've found the storage firm."

"Really?" Oates was astounded. "I'd have bet on it that they were entirely fictitious."

"No, they're not. They exist all right. It's very small, only one little office, but it's been established some time. There's one elderly woman clerk who does what work there is, and

according to her story the business changed hands just before
the war when it was in very low water. It was taken over by a
Mr. Jesso who brought in a lot of accounts of a special
kind—evacuation of furniture to the country."

"Good God!" said Oates piously, "it's coming unstuck at
last. Have they got Jesso?"

"No, not yet, sir. Apparently things are very quiet now,
and have been for some time. He comes in very seldom and
the woman doesn't know where he lives. She's quite honest,
apparently. But they have got the books with all the addresses of the various warehouses, barns and halls and other
country storage places. They're getting on to that now. And if
we're right—"

"If we're right, we'll recover the blessed lot. This is terrific,
Holly. Any more?"

The Chief Inspector did not speak immediately. A faint
smile played round his small mouth. "There's no proof of this
yet," he said at last, "but they've got a description of Jesso
from the woman and it is rather significant. Superintendent
Yeo told me to repeat it to you in her words. She says he's a
particularly small man with a very deep voice and that he
wears a small, pointed beard."

"Gold," said Campion abruptly.

Holly nodded to him approvingly. "That's what the Superintendent thought. He's arranging for a chance meeting between the two."

The Chief whistled. "We're getting very close to Carados,"
he said.

Mr. Campion stood thinking. He was remembering the
details of the last interview he had had with Gee-gee Gold
less than twelve hours before on the landing just outside
Theodore Bush's bedroom. "Johnny is *sans reproche*," he had
said, and had meant it. What exactly did that signify? Had
Gold seen Johnny as a leader to be followed blindly, or was it
possible that he might have seen him as a cloak? The Chief's
brisk voice cut into his meditations.

"Ah, here are the cars at last," he was saying. "That civilian
is the doctor, I suppose. Now we can get on."

He and Holly strode forward to meet the newcomers, but
Mr. Campion did not accompany them. He found a small
uncomfortable concrete seat between two atrocious Germanic

gnomes, and sat down. He had his fill of casualties and was not interested in the police doctor's test for death. Death was there all right. Nor did he wish to hear again the endless formalities, the apologies, and the explanations, the interviews and the sworn statements. He sat thinking that it was nearly forty-eight hours now since he had first missed his train and that there was still more trouble to come to delay him. The conviction was growing upon him that he had a duty to perform, one which demanded all his resource and experience. There was the tremendous likelihood of failure to consider, and the strong possibility of another eventuality, even more unpleasant.

He was still sitting there, hunched up in the bright sunlight, when Johnny came out of the mock-Gothic porch. He stood for a moment looking round for his car and Campion rose and went to meet him. Carados was already at the driving-wheel when the other man came up. There was a change in him, but it was not the one Campion had expected. He was no longer dazed but was still expressionless, and behind it all there was an air of determination, a grimness, almost a courage. His clear-cut, terrifyingly intelligent face was pale but he was quite steady and his voice was casual.

"Hello, Campion," he said. "Sorry to leave all this to you, but it can't very well be helped." He paused, aware that the words were too light altogether. "It's shaken me, you know," he said. "I'd known her for eight years."

"Do you know," said Mr. Campion slowly, "I rather doubt that."

Carados peered at him through the open driving window. "Yes," he admitted. "There's a lot in that. It's terrifying to think that you can see people every day and never know them. She was mad at the end, I think; utterly insane. Did you see her? Yet I came down with her this morning and never noticed anything. I didn't even think about her. She seemed just the same, efficient, you know, jolly, and unget-at-able." His voice was betraying him a little now, the edges wearing thin.

"She was insane with fear," said Campion.

The man in the car shivered. "God, how horrible!" he said.

Campion took a deep breath. "I don't want to butt in," he

began wretchedly, "but is it absolutely necessary that you should get back just at this particular moment?"

"Afraid so." Again the curious, reserved expression showed for an instant in the blue eyes. "I must. I knew I had to get back, that's why I came down in the night. I shan't touch London; I shall go straight from here. I've known about the date some time, it's vital, I'm afraid."

"But I thought that if all had gone well you were getting married this morning?"

It might have been supposed that the words had escaped Campion by accident. He coloured slightly, and apologized. "I'm sorry," he said, "it's nothing to do with me."

Carados ignored the entire incident. His reserved expression deepened and he changed the subject.

"I'd better get on," he said. "Work to do. It's a hell of a life."

"Yes," said Campion, and added with an innocence not altogether natural in him, "Doing any flying yourself?"

The other man pressed the starter. "Now and again, you know," he said above the purr of the engine. "They say one gets too old for it, but I can't bring myself to believe it."

Campion held the car door as if he would restrain the machine by force. "I'll see you at the inquest," he said.

"Eh?" said Johnny Carados. "Oh yes. Right ho."

"I'll see you at the inquest," Campion repeated. "I'm relying on you, and I think you'll come."

"Do you?" said Carados. "What a queer chap you are, Campion. I wonder why you do? Good-bye. If I can, you know, if I can."

He let in the clutch very gently, and the car rolled slowly away, shaking off Mr. Campion's restraining hand without roughness.

The other man stood looking after it as it disappeared among the trees. From the house behind him came the sound of voices and Oates and the poker-backed Chief Constable appeared in the porch. Very slowly, Mr. Campion turned to join them.

22

IT WAS ALMOST closing time at the Minoan, which, in wartime, expected its clients to eat early and be thankful. The little room on the first floor which had seen so much of the story already was well shuttered, and the light hanging from the ceiling made a bright pool on the red tablecloth. Half in and half out of the pool sat Mr. Pirri, while Stavros lurked in the dusk behind him. Both partners were unusually quiet.

Mr. Campion, whose cheekbones were beginning to show prominently beneath dark circles behind his spectacles, sat before them.

"It's a fair offer," he said.

Pirri spread out his wide hands. "We've told you all we know," he said, his shrill, angry voice rising.

"All right." Mr. Campion rose. "Party's over. We'll go the long way round. I can identify the taxi and I can swear you drove it and attacked me. My word may not convict you but it'll give you a hell of a run for your money."

The full brown eyes nearest him flickered. "That will be inconvenient," suggested Mr. Pirri.

"Very," Campion agreed. "Police everywhere worrying everybody. There must be somebody who saw the cab go out. And someone knows where the juice came from. That should be traceable these days."

Pirri reflected, and presently his teeth appeared in a brief smile. "You are not a vindictive man?"

"I'm prepared to forget and forgive a little matter between friends."

"Very good."

"I agree. Magnificent, as far as it goes. Pirri, when you kidnapped me, what were you looking for?"

179

He did not reply, but Stavros touched him.

"What does it matter?" he murmured. "Both poor girls are dead . . ."

"Women!" said Pirri, with sudden fury. "Always you think of nothing but women. I alone do the work. It is I who concentrate on the business. But for me we should be in the street. And what happens when I exert myself—when I go perhaps a little too far? You try to knife me because you think I have attacked your woman. I who did nothing but strive to help our business."

He turned to Campion almost in tears. "These restrictions, this scarcity," he said. "How can one progress? How can one supply one's patrons? At last people are willing to spend and I—I have nothing to sell."

In any other situation his rage must have had an element of the comic. His entire energy went into the exposure of his intolerable grievances. They poured from him in an avalanche of emotion.

"Since I was a child, a boy, a little helpless boy, I work to sell, and no one has a sixpence," he repeated. "And now they wave five-pound notes at me and what have I to give them? Nothing at all. It has made me a little mad, you know, and naturally."

Mr. Campion could see any brief explanation of the relationship between scarcity and cash would fall upon that soil in which such seeds proverbially wither and die. Pirri was more than ordinarily infuriated.

"It was an opportunity," he said, "and I went for it with my head bald. At first I was circumspect; afterwards I let it get me, you understand. It obsessed me, it made me wild."

Campion was abominably tired. His physical weariness was hampering and he pulled himself together irritably. He saw there was no chance of getting a coherent story here and that he would have to rely on questions if he were to find the one vital lead which would take him to the truth. He made a guess.

"Mrs. Stavros obtained a few bottles of *Les Enfants Doux* from Miss Chivers, and brought them to you to sell," he suggested. "Is that right?"

"That was the beginning," agreed Stavros wretchedly. "My wife came in here, sold me three bottles for a fair price and said there was a chance of getting me some more. It was all in the way of business, perfectly fair. And then," he added with sudden fire, "then, Pirri, you got hold of it."

"And why not?" said Pirri fiercely. "I sold one to an old customer one night. He sent for me, 'Pirri,' he said, 'this is superb. You're undercharging me, I bet you don't know that'—some such pleasantry. He made me taste it and I saw it was indeed excellent, and I realized I had made a discovery. Here was a chance at last; a real chance of making a little profit."

He spread out his hands again and his long, miserable face was pathetic in its resentment. "We were acting with complete honesty. Stavros found a good client, a nice American boy with plenty of money. We were doing nothing wrong. We offered him good stuff and he had the cash to pay for it. He said he would buy all we had and would give a little party, maybe. Very satisfactory. Then that Theodore Bush came round enquiring. But we do not want to drive any bargains, we have our client already fixed. All is arranging itself very well, and then—this—this Mrs. Moppet."

"No." Stavros protested. He was pleading rather than objecting. "Do not speak of her so. Poor girl, she's dead."

Pirri raised his eyes to heaven, where, presumably, he received inspiration, for his better nature asserted itself.

"I regret it," he said, "I'm sorry for you. I sympathize, but I have a bitter heart and I was so wild."

"You thought she was double-crossing you, I take it," said Mr. Campion.

"Naturally," said Pirri calmly. "She told so many stories. First she could get it and there was a raising of the price; then she couldn't. More talk, more persuasion from us both. Still it was impossible. On and on it went until she was one day quite definite. It could not be. She could get no more of the wine and wanted to take back what we already had. I became incensed, I admit it. I thought, I brooded, I persecuted myself, and at last I decided."

"You formed a plan," translated Mr. Campion for his own benefit.

"I formed a plan," agreed Pirri obligingly. "I said I would follow her and I would frustrate her. I would get what is mine by right, and I did. For a day and a night I followed her; she was here on Sunday quarrelling with Stavros about the stuff, and when she left I was behind her."

"My hat!" said Mr. Campion in astonishment. "In that cab?"

"Why not? It is an excellent disguise, a taxi-cab."

"So I should imagine. Rather dangerous, wasn't it?"

Pirri shrugged his shoulders. "I was wild," he said again as if that were sufficient explanation.

Campion considered. "You must have used that cab before," he said at last.

Pirri looked at him coldly. "We speak now only about the business in which we are interested," he observed.

"Yes, of course. All right. I was only checking up. And so you watched her. Where did she go?"

"To Carados Square. I waited there. I waited all night."

Campion sat up. "You waited all night?" he repeated.

"Certainly. I was determined."

"Did you see anybody?"

"No one of importance. She went into the house and a long time after another woman came out; a big woman, young, healthy, strong."

"Miss Chivers?"

"I imagine so. I don't know. She carried nothing, that was all I saw. No one else went in or out until the morning. I went on waiting. About nine o'clock the big girl came back and afterwards a lady called with some flowers, letting herself in with a key. She had been there for some time when the first woman went out again. I was tired, sleepless, hungry, but I was enraged. Still I waited."

He made it an intensely dramatic story, but looked at it all, as far as Mr. Campion could see, from entirely the wrong angle.

"You're sure you only saw these two women?"

"I'm sure. And neither of them was carrying anything heavier than flowers. Imagine my exasperation."

"I think I can—just. And then?"

"Then the older woman came out once more. She was in distress, I could see that. She went across the square on foot. The morning passed and lunch-time, and I was in danger of discovery. But I was so angry that I persisted and at last, towards evening, I was rewarded, or so I most tragically thought." Pirri was working up to his story, and was putting his soul into it. "I saw the elder woman return. Again she let herself in with her key. After a while an ambulance drove up. In my position I could not see what was loaded into it, and I dared not get out to watch, but I thought I knew. 'This is a ruse,' I said, 'and a clever one. That Moppet has seen me from the windows, and has guessed why I am here. She's attempting to deceive me but I shall not be deceived.' By this time I was in a fever, you understand. My resentment, my hunger, and my weariness were on top of me. I thought to myself, 'Here is my chance—'" He paused and peered at Campion across the table.

"You comprehend my state of mind?"

To Mr. Campion's surprise, he found that he did. The picture was horrific but convincing.

"Yes," he said, "I do. You followed the ambulance, I suppose?"

"I did, and as it turned into the cul-de-sac off Piccadilly the lights were against me." Pirri's disgust was vivid. "I dared not disobey them for fear of being questioned. By the time I and another taxi-cab entered Bottle Street, the ambulance was empty and unattended. Again I waited. Many people came to the door, some of whom I recognized, and I felt 'Ah, I am getting warm. It is to be all right. My time will come.'"

Mr. Campion suddenly saw the end of the story, and despite his exhaustion, nearly burst out laughing. "You thought Madame Stavros had sold me the wine and that it was in my two wooden cases?"

Pirri leaned forward. His shirt-sleeves rode up his bony arms and his face was woebegone. "You have my regrets," he said, "my deep regrets. You suffered, I know it. I could not revive you in the garage, but I had to take you to a little place I use sometimes where you could recover at your leisure. You were found there in the morning. I'm sorry; you were badly treated—but even you admit that the dirty laugh is on me."

In the circumstances it was most handsomely said, and Mr. Campion appreciated it. His smile escaped him. "I'm almost sorry you were disappointed," he said.

"I was not disappointed, I was annihilated," said Pirri. "After such a vigil my chagrin was unspeakable."

Stavros turned towards the door. "You will both excuse me," he said briefly. "I do not care, you see."

The note he struck was unexpected and Pirri was almost sobered.

"I'm sorry for him," he said as the door closed behind him, "but most deeply I am sorry for myself. That Moppet was a difficult woman, a worrying, nagging, importunate woman. She bothered someone so much they killed her, I expect."

Mr. Campion nodded. "I fancy you're right there," he murmured. "That's just about what did happen. Someone started to sell her that wine before they realized what it was. Then they tried to stave her off, she discovered there was a secret and tried to blackmail the stuff out of them, the secret was more important than she realized, they were desperately afraid and they killed her."

"When you say 'they' you mean Miss Chivers," said Pirri. "Why do you say that?"

The restaurateur rose. "It follows. No one else was there."

There was a silence between them until Pirri said finally:

"It is a bad business, but not my affair. After I followed you to Bedbridge Row I gave up."

Mr. Campion stirred. He felt frustrated. Pirri's story was enlightening so far as it went, but it took him no further. He got up wearily. "Thank you," he said. "That is the end then. You can rely on me not to raise the subject again."

Pirri went to the sideboard without speaking and produced glasses and a bottle. "You think trade gets better soon, eh?" he enquired blandly, as he proffered the drink and raised his own.

"Here's to it, anyway," said Mr. Campion, and still had the glass at his lips when the door edged open and a bleary, unforgettable eye peered at him through the aperture.

"I was afraid you'd gorn, sir," said old Fred, betraying his vigil by his very timeliness.

Pirri swore at him but half-heartedly. Evidently the labour shortage was another curb on that urgent but single-minded spirit. Like the countryman he was, old Fred waited until the little squall had blown over him. Then he got himself cautiously into the room.

"That young lady," he began, addressing Campion as an old fellow-conspirator, "the one who was going to marry the lord, and who went about with the American officer, and came here with you—"

"Mrs. Shering. What about her?"

"Well, she's downstairs with him now. They've been having a bit of a meal together."

"With Lieutenant Evers?"

"That's right, and they'd like a word with you. We've been shut about half an hour and they're on their own down there, waiting. I thought I'd mention it."

He stood hopefully, his head held sideways, and one eye, bright and enquiring as a goose's, fixed on the other man's face, avid for any betraying signal there.

"Right. I'll go down," said Campion, disappointing him. "How did they know I was here?"

Fred looked mystified. "Can't think," he said, "unless I might have let it slip out."

It was so well done that Mr. Campion was on the verge of being deceived. He laughed and went down, Fred shuffling behind him, outwardly at any rate as casual, as ineffectual and as disinterested as an old brown leaf in the wind.

Susan and Don were at a corner table alone in the restaurant. As usual they were engrossed in each other, and Campion envied them. He came up without them noticing him, but having tapped Don on the shoulder he was received joyously.

"Say, you're the man we want." The boy's voice rose on the last word. "Sit down, will you?"

He was deliriously happy; they both were. Delight radiated from them in a warm and generous cloud. They sat and glowed at him, so that he caught the infection and laughed. "Things pretty good?" he enquired.

"Good? They're better than that. Congratulate us, we're all set, we're getting married." Don's voice was playing tricks with him, squeaking on unexpected words. Susan nodded; she looked frightened by her own content.

"It's all right. We've got an O.K. I can't quite realize it—it's a sort of miracle."

Mr. Campion took off his spectacles, always with him a sign of concentration. "Fine," he said. "Splendid. Just the job. How come?"

"Oh it's Johnny, of course." She was shyly proud. "He's— he's pretty jolly good."

"He's wonderful," said Don with that intense admiration which dies too young. "He's a great guy."

Mr. Campion saw a piece of bread on the table and ate a pellet of it absently. He felt slightly sick.

"Oh yes?" he said. "What's he done? Made a graceful gesture?"

"I'll say. But what a gesture!" Don was enthusiastic. "We got a note today. It was sent to Susan, but it was written to me, too. I'm going to ask Susan to let me show it to you. Can I, Susan?"

"I'd like you to. I'd like everybody in the world to see it," she said, adding sweetly, "everybody nice."

Campion took the sheet of notepaper which was stamped with the address of a famous club. He held it steady with an effort, and old Fred, lurking in the background and watching his face with an experienced yokel eye, felt that perhaps he was getting something for his trouble after all. The writing was firm and very well formed, both masculine and graceful.

My dear Susan and Don,

When you are genuinely in love and you're very young and you're at war, the only thing to do is to get married at once and get some kids. Don't let any consideration on earth stand in your way. I mean this, and if it sounds didactic, then it's because I feel I'm in a position to be didactic to you two.

I think you'll want an explanation of this direction (and it is a direction, chaps, don't get me wrong) from me especially at this moment, i.e. "the evening before the wedding day." You, Susan, will want to know if I love you. The answer to that is, of course I do, who could help it, but (if you don't understand this, Don will be able to explain it, I think) the feeling I had for old Tom Shering was different, but very, very much stronger. Since you're the girl I know you are, Susan, you won't think me unduly ungallant for this, and as for you, Don, you'll follow me, I fancy.

So there you are, my dears, get on with it. Good luck,

*and if by chance I don't get an opportunity to dance at
your fête don't misunderstand me.*

Yours ever, and I mean that,

Johnny.

*P.S. I took the liberty of spying out Don's reputation
and reputed assets. Both are impressive. There again,
Don will follow me if you don't, Susan. Love, my sweetie.*

Campion put the paper down. Both young faces were
turned to him eagerly. "It's so honest," said Susan.

"It's so strong," said Don.

Susan laid her hand over the boy's. "I'll always love Johnny
as I do now," she said. "Ninety-five parts pure admiration.
The only thing I wish he hadn't said was that he might not
dance at our wedding."

"Oh that's all right," said Don easily. "That's just the
Service. You get that uncertain feeling about promising to be
anywhere at any given time. That's O.K."

Mr. Campion got up. He did his best in their delirium;
they helped him by not observing him too closely. After the
congratulations had been repeated and the adieux said, he
went out and old Fred watched him go with wistful curiosity.

As Campion stepped out into the dark, he breathed deeply
as if he needed the air. Miserably he looked up into the sky.
It was a clear curtain, threadbare with stars—a wonderful
night for flying.

23

THE COACH AND Horses, which as Yeo
had said was at the wrong end of Early Street, was a modest
little pub. It nestled shyly under the wing of a Baptist Chapel,
and Mr. Campion found it with twenty minutes to spare. As
he entered the neat bar with the nostalgic smell, his heart

sank. There was no sign of the familiar square figure with the bullet head. He was resigning himself to the prospect of a further journey when an old-fashioned barmaid with a smile and sunset hair asked him if he was looking for anybody.

"You *are* tired, aren't you?" she said. "Wait a minute." She put her head round a door behind the bar and there was a brief delay before a face appeared at a small window between a museum-piece of a bottle of Chartreuse and two dummy magnums. It disappeared again, and the woman turned to Campion.

"This way, ducky," she said, raising a flap in the counter. "I thought you looked like a friend of his. He's all alone. I'll bring you both a 'special' in a moment."

Mr. Campion felt comforted. For the first time since his return to England he felt certain that he was at home. He passed behind the bar, through the red curtains with the ball fringe and came to a small, hot room with a fire and a hanging alabaster lampshade. The Superintendent was sitting at the table, his collar loosened, his spectacles on his nose, an *Evening News* neatly folded into a wide wafer in his hands, and a tankard at his elbow.

Campion surveyed him with open satisfaction.

"Got your boots off too?" he enquired vulgarly.

Yeo raised one eyebrow. "These are my unofficial head-quarters," he explained. "Take a pew. I was hoping you'd come in. They tell me you're a wonderful marksman with a flowerpot." He permitted himself the ghost of a sniff. "Lucky they had you with them. Considering the rank of the person-nel involved, not a very creditable arrest, in my opinion, for what it's worth."

Mr. Campion sank down into a chair with a deep leather lap, and lay back gratefully.

"It wasn't too tidy," he agreed, "but the whole thing was utterly unexpected."

Yeo looked virtuous. "They always used to tell me that nothing was ever unexpected to a good cop," he said smugly. "The old man had his gun with him too, didn't he? Still," he added with growing generosity, "I don't blame the old so-and-so. I'd rather he had his job than me. God love us, what a shine the influential chap can kick up. I saw some of it, and I was glad to get the Chief back this afternoon."

"Whom are you talking about?"

"That perishing Admiral." Yeo was nearly respectful. "He's put the cat among the pigeons all right. Questions, chits, memos coming down every two minutes. You'd think we were trying to hush something up, not sweating our guts out (if you'll excuse me) to clear the mess up. I told you this case was going to be unlucky for policemen. However, we're well away now, thank God; things are moving."

"Are they?" The note of hopefulness was apparent in the words and the Superintendent shook his head.

"All in the same way, I'm afraid," he said. "Sorry, old man, I can see how you feel in a way, but the thing is too clear. It's rolling down on Carados like a thunderstorm. He's just out of it at the moment, but it can't last much longer. It's sweeping in on him."

Mr. Campion moved impatiently. "What about Gold?"

"Oh, we've got him." Yeo spoke with quiet satisfaction. "A pretty little job of Pelly's this afternoon. Gold and the woman met, as arranged; she recognized him and spoke to him and he gave himself away. It was as easy as that—no fuss, no fireworks, no jumping through the window, just a straight arrest done in the proper way. It doesn't take us much forrader, though."

"Oh, why?"

"Because he was merely working behind the woman Chivers. I've seen his statement and I've had a look at him this evening. There's no doubt about it, you can tell it. I've seen it happen again and again in this case. He knew he was working for Chivers and he wasn't sure whom she was working for. He guessed, perhaps, but he didn't know. Every single one of them has been like that. We shall work out the connection between Gold and the others we've already got in the bag, but we shan't find anything to take him close to anyone in the opposite direction, except for the woman. I know, I've seen it before."

Mr. Campion remained lying back in the chair; his eyes were closed behind his spectacles. "Quick work," he said at last.

"It was." Yeo accepted honour where he felt it was due. "We got the firm's books early this morning and I sent the boys out to the addresses right away. The only thing in a case like this is to make a big swoop everywhere before any information can leak out. The reports have been coming in ever since. There's half the treasure in England, or that's what it feels like, scattered about in safe little hide-outs all over the country. This is a feather in our cap, however they treat us, I will say that."

"It is." Campion was serious in his praise. "As an organization I suppose you're capable of putting on a greater speed than anyone in the world, except, perhaps, the Russian Army."

"That's right, for all our old flat feet," said Yeo, and he chuckled with pleasure. "We don't get many bouquets except from foreigners, and I can't say I mind one now and again."

Mr. Campion returned to the problem. "You don't think Miss Chivers could have been doing it alone?" he suggested. "Using Carados's name, but in reality playing a—a lone hand?"

Yeo met his eyes squarely. "That be damned for a tale," he said inelegantly. "No, I don't. Apart from everything else she hadn't the nerve, and she hadn't the *size*, if you get me. She couldn't keep her hands off a few odd bottles which she thought were negligible. When things began to go wrong she lost her head, started killing people, and finally broke her own wretched neck in her panic. No, the bloke we want isn't her sort. His head is like ice, and he keeps his hands good and clean."

The argument was too convincing altogether. Campion was forced to face it. The sinking fear in his heart grew.

The barmaid came in with their drinks, accepted an arch endearment from the Superintendent with tolerant kindness, and left them to it. They sat for some time without speaking.

"There's a lot I don't quite see about that first killing," observed Campion at last.

Yeo grinned. "There's a lot there no one will ever see," he said. "There'll be an open verdict when the inquest is resumed and it'll go down on that list of unsolved murders they hold against us. She did it though."

"Oh yes, she did it." The thin man spoke slowly. "The Stavros woman was a pest; she got it into her head that Miss Chivers was holding out on her and I should say she just used everything. That must have been the time when the secretary began to lose her head. The nerve strain must have been colossal for some time, and the Stavros woman's nagging was doubtless the last straw. Somehow she got her to the house and killed her. It was diabolically clever in one way, because if she hadn't lost her nerve and smothered her but had left it to the chloral, it would have looked very much like suicide; while the fact that she was found where she was just before the wedding did suggest a reason, however unfounded."

"Ah," said Yeo. "And there may have been more justification in that than you think."

"What do you mean?"

The Superintendent set down his glass. "As soon as I heard of the decease of the party this morning, I sent round to her rooms in Pimlico and took possession of all her papers," he said. "The boys are still going through them. But just before I came out tonight, one of them brought me a collection of letters which I thought curious. They were all very much the same, all just a line or two, all written on the same date in different years, and they all said 'Darling, thank you terribly, but you shouldn't,' or words to that effect. They were signed 'Moppet' and they were addressed to Carados. The last one was dated last week. What do you know about that?"

Campion was sitting upright, incredulous distaste in his eyes. "I don't believe it," he said.

"Come round to my office tomorrow, and I'll show them to you."

"Why should she have them at her private address?"

"Now you're asking," said Yeo, "but it all fits in to a kind of a theory I'm getting to have about Chivers. I'm not much of a one for theories, as you know, but I rather think I've come across women like her before. She was one of those cheerful, tell-you-everything-and-nothing kind, wasn't she? That's the kind that harbour grievances, get into emotional states and work out things that would make your hair curl, all behind those smiling faces of theirs."

"You're suggesting that she had a sublimated passion for Johnny, got no encouragement and wanted to hurt him, I suppose?" Mr. Campion put the question uneasily. He was remembering Miss Chivers, efficient and splendid at her desk such a terrifyingly short time before. Then she had been hinting at emotional under-currents said to dominate the life of the famous household. So far he had received no other evidence of them whatever. What if the tortuous depths she had referred to then had been her own?

"I don't know about that." Yeo was answering his question. "But that idea of the suicide and the wedding—that looks like it, doesn't it? And then this keeping the letters the other woman wrote. That's curious. She may even have engineered that, you know."

"Engineered?" Mr. Campion was looking at the policeman with shocked respect.

"Yes, done the whole thing herself. Sent the other girl little presents, making out they'd come from him—got a feeling of being boss out of it." Yeo was faintly amused at Campion's disapproval.

"You were laughing at me yesterday because I didn't cotton on to one or two high-class ideas," he said, "but I'm not unsophisticated when it comes to crime, you know. All this modern guff the blokes the troops call 'trick cyclists' hand out, that's only barminess of a feminine kind, most of it. We've known about that for a long time. That's about what this was. Something like that, I'll bet my pension. It's not nice and it makes a lot of trouble."

"Yes, I dare say it might." Campion spoke absently. He was uneasy; he had not forgotten Johnny Carados's reaction to the gift of a rose and some Woolworth pearls.

"That's about how Chivers got Mrs. Stavros to get into bed there." Yeo went on unbearably. "Stuffed her up with a lot of tales, I'll be bound. Nasty minds women have sometimes, you'd be surprised. I expect the Stavros woman was all excited by the publicity about the wedding, which is now off, I see. Well, they're both dead, and the old girl down in the country is lucky she's not with them. She's a one by all accounts."

"Miss Pork?" Campion came back to a happier world with relief. "Oh yes, you ought to see her, Yeo. She's one for the memoirs."

"So I understood." Yeo's smile was reminiscent. "I had a wonderful tale from Tovey. Holly won't speak about her, she seems to have dazed him permanently. I thought I might nip down at the inquest. Do you realize who the Coroner is for those parts?"

"No, I'm afraid I don't." Mr. Campion was surprised. "I'm out of touch altogether, I thought it was a very small district."

"So it is, and has need to be. It's Montie Forster's manor. Thank God travel is difficult or we'd have all the Press there."

"Doctor Forster?" said Campion. "Wait a minute—it's coming back vaguely. He's a medical legal wallah, retired, or something, isn't he?"

"Say an old publicity hound, and you'll be nearer," said Yeo with prejudice. "He knows a coroner is king of his own pub parlour, and trades on it. Thoroughly enjoys himself. There were always bits about him in the paper at one time."

Campion got up. "That's where I saw the name, then," he said wearily. "It rang only a very faint bell. Well, thank you very much."

Yeo peered at him. "You ought to get some kip," he advised. "Have you been in bed at all since you came back?"

"No," said Campion, "apparently the police don't sleep."

"It's not the police, it's London," said Yeo with ferocious good humour. "We lost the habit. See you tomorrow."

In the doorway Mr. Campion remembered something. "What about Lady Carados?" he enquired. "Is any action being taken there?"

Yeo stared past him, his round eyes deliberately vague.

"Eh?" he said. "Oh, her? No. As a matter of fact, we decided we'd pass her clean up. Your chap Lugg can thank his lucky stars for picking on a confederate who's a little too much of a good thing even for us. No, we don't want her, it's her boy we're after."

"Yes, I see," said Mr. Campion, and went out again into the perfect night.

24

HE SLEPT UNEASILY. The urge which drove him on did not lose its force despite his physical exhaustion. He was lying on the couch in the sitting-room, having avoided his bedroom since its associations were unfortunate, and he turned and twisted under the travelling rug which covered him. All the same he did not wake; his dreams led him into a fantastic world in which aeroplanes and letters and policemen chased him and themselves in headlong circles. Finally, after many nightmare journeys he became acutely aware of Eve Snow. She was sitting on the edge of the couch thrusting a paper at him, and he waved her away angrily with the other phantoms. She persisted, however, and her voice, squeaky and attractive as ever, reached him through the clouds.

"Albert! Albert! Do you know where Johnny is?"

Again and again he heard her, and at last he sat up, his eyelids peeling unwillingly apart. To his amazement she was a reality. It was morning, and the yellow London light was streaming in through windows which someone had unshrouded. It fell upon her pale face, and on the rough whiteness of her coat. At first he thought it must be raining, for her cheeks were wet. He collected himself and blinked at her.

"Hello," he said.

"Albert, where's Johnny?"

He sat thinking stupidly, and gradually the whole story flooded back into his mind, horrible as any nightmare, but far more coherent and convincing.

"Where is Johnny?" she repeated. "Do you know?"

He glanced out at the sky. It was still wonderfully clear, pale oyster through the smoke haze. His glance returned to her.

"How did you get in?"

"Lugg opened the door to me. He's out there cooking breakfast. He says he made up your bed and you never slept in it. Albert, where is Johnny?"

She was a ghost of herself, a chic and tragic ghost, with smudged eyes and a wide mouth. "Where is he?" she repeated. "Don't you know?"

"He's gone back on the job," he said with a cheerfulness which at that hour was unconvincing. "He had a call and went straight on from Chessing. Probably he didn't have time to tell you. That's where he is; at the 'drome."

"At the 'drome?" she repeated. "But I didn't think he was anywhere near a 'drome just now. Besides, he was getting married yesterday, they wouldn't have called him back yesterday. No one else has been recalled."

In her anxiety, she was like a living manifestation of his own dread, and he almost snapped at her.

"Don't be a silly girl," he said. "It's all right. He's gone back to work. His glorious country has just sent out another of her erratic commands; anyone's liable to get lassoed by red tape at any moment these days. He'll turn up. Why the excitement?"

She sat looking out across the room. "I had a letter this morning, that's all," she said.

"A letter?" The chill which ran through him was familiar, it caught him in the chest and quickened his breath.

Eve turned towards him. Her face was blank for once and her movements were very slow. "It's only a note."

She laid a crumpled paper on the rug and he picked it up. There were only three lines, scribbled in a much more uneven script than had appeared in the letter to Susan and Don. Mr. Campion made out the words with difficulty.

"*Darling, I'll love you always—anywhere. God bless— Johnny.*"

He hesitated. "It's unusual, is it?"

"Very." She met his eyes and her wide sophisticated mouth bent suddenly into an imitation of a smile. "We—didn't have to. Even when he was going to marry that child I never doubted—I always knew. I—it's gone on so long—it's so sure. One was so settled, so . . . Oh, Albert, where the hell is he? What's happened? What's he doing?" Her face was wet again and she made no attempt to dry it. "Oh, God," she said, "I am so frightened."

Mr. Campion drew up his knees and looked round for his slippers and dressing-gown. "Look," he commanded, "give me until tonight. I'll ring you this evening. It's a bet. Clear off now like a beloved angel, and I'll get cracking."

Eve bent forward and kissed him. "You're a great comfort," she said absurdly. "Maybe I'm being hysterical."

"Maybe you are," he agreed. "Very likely. Don't worry anyway, I'll phone. Eve?"

"Yes?"

"Don't go round to Carados Square this morning."

"Why?"

"Because I'm going there."

"I see." Half-way across the room she looked back. "He's been quite different these last few months," she said. "Did you know that?"

Campion regarded her helplessly. He felt he should be spared her evidence. "Frightened?" he said unwillingly. "Worried?"

"Oh no. Not frightened." Her pride in him made her a little amused. "No. Angry, I think. You don't know Johnny, everything happens underneath with him. That's why the note scared me. Do you see?"

"No," he said honestly, "not as you do, naturally."

She nodded. "You find him for me," she said. "That's all that matters in the world."

She did not look back again and he heard her light footsteps dying away swiftly down the corridor. Presently the latch clicked faintly, and she was gone.

While he was in the bathroom, Lugg tapped at the door.

"Do you want to eat yer breakfast in the bedroom?" he enquired.

"No, of course not. Bung it on the table in the sitting-room. I'll be in."

There was a moment's disapproving silence.

"Goin' to eat where you slep'? That's not quite the thing, is it, unless you 'ave it in bed?"

Campion opened the door. "What's the matter with you?"

he demanded. "Why are you here anyway? I thought you had gone down to Nidd."

"No, I ain't." Mr. Lugg was embarrassed. In his housecoat and slippers he looked more like himself; a little older perhaps, even more bald, and slightly less elephantine than in his glory, but still himself. "No, I've worked it out, see? If the bussies didn't pinch me when they 'ad me, they don't want me, and in that case I'd better get on wiv me war work. I go on me shift in a hower. I thought we'd 'ave a bite together first. I've got a tin of 'errings I've been saving up for this—you ain't 'ad much of a welcome."

Mr. Campion was touched. "I knew I was at home," he said modestly.

"Wot? The corp? I know." A shadow passed over the hillocks. "Are they pinchin' that Marchioness of mine?"

"No, I don't think they are. She didn't do the job itself and they've got their hands full, so they're not pressing the charge."

Mr. Lugg's small, black eyes widened as far as the folds around them would permit.

"I'm very glad to 'ear it, but it's 'ardly right, is it?" he said virtuously. "Someone's gettin' theirs, I 'ope."

Mr. Campion reassured him, but without enthusiasm.

It was mid-morning when they parted in Carados Square. Mr. Lugg went off to await any heavy rescue which might be required of him, and Mr. Campion rang the bell at Number Three.

Gwenda Onyer opened the door to him and to his surprise welcomed him eagerly. She had been crying, he noticed, and her affectations had vanished, leaving her a very transparent, worried little person inclined to fuss.

"There's only Peter and me here, but do come up," she said. "You haven't seen Johnny anywhere, have you?"

He followed her into the hall and answered her question as he mounted the stairs behind her. She paused, and turned to face him.

"Oh, he's gone back, has he?" she said. "How very extraordinary. But that is a relief. We didn't know, you see. We thought . . ." She let the rest of the sentence die and hurried on into the big, first-floor room where, when he had seen it last, the whole household had been gathered.

"Peter, dear." She spoke before she was well in the

doorway. "Here's Albert Campion. He says Johnny's merely gone back."

"Really? Is that so, Campion?" Onyer rose from behind the desk at which Miss Chivers had been used to sit. "I say, I'm glad to hear it. I wondered what had happened to the old man, you know. What a hell of a business down at Chessing. You were there, weren't you?"

He, too, looked much more human in adversity. His graceful elegance was still there, but it was windswept and his narrow eyes met Campion's anxiously as soon as they were left alone.

"She went completely off her head, they say. That so?"

Mr. Campion nodded. "Yes," he said. "Best thing, don't you think?"

"I suppose so." Onyer looked down at the desk where he had been sorting papers. "I am glad Johnny's got back to work. This thing will knock him endways. He trusted those people. God knows why. You know they've arrested Gold?"

"I did hear."

"Frightful." Onyer passed his hand over his sleek head. "It will shake the old man more than anything. He insisted on assuming they were loyal; I told him he was making a mistake, but he wouldn't have it. He just insisted they were all right simply because they were here. He liked them. He's got such a capacity for liking, dear silly old ape."

Campion's heart sank. Here, he felt, was the last stone there was to turn and so far the evidence beneath it promised ill. "You personally didn't like either of them?" he suggested.

"I didn't know them," said Onyer helplessly. "Nobody did. They were in the circle but not of it, if you see what I mean. Johnny never saw that. He's damned obstinate over that sort of thing—felt he understood them if we didn't. Now there's going to be the devil of a mess to clear up." He glanced down at the desk. "I don't know how long that girl's been mad," he said.

Campion began to wish he had not come, but he went on doggedly. "What's she done, cooked the books?"

"Oh no. She only handled the social stuff." Onyer sounded thankful. "No, it just looks like petty intrigue to me." He seemed to make up his mind to a confidence. "What do you make of that?" he said. "It came this morning."

Campion took the slip of notepaper from him and looked at it with interest. It bore the trade heading of a florist in St. James's, and was addressed to Miss Chivers.

"Dear Madam," he read.

"We have now completed the order entrusted to us in August, 1938:

"One dozen of Lady Forteviot roses, together with five of the thirty-five pearls (cultured) entrusted to us have been delivered regularly on 2nd September in the years 1938, 1939, 1940, 1941, 1942, 1943, 1944, to Mrs. Moppet Lewis, 12 Wayland Studios, Church Street, W., as per your instructions dated August 31st, 1938, and for which payment has been received.

"We shall be glad to hear whether you wish this order to be repeated.

"Yours, etc."

Campion handed the slip of paper back in silence and Onyer threw it on the desk.

"Damn silly," he said. "Alarming, too, isn't it?"

"It is a little. Hence the poor view taken of the parcel which arrived the other morning, no doubt."

Onyer sat up; his eyes widened. "The pearls and the roses," he said. "Good Lord, do you know that never occurred to me. Dolly Chivers sent it, I suppose. Reminding Johnny, and trying to implicate him. God, she was horribly nuts, wasn't she?"

"Yes, rather horribly. But if it was a *reminder*, you see . . . ?"

"Johnny must have known about it? Yes, I do see. Hell!"

Onyer put his hands on the arms of his chair as if he were about to rise, but changed his mind as a new thought occurred to him. "I've got it," he said. "I know. That's it. Yes, it was about then, about 'thirty-eight, just before the war. Moppet's brief appearance in our lives was just terminating. Johnny must have decided that the little party was over and have arranged to send her a string of beads and a box of flowers in lieu of a farewell lunch. That's about it. That's rather his technique. I'll ask him. Yes, that's about it. He left instructions with Dolly. She must have spun it out like this just to keep her paws on the woman. That's what she was like; that's typical of her. Small, ingenious, and somehow incredibly mucky. Do you know, Campion, it makes me sick to think of that sort of girl in connection with the old man, he's so completely above it, it's out of character."

He had spoken more frankly than he had intended and a faint colour appeared in his smooth cheek. Mr. Campion met his eye. "That's how I felt," he said.

Onyer grimaced. "The old boy's a hero," he said awkwardly. "He doesn't know it and can't help it, but that's his role, isn't it? He's just over life-size. That's why it's so bad when he gets taken in. One isn't sorry for him, one blames him. One's shocked. It's a bit hard on him, but there it is. We've shoved him on a pedestal and he's damned well got to stay there for all our sakes."

Campion sat looking at his shoes. "If he got seriously involved in anything unpleasant, it would be awkward."

"It would be a bloody tragedy," said Onyer, "but that's not possible—is it?"

The final question was put sharply and Campion looked up to find the narrow eyes watching him. "Or is it?" said Peter Onyer.

Campion got up. "My dear chap," he said, "if there's anything you can say to help, for the love of mike say it. Now's the time."

"I don't *know* anything, that's the very devil of it." Onyer was playing with the coins in his pocket and their noise made a nervous accompaniment to his careful voice. "I heard a silly frightening rumour, and I don't mind telling you I thought of Lady Carados in connection with it. In fact Gwenda and I came up a day earlier than we'd arranged for the sole purpose of making an investigation. I made a date to see Gold on the Sunday night and tried to pump him. He was one of the few members of the household left in town, you see, but I don't think we did much good except to frighten him. Then I tried to see Eve, but I gathered that Johnny was with her, and I didn't like to butt in. It was all pretty miserable and mysterious and unlike us all. This marriage upset everybody."

"It was unexpected?"

"Completely incomprehensible. I believe Gwenda tried to interfere by finding the girl another boy friend. Something idiotic like that. I was furious with her, but the marriage did seem so mad to us who knew him. Johnny and Eve—well, it's gone on for a hell of a time and they do understand each other." He sighed. "It's taken me to the fair," he said, "the old boy's so altered."

Campion pricked up his ears. It was the second time that morning he had been volunteered the information.

"In what way?"

Onyer was like a younger brother; afraid of disloyalty yet worried unmercifully.

"He's—how shall I say it? Withdrawn. To be honest, I thought he'd found out something about his mother's activities, and when she behaved in that extraordinary fashion moving Moppet, I was certain of it. But now she's come comparatively clean, and the mystery's grimmer than ever."

"She's come across, has she?"

"Oh yes. Didn't you know? As soon as she heard about Dolly, she 'told all.' She found Moppet's body in the bedroom, that's the room behind this one, in the morning when she came to fix the flowers. Dolly was in here working and apparently she threw a sort of fit when she heard the news. Old Lady Carados promptly decided to see to everything; you don't know her well, do you? Dolly did, that's the damnable part of it. She played up to the old girl, knowing she'd rise to the occasion."

He went on talking, walking up and down the room as he spoke, the coins in his pocket ringing their little alarm as they ran through his fingers.

"Dolly seems to have been diabolically clever. She pointed out to the old girl that it looked like suicide, harped on the scandal, and then proceeded to become hysterical. Lady Carados reacted as she must have known she would. She bundled the girl out of the way and proceeded to deal with the situation herself. To do Dolly justice, I don't think she had any idea of the length to which the good lady would go, but that's what happened."

Campion lay back in his chair, and faced defeat. The picture was growing too clear, the details were slipping into place, colours were taking their true daylight value, but there was no escaping the main subject. The principal face remained the same.

"Did you know he might be called back yesterday?" he enquired suddenly.

"Who? Johnny? No, I don't understand it. As far as everybody knew he was getting married yesterday, and there's no big flap on as far as I know."

The elegant young soldier shrugged in his impatience. "I wish I understood it all," he said.

Campion got up to leave. He had not forgotten that Carados had told him that he had known of the date of his recall, but he saw no point in mentioning it. Onyer had troubles of his own.

He left him, and went downstairs alone. There was no sign of Gwenda and he was about to let himself out when a head appeared round the doorway at the other end of the hall. It belonged to Ricky Silva. He did not speak, but waved his hand carelessly before disappearing again. Mr. Campion paused with his hand on the latch. Another interview promised nothing but a further strain on his already wavering hopes. It was in his temperament to be thorough, however, and his conscience stirred. Ricky was the last possible source of information; after him there was no one, not a soul. He turned reluctantly, and was advancing down the hall when the utter uselessness of the proceeding struck him violently, and he swung round towards the front door again. His hand was on the latch when the man called him.

"I say, Campion."

"Yes?"

"About my puppet theatre." Ricky was still in battle dress and sandals and he came gracefully across the carpet. "Do you think it's safe down there? Or ought I to go and fetch it? I don't want to lose it, you see. Some of it was really awfully nice."

He stood questioningly, his large youthful eyes raised trustingly.

"It's perfectly all right, I should think." Campion was annoyed with himself for being irritated. "It may get a bit damp, but that's all."

"Damp? But that would ruin it. How damp? Enough to worry about?"

"No, I should hardly think so."

"Oh well, in that case I'm sorry you told me, for I shall

worry." He stood wavering. "Oh damn," he said. Then, becoming aware at last of his ungraciousness, he smiled. "If I don't think about things like that, I'm all right," he explained naïvely, "but once I do, they get on my nerves and I get a 'thing' about them. I should never have thought of sending it away, to begin with, if it hadn't been for Dolly."

"Oh," said Campion. "When was this?"

"Within the last year. Don't ask me for dates, for I can never remember them. She had some reason, I suppose. A beastly girl, I got to hate her. I liked her at first, she was so unfeminine, but as one got to know her one saw through that. Johnny trusted her when he shouldn't have done, so I'm not alone."

Growing tired of standing he sat down on the stairs, but made no similar arrangement for his visitor. He sat with his knees drawn up, his chin resting on his palms. "She used to use me, I believe," he said. "I didn't see it then, but I do now. She used to tell me things, too. She thought I was a child, or half-witted, I believe. I used to let her get on with it, it amused me."

Inspiration came to Mr. Campion. "Ricky," he said, "what are you afraid of?"

"Me?" The big eyes were mutinous. "I'm not frightened, why should I be? I've done nothing. And it's no good your bullying me, Campion, because I won't have it."

Mr. Campion checked himself. He made a determined effort. "My dear chap, I'm sure you haven't," he said laughing. "But I do know the kind of stew a woman like that can cook up for all concerned. One finds one's been compromised before one realizes it."

"I'm not compromised!" Ricky was outraged. "Good heavens, I didn't do a thing. Johnny can't be angry with me. She only used to talk to me when he helped me with looking after my things. I'm terrified of moth, you know, and she was very good about that. I shall miss her for that. She was frightfully efficient." He paused reflectively. "But I never really liked her, you know, and I wouldn't have done a thing for her if she hadn't been very useful in her way."

"What kind of things did you do?" enquired Mr. Campion, keeping the conversation simple.

"Me? Nothing. I took a message for her sometimes, that's

all. But when I found out she wanted me to do something that was little short of burglary the other day, I just wouldn't. I kicked at that. That's why I got off a day early, though, and came up here to meet her on Sunday morning. I let it out afterwards like a perfect fool. If Johnny gets on to it, he'll be furious, I know he will, and it'll be frightfully unfair because as soon as I heard what she really wanted, I refused flatly and went off and stayed with the Bertie Lambley crowd, and they can prove it."

Mr. Campion held his breath, he dared not speak, and at last his silence was rewarded.

"Imagine," said Ricky with disgust, "she wanted me to come back here at six o'clock sharp and wait here on the stairs. Then I was to take some keys she was going to have ready for me and go round to a flat in Church Street, collect some booze without being seen, and lug it off somewhere else. I told her she was demented, and she began to cry, and said it was vital and more than her life was worth and God knows what else. I found it quite harrowing, but I made it jolly clear to her that I wasn't having any. Thank goodness. That's what I feel now." He sighed contentedly. "Thank goodness," he repeated. "I suppose you've guessed whose flat it was, that frightful woman Moppet. I didn't see what was happening until I heard she'd been found dead. Then I put two and two together. Dolly tried to put her out to get the keys and killed her by mistake, I suppose; found the sleeping stuff didn't work quickly enough and so smothered her. Then, as she thought she was a murderer anyway I suppose she just went on with it. I thanked my stars I'd had nothing to do with it. What's the matter?"

The tall, thin man in the horn-rimmed spectacles was holding the balustrade, and his knuckles were white.

"Where were you going to take this stuff?"

Ricky wriggled to his feet. "I wish I hadn't talked to you," he said. "I was to take it somewhere for her, that's all, and I didn't, and that's that."

Campion cursed himself. "Sorry," he said. "I was getting interested. She seems to have trusted you."

"Of course she did. She had to." Ricky was swinging gracefully on the banisters. "I knew things about her that the others didn't, you see."

Campion smiled at him with deceptive amusement. "Where she bought her brogues, I presume?" he suggested.

Ricky flushed darkly. "No, rather more important things than that," he said spitefully. "For one thing I knew she was secretly married and was terrified of her husband. I was to take the wine to his place. I don't know why it was so important; Theodore Bush said it couldn't possibly exist. It was some filthy red stuff I'd never heard of. *Les Enfants Doux*, was it? She said she was afraid he'd kill her if she didn't get it back."

25

THE BIG CLUB-ROOM of The Red Queen at Chessing was set for the inquest, and the landlord had done what he could. Nothing could remove the comforting smell of beer, of course, but the narrow white-scrubbed tables had been rearranged, the spittoons set inconveniently under them, and about seventy-five of the ash-trays put away. The photographs of Free Foresters secretaries and the landlord's ancestors remained.

Yeo and the County Superintendent, a delightful person, who had a smile for ever hovering on his lantern face, stood talking in a corner with a police doctor, while the jury, very solemn and tidy in its best clothes, as became its public duty, sat waiting.

At the far end of the room, Miss Pork, redder than ever in black, was nodding and glowing at Holly and Peter Onyer, who had just arrived with Theodore Bush. The secretary of the Museum of Wine looked a little pale after his recent harrowing experiences, but he still was an impressive figure and his wide tweed coat hung jauntily.

Neither Mr. Campion nor the Coroner was in the room, but they had both been seen to arrive at the inn when those of the jury who wished to do so were viewing the body, and they were supposed, by those interested, to be somewhere in the back with the Chief Constable and Stanislaus Oates.

There were a few spectators, but not many, for the victim had been a stranger, and her manner of dying, by falling from a window, was not unusual. The more extraordinary points of interest in the case had been kept under the helmets of the police and were expected to remain there. The sole purpose of the present proceeding was to get Miss Chivers decently buried, for by the law of the land interment was impossible until the local Coroner had made his enquiry and so released the parish of Chessing from its responsibility. The local authorities were curious to see so many distinguished people present, and Superintendent Beckworth of the County C.I.D. was chaffing Yeo gently on the subject.

"I see you've got plenty of witnesses, Superintendent," he said. "Hasn't the right one come yet?"

Yeo glanced up at the big moon-faced clock set over the pair of buffalo horns at the end of the room. He was uneasy.

"He'll be along," he said without great conviction. "He's R.A.F. They'll get him here."

"If he comes by parachute," put in the little police doctor a little foolishly, as he glanced at his watch. "I hope he won't keep us waiting much longer. These are busy times, you know."

"He'll come," said Yeo, but his eyes wandered towards the casement through which there was a fine view of the long straight road, rising up to the ridge a mile away.

On the other side of the room, Miss Pork was equally inquisitive, and Holly was suffering.

"We can't begin without Lord Carados, because of the formal identification, I suppose," she said. "I'm surprised the girl had no relations. I thought everyone had relations of a sort. Of course if one's mad that probably makes it less likely. Still, it makes it very hard on him; I thought he looked most upset at the time, but then we all were. He'll be very glad to see you here, Major Onyer, and you too, Mr. Bush. What are friends if they're not with one at awkward moments? It's most kind of you to come and back him up. He'll appreciate that, of course. He is late, isn't he? Perhaps he's felt he couldn't face it, but he didn't seem that sort of man."

"He'll come, ma'am," said Holly, but he, too, looked at the clock and his tone was ominous rather than assured.

Theodore Bush cleared his throat and addressed Miss Pork with a pompousness which he appeared to have decided was her due.

"In all my long experience of Lord Carados, I have never known him disappoint a gathering," he said. "A few moments late, perhaps, but absent, never."

"How nice. But, of course, you never can tell with the war," declared Miss Pork brightly. "I've experienced many wars, but this one is far more often inconvenient than any I can remember. Isn't that so, Inspector? There seems to be so much more going on in it than usual."

Holly, who was often rendered speechless by Miss Pork, was at a loss once more, and Onyer intervened.

"Yes, by Jove, there is the war," he said. "He'd have phoned if he couldn't make it, but anything might delay him. Look here, Inspector, if it's just evidence of identification I can give that as well as anybody."

"Ah, my dear boy, but perhaps it isn't," murmured Theodore Bush. "After all, he came down here with the woman, didn't he? I don't know what they'll want to go into at this juncture, do you?"

"Only cause of death, sir." Holly spoke briskly. "That's all these Coroners' Courts are concerned with. The whole thing shouldn't take above a half-hour. Oh, there's Mr. Campion out in the road, I see. No, he can't see anybody coming, either."

Peter Onyer turned. "Perhaps I'd better join him," he suggested.

"I don't think you're going to have a chance, sir. Here they come, don't they?"

Holly was right. The door had opened, and now the Coroner entered, followed by the two Chief Constables, Campion bringing up the rear.

"Just sit where you are, please," the Inspector whispered. "You'll be called when you're needed."

A hush fell over the room and Doctor Forster took his place. He was a small man, thin and shrivelled, who bore, and knew that he bore, a striking resemblance to the best-known portrait of Laurence Sterne. His lips were cruel and his eye-sockets as dark as if they had been painted, but his whole face was rendered less impressive than it might have been by an incipient naughtiness, a lightness, and a vanity which partially explained why such an obvious personality should blossom so obscurely. Before he sat down he glanced round him with brisk professional interest, not at all unlike an actor manager appraising the house on his first entrance. Then he settled himself, took up his pen with a flourish and opened the proceedings in a quiet, intentionally dangerous little voice, rather unpleasant to hear.

Mr. Campion, who had spent the last half-hour with him, was not the most attentive member of his audience. He had edged his way to a seat from which he could command a view of the road stretching out like a long grey stair-carpet towards the dark trees on the ridge. It was quite empty, and looked inexpressibly lonely in the fine rain which had begun to fall at midday and now showed no sign of clearing. As he sat, Campion's lean figure sagged, and the bones of his shoulders showed through his jacket. Every now and again he glanced down the road and at each disappointment the dull light in his pale eyes became intensified. Now that the moment had come, now that his fear was becoming a reality, he was stunned. The full story, as he saw it now, appearing in its true light, was unbearable; one of those tragedies which rankle for a lifetime. Even now with the certainty practically upon him he could not bring himself to believe it. He looked down the road again. It was unbroken and lay lonely and straight as a sword.

Meanwhile the brief inquisition was proceeding. The jury had been sworn, and as each witness made his statement it was taken down in long-hand and signed.

Mr. Campion turned from the window and gave his mind to the inquest. After all, the play was not yet over. He could see Oates sitting forward a little in his chair, and the local Chief Constable fidgeting. Yeo was uneasy, too, and Holly blinked as he strove to appear as bored as the proceedings would normally have rendered him. So far the inquest had taken its ordinary course, and even the Coroner could not make it dramatic. The ancient formula proceeded slowly and painstakingly. The local Inspector gave evidence of the place of death; the police doctor followed, and no medical Latin could hide the simple fact that a woman had fallen from a window into an area and had, by striking her head on a stone coping, broken her neck.

To Miss Pork's disappointment she was not called, and it was Holly who rose to explain the circumstances of death, together with a precise statement of the time.

Mr. Campion had heard a great deal of police evidence in his career, but he was impressed by the Inspector. The statement of fact, just sufficient for credence and not enough to make any sort of picture, was masterly.

Acting on previous information, he said, he with other police officials stood in a concealed place in the house aforementioned and observed the deceased acting in a manner which left no doubt in their minds as to her sanity. In order to prevent an act of violence offered by the deceased to the householder, he had advanced across the room and the deceased, then in a state of frenzy, had thrown herself from the window, which was closed at the time, and had fallen, most regrettably, to what was afterwards discovered to be her death.

A quirk of amusement twisted the Coroner's thin lips as he wrote, and for an instant Campion was afraid he was about to query. But the moment passed. Holly signed, and sat down.

The Coroner glanced at the statement, looked round the Court, eyed the door questioningly, and returned to murmur something to his clerk.

"Now," he said, his quiet, unpleasant voice reaching to every corner of the room, "we come to the question of identity. We are not bound to press for this in this Court. It is sufficient for us to decide how and when and where this unfortunate woman died, but in cases like this, it is always incumbent upon us to do everything we can to assist those authorities who may be in charge of any proceeding which may follow out of an incident of this kind. I understand it is generally supposed that the deceased has no near kin. I also understand that her employer, who accompanied her on the fatal occasion, was due to come here this afternoon to give the necessary formal evidence.

"Is Wing Commander Lord Carados in the Court?"

There was no answer.

The police looked wooden, and the public sheepish. The

Coroner waited, and Campion understood that he was playing for time. He did it very well, too, using his natural idiosyncrasies as a cloak.

"Wing Commander Lord Carados," he said again. "Is he here? If so, will he stand up, please?"

Again there was the long silence. The usher crossed to the Coroner's table and stood whispering.

It was then that the door opened and Tovey looked in. His clean pink face wore a startled expression, and his eyes were excited. He made an almost imperceptible gesture towards Oates, who looked away. The Coroner was watching and he sighed with satisfaction.

"I see he's not here," he said. "In that case, since I feel it is my duty to see that this question is settled, once and for all, I shall take an unusual step. I have here on my table a certificate of marriage which I have reason to believe was the property of the dead woman. It is dated June the third, nineteen thirty-eight. I see that she is described upon it as Eleanor Dorothy Chivers, spinster, born nineteen hundred and nine. The other party, the husband, is, I have reason to believe, in this Court at this moment. Theodore Bush, will you stand up, please?"

For an instant the figure in the flowing coat did not move; the soft drooping face looked as if it had become grey porcelain. In that moment, with every eye in the room upon him, he was as tense, as wooden and as withdrawn as a crouching animal. The next moment he was on his feet, ready to protest, ready to fight his way. He gathered his resources and prepared for the effort. Yeo leaned forward and passed a slip of paper to Campion, who handed it on. He saw the single line as it went through his hand.

"Your house has been searched and your papers examined. P. Yeo. Superintendent."

Bush took the message, read it, and crumpled the paper into a ball. Then he shrugged his shoulders and walked slowly up to the Coroner's table. The police closed in behind him.

*

Mr. Campion left the Court and went out into the rain.
He was bareheaded and as he walked forward down the

road, a mist settled on his spectacles, so that he wandered in a cloudy world alone with himself.

He knew that in a few moments he must go back to them, and would join with Oates and Yeo and the other good fellows in the general jubilation. He knew he would do his best to enlighten Onyer, who had played his part so well, and had brought Bush down with him so innocently. He knew that he would speak a word with little Tovey, who had been so patient with the abominable country exchanges, and had got the all-important message from Sergeant Pelly through in time. He knew just how it would be. He could hear the guarded explanations and, thanks to the Coroner, could imagine the ride home with Oates, and could see already Yeo leaning over the back seat as he thought of yet another detail and fitted it into the completed plan. He could already hear the discussions; he could hear Yeo explaining laboriously just why Dolly Chivers had attempted to kill Bush when there was no hope of her recovering the incriminating bottles of *Les Enfants Doux* before he was confronted with them; could hear him explain why Bush was so certain that the wine which Don had discovered was a fake, and was yet so anxious to prove to everybody that indeed it was one, that he arranged the little party to obtain public proof of the fact.

Campion could hear Yeo cursing himself for not realizing that the man they sought was Bush all the time; Bush, the self-confessed worshipper of the good and pretty things of life; Bush most ingenious; Bush using Johnny's employees and Johnny's name.

Campion could hear and see it all so clearly that it made him sick. As he wandered on, he allowed himself to think of Johnny, and the angry questions came unbidden from his under-mind. What did you expect, he asked himself, what did you expect from that kind of man, with that kind of background, and that kind of pride? How would you have supposed he might react to an outrageous suspicion of this kind? How long did you expect him to sit down under the constant prying, the interference with his private life? What do you imagine was his reaction to the discovery that his secretary, whom he trusted, was in league against him? What would be the effect on a man of this kind of so much disloyalty everywhere? Would you expect him to make a row about it, or would it occur to you that he might throw in his hand?

Who sent him to his death somewhere out there on that perfect night? Was it Oates? Was it Yeo? Was it the sneaking fear in the faces of his own friends? Or was it you, Campion? Is it possible that you, yourself, provided the final straw?

Mr. Campion did not attempt to answer. He went striding on, his head bent, the rain creeping closer to him, hiding him, shrouding him. He was very ashamed.

The little car nearly ran him down. It pulled up with a scream as he leapt aside and a big, square head came out through the driving window to look at him.

"Walking home?"

Campion's heart leapt. The rain on his spectacles blinded him, but he knew the voice.

"Hello, Johnny," he said, unaware that his voice was not altogether normal. "I thought you weren't coming."

"So did I," said Lord Carados. "Get in. Is the party over?"

They sat in the car for a long time, and the rain settled on the roof and made maps of Europe over the windscreen. Mr. Campion made no bones about the story. His account was lucid and comprehensive.

"Theo?" said Carados. "I did wonder. I knew he had married her, you see."

"You knew?"

"Yes, I knew at the time, or just after. She told me she'd done it and regretted it, and wasn't going to live with him, and could she carry on. I said right-ho, and shut up about it. Then after that dreadful business down here I did wonder, naturally. He married her to hold her, I suppose. It must have been part of the scheme. How devastatingly thorough those chaps are, aren't they?"

"He was very clever," said Campion. "Having his own stuff from the Museum of Wine pinched was very astute."

"That was because his committee wouldn't let him send the stuff where he wanted to. There was a tremendous row about it for weeks. He's a curious chap. What will they do to him?"

"God knows. There'll be a trial *in camera*, I suppose, unless the war ends first."

"Yes," said Johnny. "Yes."

Mr. Campion took off his spectacles, and for the first time saw his companion clearly.

"My hat!" he said. "Are you all right?"

Johnny Carados smiled through his patches. "I'm marvelous," he said. "They think I'm asbestos, but they wouldn't let me go until two hours ago. I had a little outing last night, and got back on nothing but a horrible noise and strong smell of fire. What the hell is the matter with you?"

Mr. Campion told him. He was very weary and he spoke with a frankness which is only permissable among people of exactly the same age. Carados heard him in silence.

"You're stinkingly nearly right, old boy," he said at last, "but I'm not quite as bad as that. Not quite," he added quickly. "Damned nearly. No, what happened was that some time ago I had an idea that a single pilot in a certain kind of kite with a certain kind of load might do a certain rather useful bit of damage. I can't go into it, you don't want me to, do you? But it meant a sticky job for somebody. The target I had in mind was human and was pretty well protected." He hesitated. "Don't go and glorify this," he said. "It was just a special job which, like most of them, aren't too healthy. In fact the chances of getting there were very much better than those of getting back, if you follow me."

"Well, I thought that as I'd thought of it the least I could do was to present the prize to myself, as it were, and I moved heaven and earth to get permission. That was reasonable, wasn't it?"

"Very." Mr. Campion spoke sincerely. He was feeling much happier and some of the vague affableness of his youth returned to him. "Did you get him?"

"We don't know yet. It was a lovely bouquet right on the spot. He must have heard a pop. Then the fun started. God, I was terrified!"

"This other business was nothing to do with it?"

Johnny Carados started the car. "Nothing is *nothing* to do with anything," he said. "I didn't see how I could get back, and as things were I didn't see I cared much. That's roughly how it worked out. That's why I fixed up to marry Susan; she didn't love me, you know—hadn't got much idea what love was then, poor kid. Tom wrote himself off within a week of the wedding. I'm very fond of her, but I didn't see her enjoying living with me, or me with her, of course."

Mr. Campion did not quite follow, but was too polite to say so. Presently he explained:

"Money," he said. "Money, old boy. Our family always had a packet and for a very good reason. It's all entailed; no incumbent alive or dead can touch a farthing of the capital. I couldn't do much for Tom's girl except see her decently provided for, and I couldn't leave it to her. But once I'd married her, she got an income automatically from the family bag. She hasn't a bean herself, and the Admiral isn't wealthy. I promised Tom I'd look after her and this seemed the easiest way. No questions asked, no talk, nothing. I'd timed it very neatly, I thought." He laughed awkwardly. "I didn't think it was feasible for anyone to get back from this job last night. I'd have been in a hell of a mess now, wouldn't I?"

Suddenly he stopped the car, still some distance from The Red Queen's mock Tudor towers.

"I say, Campion," he demanded, "do we have to go to this ropey old pub? I've got a date with an actress."

Mr. Campion sat up as the car began to turn.

"That's a good idea," he said, "come to think of it I've got to catch a train."

*

It was morning, sunny and cold and promising, when Mr. Campion left the tiny station which could offer him no conveyance, and walked down the lane with the high hedges on either side. For the first time for many years he was feeling hopelessly nervous for purely social reasons.

He turned at the water-mill, and took the wooden bridge. Before him the woods of the park clustered dark and friendly. He followed the rosy wall built in serpentine waves for strength, and would have turned in at the iron gates where the stone griffins kept guard had he not been stopped by a sentry. This solid stranger in battle-dress was not impressed by Mr. Campion's story.

"Not without a pass, sir," he said firmly. "I can't help it, not whoever you are."

Mr. Campion repeated his name. "But it's my house," he said.

"Not now, sir. It's an Alandel supplementary aircraft factory now, and without a pass you can't come in."

"But Alan Dell is my brother-in-law," protested the homecomer helplessly. "My wife lives in the old chauffeur's cottage, that's it over there. You can see the roof. Look."

"I'm sorry, sir." The sentry appeared genuinely regretful, "but it can't be helped. Write to the management, state your business fully, and if everything's in order you'll get your pass in a day or so, no doubt."

The lean man in the horn-rimmed spectacles turned away. He walked on, still following the road which ran along by the wall, until he came to the corner where the bank ran high. There he paused and looked up anxiously. It was all right. The beech still hung long arms to the wiry grass. He swung himself over even more easily than he had done thirty years before, and dropped lightly on to what might well have been the same heap of rotting leaves with the same exciting aromatic smell. From where he stood he could just see the house far away on its carefully chosen eminence, looking like a dolls' house or a detail from the background of an eighteenth-century portrait, but he was not near enough to observe all the changes there. He noticed the tremendous activities in the drive, and the two new roofs rising up in a flourish of camouflage from behind the west wing caught his attention, but he did not go closer to look.

Picking his way carefully among the trees, he found the narrow path which led through the rhododendrons. It took him by graceful and leisurely stages to a wicket gate and a clearing beyond, where a little house stood with its back to him.

Mr. Campion opened the gate, crossed the vegetable patch and, skirting the cottage wall, turned on to the little grass lawn which had a muddy path running through it. There he stopped abruptly, an intense emotion, three parts honest embarrassment, overcoming him.

There was a person not yet three upon the path; he was white-haired and was wearing sun glasses. At the moment he was squatting by a puddle, one discarded sandal firmly clasped in his hand.

His preoccupation was a simple one. He was trying to fit the shoe into an imprint recently made by it in the mud.

As Mr. Campion came up to him, he raised his head from his task and stared upward, and for a time they stood looking at one another in amazement.

A girl with red hair and a wide mouth came out of the cottage and joined them. She was brown and slender, and her green dress was formal and a little old-fashioned.

"Hello," said Amanda, "meet my war work."

ABOUT THE AUTHOR

MARGERY ALLINGHAM, who was born in London in 1904, came from a long line of writers. "I was brought up from babyhood in an atmosphere of ink and paper," she claimed. One ancestor wrote early nineteenth century melodramas, another wrote popular boys' school stories, and her grandfather was the proprietor of a religious newspaper. But it was her father, the author of serials for the popular weeklies, who gave her her earliest training as a writer. She began studying the craft at the age of seven and had published her first novel by the age of sixteen while still at boarding school. In 1927 she married Philip Youngman Carter, and the following year she produced the first of her Albert Campion detective stories, *The Crime at Black Dudley.* She and her husband lived a life "typical of the English country-side" she reported, with "horses, dogs, our garden and village activities" taking up leisure time. One wonders how much leisure time Margery Allingham, the author of more than thirty-three mystery novels in addition to short stories, serials and book reviews, managed to have.

BANTAM MYSTERY COLLECTION